The Sea Horse Door

by

Gina Rossi

The Lobster Cove Series

The Sea Horse Door

Cover Art by *Kim Mendoza*

The Wild Rose Press, Inc.
PO Box 708
Adams Basin, NY 14410-0708
Visit us at www.thewildrosepress.com

Publishing History
First Champagne Rose Edition, 2015
Print ISBN 978-1-62830-902-7
Digital ISBN 978-1-62830-903-4

The Lobster Cove Series
Published in the United States of America

"Can't you postpone your trip?"

"We're decommissioning a rig in the North Sea this week. One of the legs needs urgent assessment. There's a corrosion problem. It's an emergency so, no, I can't postpone my trip."

"Well, I can't stay."

He shrugs. "Then you will be responsible if that platform collapses, dumping everyone in the sea. Their chances of survival will be zero. Husbands, sons, brothers, fathers of children will be drowned—"

This is not jolly. "It's not my fault that Ocean Kazang has a wonky leg!"

"Ocean Zen. And as it happens, it is not an Ocean Zen rig that has the problem. It's the Trident 202. It's not your fault, of course, but it will be your fault if I have to delay my departure and something bad happens."

Blackmail! "How ridiculous to design an oil rig with corrosive legs."

"Corrodible."

"There's no such word."

"Corrodible. Believe me I know."

Honestly!

He sits again, opposite, and rests his jaw in his hand, the one with the scars, and studies me. "The ocean is a hard taskmaster, Lara Jasmine Layla Fairmont. We fight a constant battle."

Well, at least he's read my CV.

Dedication

For Jonathan, always a hero,
and
Sophia Jean Harrod-Pike (b. 2013),
always adorable.

Chapter One

Some people have no compass, no geographical clue.

"Maine? Where's that?" Holly asks. "Please, Lara, tell me California because at least that would be dead cool."

Holly's so agog at the news I'm going to America, she called an urgent meeting at our favourite wine bar, Mel's Garden, in South London.

Seriously? "Holly, didn't you study geography in high school?"

"I failed."

"Figures."

"So where is it?"

"Do you know where Boston is?"

"Um, south of New York?"

"North! Maine is, roughly, north of Boston up toward the Canadian border," I tell her. "Mountainous interior, craggy coastline, really beautiful."

"Why there?"

"Because, Holly, that is where I have found a job."

"What kind of job?"

I search in my bag for the email I printed. *"Companion to Liz Dalton,"* I read, *"seventy-four, resident of Lobster Cove, Maine.* She lives in a place called Blue Rocks."

"What? Like a nursing home?"

"Hardly, or she wouldn't need a companion, would she?"

Holly's laughing at me. "Oh my God, you're going to end up in a nursing home, sleeping in a single bed with an old lady in an adjoining room!"

"Am bloody not. Blue Rocks is a mansion on the beach." I made that up, but I let it go.

Holly frowns at me over her empty glass. "Seventy-four is quite old, isn't it?"

Is it? My own parents are in their mid-fifties, fit and healthy as you like, both PhDs, working on a research vessel in the southern Indian Ocean. Will they be old in twenty years? I don't know.

Holly leans closer, elbows on the table. "I can't understand why you're doing this, Jazz."

My name is Lara Jasmine Layla, surname Fairmont. Holly frequently calls me Jazz, Jazzy and other things. My parents never call me anything other than Lara Jasmine. What can I say? Both were students in the seventies—one foot grooving on the hippy trail and the other firmly nailed on the highway to Academia. With Holly, it's open season on names, and has been since we started boarding school, aged ten, at St. Anne's in Hampshire.

"I'm doing it, as you very well know, because my fledgling darling business, Hampers, went *bust*. Believe it or not, a mail order, posh picnic company cannot survive the tail end of a recession in a country where summer lasts a brief three weeks. With rain. I worked my butt off, and still, it failed—"

"I know, Jazz. I know all that." She flaps a hand. "And I know the whole Hampers thing is a real bummer. I feel for you, I do, but why Maine?"

I thrust the email at her. "The money, sweetcheeks. I have debts. I narrowly missed going under."

She takes the page and scans the text, eyes widening. "Oh. Wow. I see."

Lucas Dalton, my employer, the old lady's son, has offered me two and a half times what Hampers would have had I delivered on every picnic order at Ascot, the Henley Royal Regatta, Glyndebourne, the Hampton Court Flower Show and many more, Cristal and beluga option, ten times over.

"I can't afford to say no, Hols." Two can play that game.

"I can see that, but—" She waves down a waiter and orders two more glasses of chilled rosé. "—what if it's a horrible job? I mean, what if the old girl is a right bitch, or throws fits or something?"

"If you read all the way down, you'll see the agency confirms she exhibits normal behaviour for her age. There are no special requirements. It's easy money. I mean, how hard can it be to look after an old lady for a few months? Go to the library, take her to tea, to visit friends, to the post office, drive along the coast, all that stuff."

"I bet there's a catch. I bet there's a smelly little dog you'll have to walk."

"For that money—" I point at the email—"I will walk the smelly dog. The smelly dog may even sleep on my bed."

"Yech." Holly reads further and throws her head back in a squawk of husky laughter that turns every head in Mel's—like it always does.

"What?"

"You've been approved by the Child Protection

Services Authority."

"So? It's routine. In case the grandkids come around, and I herd them into the broom cupboard with dastardly motives."

"*What*?" She looks at me, shaking her head. "For God's sake!"

I shrug. "The world we live in." I open the menu as our wine refills arrive. "Come on, let's order something to eat before we fall off our chairs." I scan the list of salads because, to be honest, I could lose some weight.

****

Right now, standing here in the wet gloom a few days after my lunch date with Holly in sunny South London, it feels strongly like the Canadian border end of things—like where Quebec meets Newfoundland in the north. Firstly, it's pouring: cats, stair rods, dogs and rats. Secondly, this place, Lobster Cove, is also, in addition to the rain, cloaked in thick mist. I can't see my hand in front of my face unless it's *on* my face. Thirdly—and most sadly—the vibrant memories of my glittering few days *en route*, in New York City with Dad's cousin Lauren—editor of glossy foodie magazine *Filo*—have sloshed down the road in the wake of the cream Bentley driven by Lauren's strong, silent driver—a woman. I'm a city girl, a Londoner. What the hell am I doing in a place like Lobster Cove? At the very least, I want to—make that I *wanna*—go back to New York!

Where, I would like to know, are the pastel-hulled rowboats and dinghies bobbing at their moorings while their halyards sing in the gentle breeze? Where are the puttering lobster boats I've read so much about? Never mind that, where's the pier? Where am I?

What do I do next? I have no idea what's supposed to happen, bar the curt text message from Lucas Dalton: *Maggie's Diner, 8 p.m. latest.*

The taillights of the Bentley, my deliverance, vanish into the drizzle-mist. Within the hiss of the rain, there's the faint yet unmistakable sound of the ocean and the more insistent slap and slop of small waves against a dock, somewhere to my right. I take a step toward the sound and think again. Visibility's not great and I don't want to get lost, or end up upside-down in the harbour, first off. I peer left, groping my way to a blue sign flashing *Maggie's Diner* in retro neon—apart from the second G, which has blown—up on the mist-draped gable of a grey shingle, weather-blasted building. Easy to see why Dalton suggested Maggie's. It's the only place open. Seems to me it's low tide in Lobster Cove in oh so many ways.

How I miss Lauren's driver, while I lug my bags through the entrance. I abandon them next to the door and look around: blue checks, blue vinyl and a lot of cream and chrome.

"Hi." A young waitress approaches. "I'm Sally. How may I help you?" She ushers me to a booth next to the window with a swirly, white view onto the deserted main street.

"Thanks," I say. "I'm Lara F—"

"The new help for the Daltons up at Blue Rocks?"

"That's me."

She hands over a laminated menu the size of a broadsheet. "Lucas asked for us to call Skeet as soon as you arrived. I just did that."

Skeet? What is a skeet? Sally reads my expression and smiles. "Skeet's our local cab driver. He'll run you up to Blue Rocks. Lucas can't leave Liz. Wouldn't wanna bring her out in this." She pulls a face at the window. "You wanna order something while you wait?"

Our local cab driver? One? Didn't Boris Johnson say in a BBC interview last week that there were close on twenty thousand licensed taxicabs in London? Maybe I misheard. Maybe Sally said, "Skeet's *a* local taxi driver." That means there could be more than one. That means there could be two. I swallow a despondent sigh and order tea, handing back the giant menu, aware I'm not hungry, nevertheless feeling a tweak of guilt for the unchallenged chef waiting through the blue door behind the counter. "Thanks."

"You're welcome."

I gaze around the diner: no one. I get my phone out of my bag: no messages. I look through the window: nowhere. I message Holly. *Arrived safe in Lobster Cove, Maine. Yet to meet my gracious charge. Remind me, what am I doing here? Will call soon. Love xxx*

No answer.

Sally arrives with my tea. "How long you gonna stay?"

"My contract with Mr. Dalton is for three months, then we'll see."

"*Mr. Dalton.* You English are so cute! He's gonna love that. Do you know anything about Blue Rocks and the Dalton family?" She places cup and saucer in front of me, and a small jug of milk and bowl of sugar to the right.

"Not really."

"They're okay, I guess, though it's not what I'd call a normal household."

"Why's that?"

Sally looks at me for a few seconds, considering. "Lucas is real nice in spite of what people say, and think, but things ain't the same at Blue Rocks since Liz went. She was the glue."

"I see." Alarm bells! I pour a little milk into the teacup, followed by tea.

"Then there was that whole murder business."

I sip, calm, like murder is a daily event for me. My heartbeat changes gear. Alarm bells develop into the whole of Scotland Yard gunning down Regent Street in squad cars, sirens screaming. "So—" deep breath, and first things first—"you say Mrs. Dalton *was* the glue? What do you mean *was*?"

Sally smiles, head on one side, eyes distant. "She died last spring, honey. She's gone."

Add some fire engines. "She was *murdered*?"

"No. No, not Liz."

"I see." I do not see. "So why…" I'm about to ask Sally whether I've crossed the North Atlantic to work for a dead woman—and, PS, what's this about a *murder*?—when the door opens and a giant man pushes his stomach into the diner.

"Miz Fairmont? You ready? Gotta do a pickup at the station for the sheriff in forty," he says.

Abandoning my too-hot tea, I jump up and follow him to the door. He lifts my bags in one hand—the size of a Christmas turkey—and backs outside, his heavy tread rattling a display of blue and white porcelain lobsters on a shelf above the window.

I try to pay Sally, but she waves me off. "On the house, honey. In any case, I'm sure to see you around in the week, when you bring Alice in to town."

Alice? No time for questions because Turkey Hands has blown his hooter, I mean *honked his horn*. Listen to me. I'm American already. Maybe Alice is that little smelly dog? I dash out into the rain and dive into the back seat of his Chevy.

****

God, I'm tired. I yawn and look at my watch: five past eight. Hardly late and not quite dark—at least I don't think so—but there's nothing to see in the gloom. Skeet clearly has talent for driving blind. All I can gather is that we drive away from Maggie's, up the main road, turn right and start climbing, then it's downhill for a bit, then up, then down, and I don't see a single car coming or going in any direction.

"Pretty quiet around here," I remark to the back of Skeet's neck. To be frank, it's not so much a neck as an extension of his broad, bald head downward into mighty, pudgy shoulders.

"Yeah," he says, after a while. "Fog keeps folks indoors. Keeps the tourists away. Delays the season."

"For how long?"

"It'll clear soon enough."

I doubt Skeet's soon enough is the same as my soon enough, but I keep that to myself. No wonder poor old Liz Dalton needs a companion. Who could live in a place like this without one? I imagine a cosy scene, me and Liz locked in by mist, toasting tea cakes by a blazing fire. Only, it's not cold, so a blazing fire, so…no, wait, I need to ask Skeet about Liz being dead, although…although it could be another Liz, a cousin perhaps. Too bad she's dead. Sad. No toasted teacakes and a blazing fire for her, uh…

"Blue Rocks," Skeet proclaims, like he's unveiled

a remodelled Pentagon, waking me. Damn. I had meant to ask all sorts of questions about the Daltons, but Skeet's laid-back attitude lulled me to sleep. Sleep! I yawn and rub my eyes fervently hoping the Daltons will let me go to bed immediately on arrival. I look at the time on the dashboard clock: 8:25.

"Hey, Skeet," someone calls from the house—a man. Skeet's already out of the driver's seat with the boot open and my bags on the driveway.

"Hey, boss. Still okay for eleven tomorrow morning?"

"You bet." The man, in jeans and a long-sleeved tee-shirt pushed up to the elbows, leaves the shadow of the porch and walks, barefoot, out onto the drive.

My, my. And just who is this?

Chapter Two

I stare through the window. At the very most, I am expecting a robust man in his fifties and his sweet, tottering—living—mother. We must be at the wrong house. I get out and open my mouth to suggest this to Skeet.

"Don't worry," Skeet says to me. "Gotta go. I'll settle with the boss tomorrow." He bangs the boot, gets in the car and zooms off, leaving me open-mouthed with confusion.

"Hi Lara," the guy says. "Welcome. I'm Lucas Dalton." His eyes are so dark I swear they're black. There's no smile whatsoever, but his expression's polite.

"Um," I say, "hello."

He looms, head and shoulders—non-pudgy—above me, wisps of cloud clinging. Not large and soft like Skeet, but I notice in spite of my zombi-esque state, lean and muscly, ultra-fit. We shake hands. Big, warm, firm handshake. Strong. He, like Skeet—not turkey-handed, however—lifts my bags like they're packed with one sheet of tissue paper each. He strides to the house, and I follow. By the time I get through the door, he's across the hall and up the stairs. He turns right and goes along a gallery. There's some banging and crashing and he yells, "Liz! Come say hello."

Well, that's no way to talk to your elderly parent,

or is she his grandmother? Cheeky lad, in that case. Maybe Liz is deaf. Seventy-four isn't that old, but it's hardly young. However, anyone can be deaf, it's not always an age thing. I close the studded door noticing its width and weight. The bronze handle is the shape of a tall, elegant sea horse, as is the knocker, only smaller. The bell-pull on the doorframe is a chain of sea horse babies, and the door hinges graceful branches of seaweed. A work of art.

Inside the house, on the one hand, something doesn't sit right. On the other, I'm having a second wind thanks to the involuntary power-nap in Skeet's car. I've entered an unbelievable space. A huge hallway, with that handsome, focal-point set of broad, bare stairs up to said gallery. It's borderlining *Gone with the Wind*, beach-house style, with a little scuffing and no carpet. I turn around, full circle on a vast, faded, thin rug that's worn bare in large spots, the only item of furnishing I can see apart from a pair of big, dark oil paintings of old Boston harbour. There are wide window seats—minus cushions—and no less than two fireplaces, one with—unfortunately—a moose skull and antlers mounted above the mantel.

"Sorry," Lucas says, coming down the stairs. "We've been having a tooth-brushing argument." He glances at his watch and looks up at the gallery. "Quit fussing and get down here, Liz!"

A shriek from above. "No!"

"Okay, you go to bed without meeting Lara."

"Wh—" I say. What's happening here? I look from Lucas to the gallery and back again. He's watching the top of the stairs. There's the patter of little feet and a smile spreads across his face, bringing his eyes out of the darkness.

"Good girl." He looks at me, eyebrows raised and then back at the little figure on the stairs. "Progress," he says, nodding.

"Um—"

A little girl, three or four years old—actually I haven't a clue—dressed in blue pyjamas with most of the buttons missing, jumps down the last step. "Look at my big jump!" she says, and runs to Lucas. He goes down on his haunches, catches her, and levels his eyes on hers.

"Lara, this is Alice, and Alice, this is Lara." He points up to me. "She's come all the way from England to look after you while Daddy's away, okay?"

"But, um," I say. "Hello, Alice." I bend and scoop a handful of curly hair out of her eyes. It looks clean enough, but could do with a thorough brushing. She smiles back, all dimples and then, overcome by shyness, she moves close to Lucas, peeping up at me over a not-too-shabby bicep. Plenty of room to hide there. He stands, picking her up. She buries her face in his neck.

"What about a goodnight kiss for Lara?" he asks. She shakes her head. "What about tomorrow night?" She nods. "Good." He backs toward the stairs. His eyes meet mine. "I'll be with you in a few minutes."

"So—" I begin, but he's turned his back.

"Ten at the most." His voice floats down from the gallery. "Kitchen's straight on through. Help yourself."

I am thirsty, so I go across the hallway and open the double doors in front of me. Not the kitchen it turns out but a long, narrow conservatory-style studio of some kind. There are three workstations illuminated by low-level industrial lighting. Technical drawings and printouts are pinned and stuck to every wall. I go into the room and look at the high-tech drawing board beneath the central skylight. There's a computer-generated diagram on it of God knows what: pipes and tubes and cubicles and ladders and tanks and a lot of criss-cross metalwork like a crane. I look at the logo in the corner. *Ocean Zen*, it says, and underneath *Ocean Zen 14, Fixed Platform 1500 metres, Leg 3.*

In the corner of the room, away from the windows, there's a functional spiral staircase that ends against the high ceiling, leading nowhere.

None the wiser, that's me, and I doubt I should be in here. I turn to go, and my eye falls on a work surface against the wall of tall windows. One of the desks. There's a letterhead. *Ocean Zen*, again, and an address in Boston. At the bottom of the page I see *Oil & Gas Platform Design & Maintenance* followed by a list of names, directors, with plenty of letters after their names. There's even one I recognize: *Lucas Dalton, Owner, Harvard and M.I.T.* I touch the paper and it moves slightly, revealing a professional headshot of me—the one I sent Clarkson's Careers with my CV. I stare down at my groomed, dark brown hair, smoky-but-subtle eye makeup, and lips helped to full quirkiness by neutral lip pencil and Mac's *To the Future.* The way I feel right now, that person is not me. I'm looking at a stranger. What happened?

Unsettled, I leave the room, pulling the doors shut. There's no sound from upstairs, so I explore further and find the guest toilet—not too clean but I'm desperate—and *whoa* mirror! *That person is not me.* My hair is thrilled. It's sprung, joyous, from the confines of

Lauren's industrial strength, New York salon-brand products and hair-straightening tools, which she thrust upon me with concern and alarm in her eyes, while nervously fingering her bob by Mizu—as round and shiny as a liquorice lollipop—already licked. I'm pale and my eyes are over-bright. I blame the fog. Where's *To the Future* when I really need it? I find a tube of clear lip-gloss in my pocket. It doesn't help. I look like a rough sketch of Plain Jane by Botticelli—one he crumpled up and threw away.

Finally, the kitchen. A lovely room, high-ceilinged with tall windows and spectacular views of fog. Why doesn't someone draw the blinds? I look around. There's mess on every counter. The dishwasher's open, overloaded with dirty stuff and the recycling bin's overflowing. The sink's piled with plates and glasses and there's a huge black beast, a cat—I think—on the draining board, his head inside a pot, licking away to his heart's content. I shoo him away, except he doesn't move. He lifts his head, looks at me with utter disdain in his yellow eyes, licks his fabulous whiskers and carries on. Thank God I'm not the cleaner in this place.

Deciding not to trust the bottle of chilled tap water in a fridge full of empty containers and limp vegetables, I cross the kitchen on a sticky floor and hunt for a glass in the cupboards. No luck. Every receptacle is used. I rinse a coffee mug—thoroughly, under very hot water—barely able to move the mixer tap over the stack of washing-up in the sink.

Lucas comes into the room. "Scram, Buster," he shouts, clapping his hands, and the giant cat scarpers. "Meet Buster the Eunuch," he says.

"Buster the…"

He grins, shooting brief light into those sombre eyes. "Alice's cat. Her best buddy. Bit of a party animal in his youth so, in spite of his pedigree, he had to be fixed."

"Oh."

"So Alice is down. She's a goner. She was really looking forward to meeting you, so that shy act was a surprise. Drink?" He opens the fridge, pulls out a bottled beer and holds it up.

"Er, no thanks."

"Glass of wine, maybe?"

"Well, if you have."

"Sure. Have a seat." There's half a bottle of red on the counter. He opens it, somehow locates a rare clean glass, fills it, and hands it over. "Cheers." He downs a third of the beer in one glug. I sit, and sip the red. It's disgusting. Worse, there's black-confetti residue, a clue to how long the bottle's been open.

Lucas doesn't notice. He's standing on the other side of the table, beer in one hand, phone in the other, intent on the screen, texting with his left thumb. Eventually, he tosses the phone onto the table, pulls out a chair and sits opposite. "Sorry," he says. "Business. Do you have any questions?" He looks at his watch.

"I do."

"Fire away."

"Um, when do I meet Liz?"

"Who?"

"Liz Dalton, the lady I'm here to look after."

"But you're here to look after Liz."

"I am, yes."

He's looking at me with wary eyes. "You met her. Alice. My daughter. She calls herself Lis. So do a lot of people."

"Lis? No. I don't understand." I reach for my bag and take out the printed contract and job description forwarded to me by Amy, my top contact at Clarkson's Careers. "Look." I flip the pages and fold them back on one another. "Here." I point, showing him. "*Liz Dalton, seventy-four,* and here, further down, *general care and companionship while son,* I skip, *widower—Lucas Dalton, thirty-five years of age*—oh? I didn't see that. I had fifty-five in mind. Perhaps I should have read the contract better—*a frequent traveller away from home, conducts his business affairs in*—"

Lucas takes the papers out of my hand and reads the page, frowning, his beer forgotten. "Shit," he says, at the end.

"What?"

He gets up, turns his back, spits out a monumental sigh, and swears again.

"What?" I get up, sit back down. He's gone to stand by the window, where he's staring at nothing, both hands jammed into his hair.

"We've screwed up," he tells the fog on the other side of the pane.

He yanks down his hands, leaves the room, returning seconds later with a small laptop in a durable cover. Like his watch, it looks like it works a hundred metres underwater. He sits again, at the table—next to me this time, opens the laptop and scrolls quickly through his emails. "Fuck."

I push my wine glass away, and wait.

After a few minutes, he sits back and looks sideways at me, eyes anxious. "I had over fifty applicants for this care job."

Well he would, wouldn't he? The salary's amazing. I nod. "So?"

"I chose you. You were the third attachment I opened and you stood out, waist, head and shoulders above any of the others."

"Thank you."

He turns the laptop to face me. "Read that email."

I do. It's from Amy, at Clarkson's.

Dear Mr. Dalton,

*We are delighted to confirm that Miss Lara Fairmont is available to care for your daughter, Alice, aged four years from 20th June...*blah, blah, blah. We've screwed up all right! Hang on a minute. *We*?

I stop reading, and swivel the laptop to face him. "Look, I'm definitely not caring for a four-year-old. I—"

"The glitch happened in the contract. I didn't read it."

"You what? How can you not read contracts?" Aren't I the one to talk? "You're the owner of a company!"

His eyes sharpen. "How do you know that?"

I look away. "I went into your office by mistake. I thought it was the kitchen. I saw a letterhead on the desk."

"On the desk? That's quite a way in."

Guilty! I stare at my wine glass. "I was lost." I was. I am.

"What else did you see in there?"

"Nothing I understood." Not even the photo of that me-woman among his documents.

He lets it go. "How's your wine?"

"To be honest," I say, to change the subject and

17

swing the blame. "It's vile."

"Sorry." He grins, gets up, snatches the glass off the table and pours the contents into the heap of pans in the sink. He goes to the fridge and opens it, studying the scummy contents from top to bottom. "There's a bottle of white."

"Don't worry. I've got water. I'd rather sort out this problem—"

"Which problem?"

"I'm here to care for a seventy-four-year-old woman. That's the job I agreed to do. She doesn't exist, so I need to contact the agency, get back to the UK, probably, and start over. Unless Amy can transfer me to another job in the US."

"But I've, er…" He's hunting everywhere for a clean glass. Finding nothing, he rinses the black confetti out of my old glass, glances around for a tea towel, I presume, gives up, shakes the glass upside down a few times over the pot mountain, and fills it with white wine. "I've paid your airfare."

"The contract states—"

"I told you, I didn't read the contract. I've been working with Clarkson's for three years, and it's always the same contract. I sign it, and they send someone. That's how it's worked ever since Lis and I have been alone."

I'm done with treading lightly. I take the offered glass of wine and put it on the table, "What happened to Lis's mother?"

"She died. When Lis was a year old." He sits down.

"I'm sorry." I am sorry, but it's not my problem. "Where," I ask after a suitable moment or two, "and who is Liz Dalton?"

"My mother. She died last year. Heart problems. Clarkson's helped me out with her care. Dad couldn't cope."

"I'm really sorry." Is everyone in this family dead?

"Dad went through a bad patch, but things are a lot better now. He's met someone and moved out of town. She owns a B&B in the Florida Keys. They're planning to get married next year."

I sip my wine. It's chardonnay, but hey.

Lucas sits up, like he's waking from a dream. "What are we going to do? I have the person I chose for the job I need done. You have, apparently, been led astray."

"Yes, um…"

"What are you going to do?"

"I should probably—"

"Look, how different can it be? Caring for a kid can't be that different from an older person. A kid's a person, after all."

"But I have no experience, no training." And no desire whatsoever to get involved in the sticky realms of childcare.

"Oddly, experience and training aren't always the best qualities. At least, that's what I've discovered over the years I've been trying to balance career and childcare."

I have *never* heard a man say something like that.

"It's more the type of person," he goes on. "More about personality, less about convention."

"It's…it's not what I want to do. I'm sure Alice is a lovely little girl, but we should sort this out and I should go home."

Lucas is anxious, and irritated—who wouldn't be?—and there's a trace of distress in his eyes. Is he hurt because I haven't fallen at his beloved daughter's feet? Also, there's something about his mouth—the way he won't let it soften even when his eyes do—that tells me he's not as hard as he makes out.

"I'll pay you more," he says. "Double."

I hold my breath. He doesn't mean that. "Mr. Dalton, I—"

"Lucas."

"I'm not—"

He raises a hand, to stop my words. "Listen, you're here now. You've come all this way. I leave tomorrow morning and I'll be gone six weeks at least, so, would you be prepared—" he looks straight at me—"to help me out for now?"

"This is not the job I want. I know nothing about children." I don't, apart from the fact that they make you sick and tired before they're even born. My sister, Julie, is expecting her first baby and spends all her time with her head in the toilet or asleep.

"I don't need this," Lucas says. "Please? Help me out."

"*I* don't need this."

"Yeah." He puts his face in his hands and rubs his eyes with his fingertips.

"Amy will sort you out with someone fabulous. I know she will."

He drops his hands and looks at me, eyes empty. If I hadn't seen those letters behind his name on that letterhead lying on the desk, I would say he'd graduated M.Sc and Ph.D *cum laude* from the University of Brutal Knocks. "And will that person be available, suitable, *here*—" he spreads out his hands—"before I leave tomorrow morning?"

"Well—"

"I put a great deal of effort into finding the right person. I don't leave Lis with anyone. She's all I've got."

Okay, no need to make *me* feel guilty. None of it's my fault. I refuse to feel bad. I also have no idea what to say. I drink wine and ask for ice.

He brings it from the ice machine in one perfect hand—apart from a scar running across all four knuckles like someone tried to chop off his fingers—and drops it into my glass, bringing the level up to the brim.

"Thanks," I say, looking at his other hand, unmarked and big, with the teeniest trace of hair, strong fingers and healthy, short rectangular nails. His hands match his teeth: perfect, with character.

Why am I even thinking about these things?

"Look," he says. "All Amy did was get my mother's and Lis's names mixed up."

All? What about the seventy years separating the two? "Can't you postpone your trip?"

"We're decommissioning a rig in the North Sea this week. One of the legs needs urgent assessment. There's a corrosion problem. It's an emergency so, no, I can't postpone my trip."

"Well, I can't stay."

He shrugs. "Then you will be responsible if that platform collapses, dumping everyone in the sea. Their chances of survival will be zero. Husbands, sons, brothers, fathers of children will be drowned—"

This is not jolly. "It's not my fault that Ocean

Kazang has a wonky leg!"

"Ocean Zen. And as it happens, it is not an Ocean Zen rig that has the problem. It's the Trident 202. It's not your fault, of course, but it will be your fault if I have to delay my departure and something bad happens."

Blackmail! "How ridiculous to design an oil rig with corrosive legs."

"Corrodible."

"There's no such word."

"Corrodible. Believe me I know."

Honestly!

He sits again, opposite, and rests his jaw in his hand, the one with the scars, and studies me. "The ocean is a hard taskmaster, Lara Jasmine Layla Fairmont. We fight a constant battle."

Well, at least he's read my CV.

Something occurs. Could I be at the wrong house? Is there a sweet elderly lady waiting for me in mist-shrouded Lobster Cove, wondering where the hell I am? If only.

"Um." I look in my bag for my phone. "I'm going to call Amy." Amy's given me a twenty-four-seven emergency number—the kind of thing you think you'll never need. It's terribly late in the UK now, but I'm going to ring her. An emergency's an emergency, after all.

Amy answers the call on the second ring, wide-awake. She knows exactly who I am. There's no blank pause while you have to explain who you are. She sounds absolutely delighted to hear my voice. I apologize for phoning so late and explain what's happened.

"Give me a moment," she says, unfazed. "Let me get my laptop up and running. Please hold." Music comes down the line, spilling soft, soothing notes into my ear. Everything's going to be all right.

Amy's awesome. Once the writing appeared on the dinky, blackboard-paint wall of Hampers, I made an appointment to see someone at Clarkson's Careers and—lucky day in six months of disastrous ones—I ended up with Amy. Imagine Oprah, but Asian, with a chignon, and you've got Amy. She's calm, professional and immaculate. She puts the world to rights—that's if it could ever get to wrongs with Amy in it.

The music gives way to a bit of promo. "Clarkson's Careers is here to help *you*. Give us your problems, and we will solve them. Relax, while we partner you with the perfect solution for your care requirements."

"Bear with me," Amy says, super-calm.

"Whether your loved one requires live-in or live-out care, professional nursing or merely a caring, responsible companion, we are here to meet your *every* need."

"One moment."

Music again, then, "Contact us now, without delay and put your mind at rest—"

Amy wails. I almost drop the phone. Amy is so *not* a wailer.

"Hello?" I say. "Amy? Hello?"

"God!" she cries. "I am *so* sorry. Sorry, sorry, sorry!"

"What?" I know what. My sweet old lady friend dissolves—finally and forever—into the mist along with her little dog. I miss them badly.

"Just a moment."

How long is a moment? How much is this call costing? I hear the furious tapping of laptop keys. Lucas gets up, tosses his beer bottle onto the foothills of the recycling mountain and goes to the fridge for a second one. He stands at the sink, tapping the neck of the bottle against his chin, one hand sunk in his jeans' pocket, staring at the mountain range of dirty dishes.

"I have *totally* fucked up." Amy groans. "Totally. I had such a crap day that day you and Lucas exchanged contracts. I knew something would go wrong. I knocked someone off their bicycle on the way to work that day. No damage done, and he admitted it was one hundred percent his fault, but it *really* tipped me. Worse, come lunchtime, I get a call from my hubby telling me he'd been bloody retrenched. Then, a call from my son's school to say he'd been suspended for selling cigarettes. It's not professional to let these things intrude, but it was just one of those ghastly days when everything, *everything*, went wrong. And now this comes along to haunt me."

OMG, Amy swears? Amy has a life? A messy life, a bit like mine? Amy has *problems*?

"Look," I say, "it's not a big issue." How, exactly, did that remark arise?

"It isn't? Thank God! Will you be able to help Lucas out? He's a great guy, honestly, our best client."

I hesitate. Amy, during the worst time in my life, made me feel like I could rule the world—my pearl-crammed oyster—from a gilded balcony; all this through the humble calling of care, while paying off my sordid debts. She made me feel like a rare, precious resource, like my total failure at Hampers was a mere, yet necessary stepping stone to greater and glorious things. She never looked at me like the bank manager did. She complimented me, built me up when I'd felt like a sorry drudge. Amy made me feel better about *me*. Because of all this, because it's Amy, who also has a life, who is normal, I say, "Yes, I'll do it. No problem."

For a moment, I'm sure she's fainted, but her voice comes back, wobbly. "I'd better speak to Lucas."

I hand him the phone, confused. What have I done? More important, why? I'm regretting it already. But I won't go back on my word because I'm not stumbling, again, on something that's behind me.

Lucas chats away to Amy, smiling like they're the best old mates, smiling until his eyes crease so much he's got deep crinkle-grooves way past his cheekbones. I can't follow what he's saying, his back's half-turned now, and he's wandered to the far end of the room, talking softly. He looks pretty happy with himself, one way or another. Me? I'm wondering what the hell I've let myself in for.

"Right." Lucas hangs up and drops the phone on the table. He rummages in a pile of papers on the counter next to the fridge and comes back to the table with a red file.

"Lis's program, day by day. Emergency numbers, various contacts, all the info you'll need. Any questions?" He checks his watch.

I bend my head to the file. Poor little Alice. She's already at school five mornings a week and has after-school activities on three of those five days. Art, tennis—*tennis?*—and Green Club. Is Lucas a tiger-dad?

"What's Green Club?" I ask.

"A nature group thing run by the school. They go

on mini-hikes, learn about the environment, collect stuff. Lis is mad about it."

"No more than two play-dates per week," I read.

"There's a list of Lis's special friends and their numbers on the next page."

"Does Alice go to their homes, or do they come here?"

He hesitates a fraction. "She always goes to their houses."

I look around the kitchen. If I were a mother I'd probably worry about my child coming here and catching something. It's hardly hygienic. Blame me for working in the food industry. I know about health and safety.

"What day does the cleaner come?" I ask.

He looks straight at me. Do you get brown diamonds? Because that's what his eyes are—smoky-topaz gems. They're large for a man, but deep set, so, at first, you don't notice their size and colour. It's more of a gradual discovery. Heavy lashes cast shadows, deepening the darkness.

"Cleaner?" he says. "There's no cleaner."

I sit back in my chair. This seems like a pretty big house. "So…" I wave a hand at the kitchen.

"I'll fix this up before I go."

"And the rest of the house?"

He shrugs. "Lis and I pick up as we go along. There's nothing to do, really." He smiles and the brown diamonds sparkle. "Leave the doors open. Let the wind blow through."

"I'm not cleaning this house."

"You don't have to."

I like to live, and prepare food and—lately—care

for a four-year-old in a clean environment. It's a prerequisite.

He clocks the way I'm looking at him. "If you can get anyone to come up here and clean this place, good on you." He holds out a card. "Here. It's a debit card. Cash, basically. Use it for household expenses and—" he grins, but it's a mocking kind of grin—"that cleaner you're going to find." He grabs a pen off the counter and scribbles the pin code in the front cover of the file. "Anything else? I must go pack."

"Do's and don'ts regarding Alice? Anything specific?"

"The usual. It's all in here." He taps the file.

Usual? I have no idea. I mean if I were looking after a dear old lady, she could tell me these things. Can Alice do that? I flip the pages in the file, scanning.

• Brush teeth after meals
• Maximum one hour of TV per day
• Two bedtime stories and lights out by seven thirty

And so on. It's common sense, really. My eyes fall on the last page, the very last item on the list, typed in capital letters. I read it aloud: "NB. ALICE MAY NOT GO TO THE COVE. THE COVE IS OUT OF BOUNDS."

I look up. "What's the cove?"

He looks through me. "The private beach below the house. Bonny drowned there."

I frown. Bonny? Another dead person?

"Bonny. My wife."

"I'm sorry. It must be very dangerous."

"Was for her." He pauses, opens his mouth to say something else, clams up, thinks a moment, and then goes for it. "You should know...you should know some people in this town think I killed her."

I wait for him to say *I didn't*.

He doesn't.

"Why?" I ask.

He rubs his eyes that way he does, like he's clearing his vision, like he's a man so tired he can't see straight. "Did you eat anything tonight?"

"No."

He goes to switch on the oven and open the freezer. I hear the crack and crunch of ice as he rifles through the contents. He pulls out a couple of pizzas and prises them out of their frozen boxes. While the grill heats, he loads a few more things into the already over-full dishwasher and switches it on. He slides the pizzas into the oven, pulls a third beer out of the fridge, pops the lid and places it on the table.

"More wine?"

My glass is half-empty. Or is it half-full? "No thank you. Can I help?"

He looks at me, calculating something, and then he picks up his beer and pulls at the label with a fingernail while the kitchen fills with the smell of an oven that hasn't been cleaned in a long, long time.

Why? There must be good reason, but the moment's gone. He's not answering that question. He leans against the counter and picks, picks, picks at the label, lost in thought, easing the corner off the glass.

The oven's smoking. He switches it off, slides the pizzas onto plates and brings them to the table. They cool for a minute or two, during which time we don't talk. In the uneasy silence—or is that just me?—he slices pizza into equal wedges. Judging by his expertise, something tells me there's too much pizza eaten in this house.

Who knows why, indeed? Why would you murder someone by drowning them? I'm not an expert, but surely that's one of the messiest, noisiest ways to kill somebody? Would Amy know anything about this? Is it the best idea in the world to be sharing a house with a possible murderer? As long as he doesn't murder me, I suppose. Anyway, murderers are shoved in jail, so it's likely a rumour.

"Help yourself," he says.

I take a slice and nibble, ignoring the calorie intake. The silence stretches.

My phone rings. It vibrates across the table. It's Holly, checking up on me. "Hey, Jazz!" Whoops, it's on speaker. "You sounded very low, in your text." I fumble with the keyboard to mute the call, spreading cheese. "I wasn't! I'm not! Everything's great. Awkward to talk now. Let's talk tomorrow." I ring off.

He's looking at me, pizza wedge drooping at the point, halfway to his mouth.

"Jazz?"

"A nickname."

"Why are you low, Jazz?" He eats the slice in three bites, watching me.

I hesitate. Here is a man, a single father, whose wife is dead, whose mother is dead, and who surely, whatever happened, carries a burden of loneliness, sorrow, guilt and regret. Trouble shadows his eyes. Eyes that are as dark now as one of those brown sugar crystals you get on a stick—in posh Italian cafés in West London—right after you've dipped it in black coffee. "I'm not low. Perhaps a little homesick, that's all."

He pushes his plate away, folds his arms on the table and leans closer to me. "I'm sorry. I hope it passes soon. And I hope you like Lobster Cove."

If nothing else, murder is off the agenda. However, there's bound to be gossip down in town. I'll get Sally to elaborate, after all she let slip.

We finish, not saying much, apart from the odd stuff about Alice and various housekeeping issues.

He talks me through the keys. "These are the important ones. Keys for my Jeep, the back door key and—" he singles out a strange, long, curved key and holds it up. "—don't lose this one. It's the only one. There used to be a second, but it's lost." His voice cracks.

"What's it for?"

He clears his throat. "The sea horse door."

"The what?"

"The front door. It's a special design with a unique lock. There's not a locksmith in the world, apparently, who can make a replica."

"I'll take great care of it," I promise, smothering a yawn. I'm more than ready for bed.

"Anything else?"

"Um, can I do anything?" I survey the kitchen, doubtful. Frankly, I wouldn't know where to start.

He stands up, hands on hips, and looks at me. "You must be beat. Go to bed."

"Are you sure?"

"Go on. Up the stairs, turn right and it's the third room left, next to Lis's." He turns away to tackle the recycling pile.

I tramp up the stairs, defeated. Meet me—business owner to babysitter in a few short weeks.

Chapter Three

Bam! Bam! "I'll be back in forty."

Whazzat? I sit up, startled and disorientated. Who's that American shouting in my dream, bashing on my door? Mmmh, right, I remember. Four is to seventy-four as Lis is to Liz. I hear Lucas—I suppose—bounding down the stairs and the resounding crash of a front door slamming in a house with hardly any furniture. I guess that means I'm on duty. I look at my phone to check the time. Six a.m. On a Sunday.

However rudely, I have—glory be—woken in heaven. I fell asleep last night in this giant double bed with the inside shutter-things open because I couldn't find any curtains and was too pooped to wrestle with the hooks and hinges once I'd pinched my finger on the first attempt. Now, tempted by the bright, golden light streaming into the room, I get out of bed and go to the window.

Oh.

The drippy mist's gone, and the sun's coming up over the sea. The sky is pink and gold, and the sea is silver. It's possibly the most beautiful sight I have *ever* seen. I open the window to the fresh, cool, salt air and the sound of surf on rocks and that first-day-of-holiday sensation fills me with such excitement I break out in goose bumps. A deep breath brings a warm rush of memories—rock pooling with my grandparents at

Belcroute Bay, on Jersey, in the Channel Islands.

But holiday it isn't. I wallow for a moment, turn away from the window, and go next door to Alice's room, still in darkness. She's fast asleep on her tummy, legs and arms splayed, toys and books all over the bed. I walk away quietly. Better shower and get dressed before she wakes up. When does she wake up? I wonder if there's a child-rearing book somewhere in the house? Something tells me there isn't.

Half an hour later—showered, hair washed, dressed—I'm finishing my unpacking when a movement in the doorway catches my eye. It's Alice in her blue pyjamas, carrying a storybook.

"Good morning, Alice," I say, in my best, bright voice. "What's that you've got?"

She holds out the book. "Story?"

Is it story time? I thought bedtime was story time. I read in bed at night, but then again I read on the train, at the bus stop, in the bath and everywhere in between, so I reckon six-thirty in the morning is as good a time as any for a body to read.

"Okay." I take the book. Alice climbs on the bed I've just made, pulls back the duvet, bringing the cushions with her, tosses them about into a crooked pile against the headboard, wriggles under the bedding and tells me to get in.

I do, and it occurs that I haven't been in bed, fully clothed at six-thirty in the morning, since my student days. Alice, shy, kneels next to me, a skinny little knee poking through a hole in her pants.

"What's this?" I put a fingertip on her kneecap.

"Broken," she says, mournfully, stroking the frayed fabric.

"Shall we mend it?"

She nods, smiling, eyes huge and bright and happy, and pushes the book toward me.

It's *Winnie the Witch*, and I *adore* Winnie. I could be her, no problem. She's got a fabulous house and hair not dissimilar to mine. She's so together it's not fair. Magic helps, of course. We read the story about how she offends Wilbur—her black cat—by making him rainbow-coloured because she keeps tripping over him in her black house and falling down the stairs. Alice absorbs the story like it's the first time she's heard it, but I can see it's a well-read, well-loved book, falling apart at the binding.

"Shall we fix this too?" I run my fingers up and down the battered spine, after we've read the book three times.

"And pyjamas." She smiles at me, puts her arms around my neck and hugs. "More story?"

"Have you got another one? Another *Winnie* book?"

She jumps off the bed and runs out of the room. I wait, staring through the window at the blue sky, listening to the sound of the sea.

I could do with a little magic in my life.

Alice's back with an armful of books, dropping one on the floor with every step. She climbs into bed, dumps the remainder on my lap and we read, showing each other Winnie's hat, her stripy stockings, her pointy toes, her curly eyelashes and Wilbur's whiskers, which Alice calls "whispers."

"Must fetch friends," she says, when we have read every book. She scrambles out of bed and runs to her room.

I get up and look through the window. There's a solitary runner on the distant shore, coming closer. Lucas. He's leaving today, enjoying the last of beautiful Maine before he holes up—I imagine a narrow, steel-walled cabin in a rig like a storm-tossed lobster trap bobbing on the vicious ocean, with no landscape to love, incarcerated between dark, hostile skies and spitting seas. How can he leave this? How can he leave Alice? Why?

He disappears behind the low headland to the east of the house. Is that the location of forbidden cove? Does he spend time there, reflecting on the tragedy that changed his and Alice's lives forever? No, not today, because he's popped up on the lawn—or whatever you call the shaggy half acre or so of wild and weedy grass between the house and the sea. He's in good shape, is Lucas Dalton. I force my imagination into neutral. My mind blank, I merely witness the fitness until he disappears from sight, pulling back from the window as he approaches the big porch along the front of the house. I wouldn't want him to see me.

"Who are you waiting for?"

I jump. Turning, I see Alice, arms full of teddies, bunnies and a knitted sea horse with stuffing oozing out of a hole in his tail.

"Get in bed," she says. "We not finished."

I obey. Seconds later Lucas strides past my wide-open bedroom door, head back, downing a carton of juice as he goes.

"Daddy," Alice says, without looking up, arranging her toys around the bed.

We turn our attention back to Winnie and are halfway through a repeat routine when Lucas roars,

"*Alice?*" I look up at the doorway. He sounds terribly close, and cross.

With a little shriek, Alice dives under the duvet. A moment's silence. I'm not sure what to do.

"Lis?" he calls.

Smothered giggle way down in my bed.

He lowers his voice to a menacing rumble. "Lis, are you hiding from me?"

She flings back the bedding. "Yes, Daddy! I hiding in Lara bed!"

Oh.

"Well then, I'll just have to come and look for you." He steps through the door.

Wow. Showered, not very big towel around his waist, he comes into the room, stands at the end of my bed, raises his eyebrows at the squirming lump under the duvet, puts his hands on his hips, and says, "Hmmm. I wonder where Alice is? Could she be under the bed?" He bends to look. "Nope." He turns to face the window. "Behind the shutters? Nope." He winks at me. Oh my eyes, he looks naughty. His hair, wet, is up in dark spikes, his frankly mind-blowing shoulders speckled with drops of water. "I think," he goes on, "I think Lis is *in Lara's suitcase.*"

Squeal from deep in the bed.

He rushes across the room, rattles my suitcase. "Hmmmm," he says slowly. "Not there. Hmmmm. Lara, do *you* know where Lis could be? She has to get dressed real quick."

I shrug. "I actually haven't seen Alice for a while." I pull the duvet up to my chin, fists clenched.

"I don't believe you." He grins, his eyes gleaming like a hungry wolf's. "What's that in your bed?" The towel slips. He grabs it, folds it around his waist and tucks the end back in.

The bedding heaves as Alice rolls herself into a tight ball. She's laughing now, barely able to catch her breath.

"Um, I think it's a…a little mouse," I say, my heart beating in my throat.

"A little mouse! If there's a little mouse in your bed, I'm going to have to catch it because I'm very, *very* hungry."

"Nooooooo, Daddy!"

Lucas lunges. We are doomed.

"Waaaah!" he roars, throwing back the bottom of the duvet, exposing the both of us—lucky I got dressed. "Waaaah!" He grabs Alice's kicking feet and drags her off the bed, toys flying everywhere. "Oooh, yumyumyum," he growls. "What tasty bit shall I eat first?"

Shrieking with laughter, Alice can't fight Lucas's strength. "Help me, Laraaaa, help meeee!"

I abandon her, and reverse up the pillows piled against the headboard. There's a kind of exquisite terror. Also, I'm very ticklish and Lucas is tickling Alice, making *me* laugh. I can feel it everywhere.

"Help," she shrieks.

"I can't!" I wouldn't know how. My knees are under my chin, clamped to my body with both arms.

"Come on, Lis," Lucas says. "I'll eat you in the bedroom while we get dressed." He picks her up, slings her over his shoulder in a fireman's lift and lets her slide down his back. He carries her out of the room, by the feet, upside down. She's giggling so hard I'm surprised she doesn't wet herself. I grit my teeth as her head swings wildly, missing the doorframe by a half a hair's breadth.

And oops, there goes the towel. Clearly, Lucas dives in warm waters for a large part of the year. There's no white bum revealing the size of his swimming trunks. He's nicely tanned, all over.

They go off, down the passage. "Do it to Lara, Daddy! Do it to Lara! Eat Lara too," Alice begs.

"Not now, sweetheart. I'll eat her later."

"Why? Why?"

"Because I won't have room for breakfast if I eat both of you now."

Their voices fade, Alice laughs again, delighted at something her daddy has said. I slide off the pillows and stretch out on my ruined bed. For a moment I lie on my back, hands behind my head and listen to the thump of my heart, my mouth curving in a smile. I'm glad I didn't flounce out last night. This will be way more fun than looking after an older person, no offence. Lucas is, well, nice—let's leave it at that for now. Alice is adorable and her cuteness will more than make up for what I'm missing by not being a companion to an intellectual grand old dame of Maine. There's potential for great happiness in this house. It's everywhere, in spite of the shadows, waiting for the right moment to come out.

I hope.

Chapter Four

Breakfast. There's absolutely nothing apart from milk in the fridge and some sugary cereal in one of the cupboards. Someone—it had to be Lucas—has been shopping and dumped a bag on the kitchen table. I look inside. Doughnuts and orange juice.

Alice, hair unbrushed, skips in wearing odd socks, a blue smock printed all over with white daisies and a red and green striped cardigan with one button done up. She goes straight to the bag of doughnuts and takes one out. I pass her a plate and ask her to sit at the table.

"Would you like some orange juice, Alice?"

She nods, mouth covered in sticky icing. Like I said, I'm no childcare expert, but I don't think doughnuts constitute an ideal breakfast for a four-year-old.

Here's a positive: while the kitchen remains destroyed, the dishwasher contains a load of clean stuff. I get out a Hello Kitty mug and fill it with juice, handing it to Alice.

"What shall we do today, Alice? Shall we go to the beach later?"

"I show you the oyster tractors."

"Oyster tractors?"

"No. Oyster tractors."

I don't see oyster beds anywhere, so why would we need tractors to pull trailer-loads of oysters? Maybe she means oyster crackers, giant crabs that crack open oysters? Do such creatures exist? Or crackers, like biscuits you eat? *Maybe* she means tractors driven by oysters. Okay, that's rubbish.

"What are oyster tractors, Alice?"

"Birds. Lis means oyster catchers, don't you sweetheart?" Lucas dumps a giant holdall on the kitchen floor. Here is a man ready for long-hauling it to the oil and gas fields of the dark north. On top of the holdall is a fur-lined jacket that would fit King Kong. On the table, that underwater laptop, smartphone, headphones, fat passport with extra pages and a pile of documents.

He pours coffee and knocks it back standing up, going immediately for a second cup. "All okay? Sleep well?" he asks me.

"Yes, thanks."

"Lara was waiting and waiting and *waiting* for you, Daddy, by the window, when you were running." Alice grins at him, and then me, crumbs everywhere.

"She was?" He studies his coffee.

Want to know something? I am not a blusher, but my cheeks ignite. "Ah hahaha," I trill, "I was looking at the view. It's beautiful." None of that is a lie. I wish I could shove my face in a bowl of ice.

"Any questions before I go?" Lucas is looking at me now, but no way am I looking at him.

Yes. To kick off, what am I doing here? "Too many."

There's a bit of a silence, and then he says, "Know something?"

"What?" I ask, eyes down.

"You're a natural."

Is that so?

"Look, it's easy." Lucas reaches for a doughnut. "You have Lis's program."

Is that all there is to childcare? Programming? "But what's the…the essence of a good relationship with a child? How do I reach out and connect?"

He bites into the doughnut, chews and swallows. "Nobody's ever asked me that."

Damn right they haven't, because everybody, up to now, has known what they're jolly well doing!

I wait. He thinks, drinking coffee. Eventually he says, "I guess every kid is different, but, with Lis, tell her what's going to happen, or what you're going to do, and do it. That way she'll always trust you. And always tell her the truth. Other than that, keep to her routine, be strict about manners, bedtime, TV and blasphemy. That's about it."

"Blasphemy?"

"Yeah. I sometimes, you know, make a mistake." He shoots me an apologetic look, a sudden, rich glint in those sombre eyes.

I glance at the sheaf of papers he's shuffling on the table, spotting British Airways First Class boarding passes.

"That's nice," I say.

"Yeah."

I look at him, with envy. Holly and I often discuss what we'd do if we won the lottery: buy a huge house on the beach, have our shoes handmade and always, always, travel First Class. I can't comment on his shoes, but he scores on the other two, lucky, lucky man.

He grins. He's got unusual teeth for an American insofar as, while they're white and healthy, they're a little crooked, each and every one. It's lovely.

"I go First Class because—" he finishes the last of his coffee. "—you can't take your money with you."

"You can't." I agree. I won't have any money to take with me, after the Hampers disaster. Problem solved.

He sits, puts his elbows on the table, rests his chin on clasped hands and looks at me. "The day after I get to Aberdeen, weather permitting, I have to get into a rubberized body bag and fly for three hours in pissing rain and gale-force wind, in a rusty, storm-battered helicopter with grim, silent, oily men. When I look down at that heaving rig, at the tiny, postage-stamp trampoline of a heliport, awash with seawater, without a guardrail, I think, fuck, if I ditch here at least I spent my money on the way, drinking champagne at thirty thousand feet in a leather chair, having fun."

"Quite." What was that about a body bag?

Honk honk. Skeet's here. Lucas digs in his jacket pocket and hands me a folded cheque. "The Morgan Bank in town has a series of post-dated cheques for you. Go see them about an account."

That's a quaint way to bank in this day and age. I pocket the cheque without looking at it. "Thank you, and, um, don't worry about anything. Everything will be fine here."

"I know."

We go outside. Lucas dumps his stuff in the boot of the Chevy, picks up Alice and hugs her tight. "Goodbye, sweetheart. You be a good girl now, see?"

"Bye, Daddy!" she chirps, happy as you like.

He is not happy. It's really, really hard for him to leave her. Why, why does he do this? A lonely man, leaving his daughter alone. I swallow the soppy lump that's gathered in my throat and watch the softness in his eyes as he lowers her to the ground and goes down on his haunches, straightening her dress, re-buttoning her lopsided cardigan. "I love you, sweetheart."

Skeet's back in the car, engine running, seatbelt on.

"Love you, Daddy," Alice says. "Now kiss Lara."

I smile. He gets to his feet and I hold out a hand for him to shake. He takes it and leans in for a formal peck on the cheek. We press faces and air kiss.

"No, Daddy, silly. Kiss properly, and cuddle!"

He lets go my hand and looks down at her. "I did."

Her face falls. "Didn't, Daddy. You must, or Lara will be very sad."

Lucas looks at me, shrugs and holds out his arms. "C'mon, Lara Jasmine Layla, cuddle time!" We hug. He's laughing, but as his arms go around me I can feel, against his chest, that he's trying not to cry.

We break apart. I look at the ground, blinking my own tears. This is absolutely, ridiculously, over-the-top sentimental. Lucas must go now. I grab Alice's hand and step back, well back, into the small porch at the front door—the one Lucas calls the sea horse door.

He's standing by the taxi, feeling his pockets, thoughtful. Out comes the set of keys he showed me last night. He looks at them for a moment, rubbing a thumb over the oddly-shaped key. "Let me not forget to give you these." He flashes a brave smile that shoots a squiggle through my stomach. "All the keys. You'll need those." He tosses them in my direction. I lunge and miss. They clatter to the ground, scaring Buster.

I pick them up. "Bye now, Lucas. Take care."

Alice waves. "Love you, Daddy!"

Lucas gets into the car. "Be in touch every day, okay? Email's best."

"I will," I say.

"All my details are in the red file."

Skeet, thank the gods of each and every universe in our solar system and beyond, puts the Chevy in drive and rolls away through the gate.

"Daddy?" Alice, plaintive, puts a finger in her mouth.

I pick her up. "Wave, sweetheart, wave!" We wave until Lucas's big hand, waving high over the roof of the car, is obscured by the trees on the drive. All of a sudden, it's very quiet in the vacuum of departure. We can't hear the sea from this side of the house. Nothing moves, nothing happens until a bird lands close to our feet, and takes off immediately, with a cheep of alarm.

Alice points. "Look! Buster."

Praise the Lord for Buster, truly. He waddles back out of the house, and I make much of him. Together, Alice and I shoo the bird to further safety while Buster lies on the bottom step of the porch and eyes us with hungry misgiving, like he'll never eat again.

I ask Alice to show me around. The pinks, golds, and silvers of early morning have been overrun by blue, blue, and more magnificent blue. We wander right around the house in the sunshine, holding hands, Buster following. The house, viewed from the scruffy garden from a little distance, my back to the sea, is a great, gracious, magical pile of mellow grey-blue planks—clapboard, clinker? I don't know the name. It's the same colour as the Paul Revere house, and the Witch House in Salem, that I visited only last week, but the windows are bigger, the doors wider, and there are square porches and stoops and balconies, even a cupola, but square. Above and behind the house, there's a hill cloaked in dark pines. Here and there, big roofs of what I'm sure are grand old Maine mansions stand clear above the trees. Turning, I look at the sea, the view that must be visible from every south-facing room in Blue Rocks—that immense blue sky underscored with a bright pewter band of ocean. It's glorious.

"Look, Lara, look!" Alice tugs my hand, pulling me around to face the house again, pointing to something on the roof.

I shade my eyes. A weather vane.

"It's a mermaid," Alice says.

It is. It's a mermaid curled around a trident. Only, it looks more like a mermaid *pierced* by a trident. If this were my house, I wouldn't change much, but I'd change that.

****

Later, when we're home from the beach, Alice falls asleep on her bed, browsing through her pile of Winnie books. Is she supposed to sleep now? I have no idea. The program says nothing about an afternoon nap. I call my sister Julie on Skype. "How long does a four-year-old sleep?" I ask, when I've explained what I'm doing in the first place with a four-year-old.

She yawns. "I have no idea. God knows, but I hope it's more than me."

"Oh, right. How are you feeling?"

"Don't ask," she groans. "I'm exhausted. During the day I can't stay awake, and I can't sleep at night. All I can eat is chocolate ice cream. I've burst out of all my clothes. I can't wait for this pregnancy to be over, so things can get back to normal."

Normal? What is that? I look around the half-sorted kitchen, at the colourful Kilimanjaro of washing tumbling through the laundry room door, at the books and toys strewn across the floor. I think about the bookshop jumble of documents, plans and sketches in Lucas's office, the bare house, and the gone-wild, run-to-seed garden outside the tall windows—and ponder *normal*.

We chat about this and that: her blood pressure, nausea, and back pain, and after about half an hour she tells me she needs to take a nap. Well, that would be about six p.m. in the UK, so things are back-to-front if you ask me. We ring off. Come to think of it, I'm pretty sleepy too. A little delayed jetlag, a week partying in New York, and a few hours in the sun will do this to a person.

But there'll be no nap for me. There's work to do. I'm not on holiday. I drink a glass of iced water and get started on the kitchen. It takes me an hour to clean up. Funny, there's no way I'd normally do something like this—I like to stick to a job description and as far as the Blue Rocks job goes, I've deviated quite enough, thank you very much—but I don't mind doing it. After all, it's me who's got to live in the house.

And there's still no food. That aside, the soap I used in the shower this morning is so brittle and cracked it could be prehistoric, never mind the three sheets of loo paper dangling on a battered roll. We'll have to go shopping as soon as Alice's awake.

I move through the house, straightening what little there is to straighten, and wiping down the guest loo and upstairs bathrooms. If I were the stay-at-home mum of Alice, at this moment, in this house, life would hardly be normal! Quite apart from anything, I can see life is going to be really busy. I'm referring to the physical side. As far as the emotional side goes, of caring for lovable, delightful Alice, I worry I haven't got what it takes. Has Julie got any idea what's heading her way?

In the end, it's easy. Alice wakes the minute I come inside from pegging out a load of washing, and says she's hungry, so—leaving the food desert of Blue Rocks—we go to town. First, I acquaint myself with Lucas's dark blue Jeep thingy, which is totally ridiculous. It's as wide as a combine harvester with a double "cab"—as Alice informs me—furnished with deep leather seats and all things luxury. It has the words *Trailhawk* and *Renegade* on the rear, but I've no idea what it is, apart from a four-by-four vehicle of whatever origin. The back is so big you could fill it with water and keep a whale there. I suggest this to Alice, and she decides it's a brilliant idea. You could go to the moon in this thing, whale and all. Luckily, there's an instruction book because I have no idea how to turn it on, and luckily, I've driven my parents around Spain on the wrong side of the road, and surely the airbags on this thing would be nothing less than the arms of Jesus.

We kick off at Maggie's Diner, with Sandwich of the Day—I have to scrape some of the basil pesto off Alice's—plus apple juice, and watch the Lobster Cove world go by for an hour or so. Alice insists on keeping some panini crust.

"For Queenie to eat, Lara."

"Who is Queenie?"

"A chicken."

"Where does Queenie live?"

"At the gas station!" she exclaims, like that's the silliest question ever.

Lunch over, we go back to the Jeep, and I drive the long way around town, to see what's what and where, before going to the grocery store on First Street to stock up on basics. That done, we go home, but as I'm turning right off Main Street, to head north out of town along the bay to Blue Rocks, Alice says, "Stop, Lara, stop. Pleeease. Queenie's gas station!"

I turn into the forecourt and stop. Jay's Automotive—repairs to all makes and models—has a clearly demarcated way in and, likewise, a way out. In between those, a white picket fence with a little gate encloses the husk of an old Model T Ford, without doors, painted powder blue and hung with baskets of petunias and fuchsias, drawing the eye away from the modern petrol pumps in front of the station. Inside the car several chickens with scarlet combs and beaks, and black and white barring, a bit like guinea fowl, peck about, looking impossibly picturesque. Alice retrieves the crust from the pocket of her dress and, arm stretched between the pickets, crumbles it on the ground much to the delight of Queenie, I presume, who most definitely rules the roost, strutting with confident grace to peck elegantly at the offerings.

A man comes out of the workshop in ancient white overalls done over by Picasso in every shade of grey, black and brown. "Hiya, Alice. You wanna egg?"

Alice, shy, hangs back, an arm around my leg.

"C'mon! Queenie laid this morning, and she'd sure like you to have one of her eggs for supper."

He ducks into the old blue Ford and holds up a large brown-pink egg, smooth as a beach pebble. "Hold out both ya hands, Alice."

She does, and he gives her the egg like he's handling fine china.

"Careful now," he says.

She nods, eyes shining.

"What's the magic word, Alice?" I ask.

"Thank you, Jay. Can Molly come and play?"

The man glances at me. I remember the name Molly Sawyer on Alice's list of special friends in the red file.

"I'm Lara Fairmont," I say. "Alice's nanny."

"Jay Sawyer." He doesn't offer his hand. Maybe it's greasy. "Is Dalton away?"

Dalton? "He is, yes."

"How long for?"

"About six weeks. Would Molly like to come home from school with us on Wednesday?"

He hesitates. "Sure. Okay." He rests a hand on Alice's head. Did he mean to say no?

We say more thank-yous for Queenie's beautiful egg and leave. Alice won't give up the egg so I strap her into her car seat, telling her to hold it tight, yet not tight, hoping the Jesus airbags will do the trick if sudden braking is required.

The rest of the way home I run the day's experiences through my mind. Maggie, owner of the diner, was sweet to us. There's no ulterior attitude there. Helen at the grocery store came across as remote—but perhaps she's always like that. Sawyer was reluctant. Is it because I'm a stranger, or is it to do with Lucas? Am I working for the black sheep of Lobster Cove, the pariah? Do people hold back?

Or maybe they're not used to me yet in Lobster

Cove because I'm an outsider. I'm foreign and talk funny.

I hope it's only that.

Chapter Five

The clear blue afternoon darkens, and rain spatters the windscreen. By the time we get home it's pouring. A sudden squall rattles along the cliffs, passing as fast as it arrived. The sun comes back, bathing the clean-rinsed world in mellow afternoon light. Alice and I are out on the sea porch admiring the golden sparkles on the water when I remember the washing. I bring it inside, cross with myself. What the hell use is that? All that trouble to hang washing in the sunshine and then to bring it in wetter than it started out. There's a brand new tumble dryer in the laundry, but it's still crated. Briefly, I consider breaking it open but unfold the drying rack instead and peg the sodden items to that. That'll do.

Alice has her egg, scrambled, for supper, along with green beans, carrots and some cucumber and tomato salad.

"I never tasted this." She points to everything except the egg.

"What does Daddy cook for you?" I ask.

"Pizza."

I thought so. Although, taut and toned Lucas is living proof that a pizza and beer diet has merits. Mmm.

After supper we go upstairs and run Alice's bath, adding liberal amounts of bubble bath. She spends ages playing in the water and chatting to me and her bath toys until, eventually, the bubbles melt away and it's time to get out.

"Where are red pyjamas?" She glances at the yellow and pink ones I've laid out on her bed.

"You mean the blue ones you had on yesterday?"

She nods, watching my face with worried eyes.

"I washed them today, Alice, so they're wet."

"But I want them."

"You can have them tomorrow."

"I want them!"

"Tomorrow. You can have them tom—"

She bursts into tears, and this is an understatement. It's more a tantrum of profound grief, an anthem of heartbreak.

Alarmed to say the least, I try to gather her in my arms but she fights me.

"Want my red pyjamas."

"Alice. Alice! *Alice.*" Eventually I break through the vicious cycle of full-on weeping. "Be quiet and you can have your pyjamas. I'll make a plan."

Now what have I said? She looks at me, everything streaming. I dry her face with a towel unable to meet the unbearable distress in her eyes.

"First…" I hold up the rejected pink and yellow pyjamas, you must put these on."

She won't.

"Just for now, Alice. Then we can go downstairs to see if your blue pyjamas are dry."

She won't, and that's definite.

I think, fast and wild. "What about one of my tee-shirts? That will be fun!"

"No."

What now? Shall I take her in the damp towel?

And what are we going to look for anyway? The pyjamas are still wet, wet, wet. I know it.

"Okay then. What about one of Daddy's tee-shirts?"

She considers this and nods her head. Phew. We're hardly progressing through this crisis in leaps and bounds, but here is a glimmer of hope.

We go into Lucas's room, and Alice shows me where he keeps his tee-shirts. "You choose one," I suggest.

"Red one." She points to a black one and I pull it out of the pile, shake it open and put it on her before she changes her mind. Of course it's vast, pooling around her feet, slipping off her shoulders. I bunch the fabric in her hands and she follows me back to my bedroom, tripping up like a desolate baby penguin. It breaks my heart, even though she's stopped crying. The large safety pin I find, left discarded in the bottom of my suitcase is a godsend. I don't know how it got there, but it's been there forever, like a weird kind of talisman and now I know why. It's a sign that life may possibly return to normal, one day. I use the pin to make the tee-shirt neckline smaller for Alice, hooking up the back hem like a mini bustle.

"Let's take a picture to show Daddy." I take out my phone, take a picture of Alice drowning in Lucas's tee-shirt, and send it to Lucas's email address with the title *Blue Pyjamas Disaster*. Alice even manages a watery smile.

That done, I say, "Let's go and have a look in the laundry room. Let's go see how your pyjamas are doing."

We hold hands and go downstairs. As I thought,

the pyjamas are wet. In fact I'm pretty sure they are *wetter.*

"Alice, I think you must sleep in Daddy's tee-shirt tonight." I show her how wet the pyjamas are.

"Noooo!"

What now? I glance at the crated dryer. "Does Daddy have tools?" If I'm going to break into that baby, I'll need more than a teaspoon.

Alice shakes her head.

Uh-oh. "Does he have a hammer?"

"Yes."

"Let's go and get it, shall we?"

She takes me into Lucas's studio and shows me a cupboard at the far end containing man-stuff.

"Oh, Daddy has many tools! Look at these lovely hammers, Alice. These will help us get your pyjamas dry."

She nods, but her forlorn eyes convey the message that I have let her down badly, that it might take forever to deserve forgiveness.

I select my weapon and we go back to the dryer. I put Alice on the counter, well out of harm's way, and attack. It's like prising a reluctant oyster from its shell. I use the opposite side of the hammer—that double-pronged thingy, to haul huge metal staples forth, screaming, from splintery wood, straight into my splintery hands. My nails split. I break out in a sweat, but I'm on it. I will do this. Eventually, I expose the back of the machine. Yay, cord and plug. We're on the home straight, except there's no way I can shift the machine by myself, or can I? Because the plug won't reach the wall-socket. I face my nemesis, pushing and shoving, ramming it with my hip, my other hip, even my bum—at least it makes Alice laugh—until the plug can be plugged in.

Done. I cut the thick plastic away from the front of the machine and twiddle the dials. In seconds, the machine's going with the pyjamas inside, the lonesome remaining buttons pinging against the drum. We are not exactly saving the planet by putting a tiny set of pjs into a tumble dryer on the hottest setting, but when needs must, the devil drives. I'm going to put Alice to bed now, phone Julie, and have a big glass of wine. Except I'm not. She won't be left. In the end after much—failed—cajoling that only makes her cry all over again, I get into bed and cuddle her. After a while, her sobs turn to hiccoughs, her breathing evens out and she goes heavy in my arms. Asleep. Asleep and peaceful at long last, poor little thing. I stroke her back, murmuring "Shhh, shhh," again and again until she is fast asleep.

Alice has framed photos on the shelf next to her bed, and I gaze at them in the half-dark while she sleeps, her face pressed into my neck. They're all of her and Lucas—one when she was a baby, one at about a year old, she with a ponytail on the very top of her head, the hair falling outwards like leaves of a pineapple, he with suntan, shades and a big grin, and so on. He's nice. I could like him. A person, a woman, could love that sort of man, they could. Coupled with what little I know, I can see the type of man he is. A keeper, as Holly would say, I bet. There are several more photos, always the two of them, Alice and Lucas, hugging each other, father and daughter. Alone.

Why no pics of Mummy? Why no mention? Alice never mentions. What would I say if she did? I'm certainly not going to mention. There's no evidence of

Mummy anywhere, no reference, no clues. Whatever, I'll steer well clear of the subject. I'd hate to risk releasing another torrent of despair. What would that be like, given the pyjama anguish? I close my eyes, emotionally exhausted. I'm tired, arms and back aching from carrying Alice. She shifts, moves her head and snuggles closer, if that's possible, her light breath warm on my shoulder. I don't think about it, but it's there…the fragrance of Lucas all around me, that clean man smell when I opened the closet door and placed my hand on the cool cotton of the tee-shirt pile.

Ah. Ooh. Pins and needles. My arm's numb. Where? What? I try to sit up, but Alice is lying on my arm. The Hello Kitty clock next to her bed says 02h30. I extricate myself, taking care not to wake Alice, but no worries on that score—she's like a big ragdoll. She flops onto her pillow. I cover her and go to bed.

If I weren't so tired, I'd ring Julie and tell her how tired I am.

Chapter Six

Alice wakes me early, a good half hour before my alarm is set to go off. It's Monday, it's school—and Alice is enthusiastic about school, long may it last.

There's a message from Lucas on my phone, a reaction to the photo I sent. He's not amused, and I get a cryptic little lecture on making a joke out of his child's distress. Like I would do that! I'm at a loss for words, so even if I shouted back at him—which is what I feel like doing—I wouldn't know what to say. I stare at the letters of his text considering my feelings Actually, I'm mortified that he's taken it the wrong way. I look at Alice, curled next to me, studying the detail of a *Winnie the Witch* illustration. I touch her on the shoulder.

"Come here, Alice."

She slides up the pillow next to me and puts her arms around my neck.

"Look up," I tell her. "Smile." I hold the phone at face level and take a selfie.

"Why did you do that?" she asks.

"It's for your daddy."

"Why?"

"To show him how happy we are."

She hugs me tight. "I love you."

"I love you too." It's the truth.

"I love my daddy. Do you love my daddy?"

I take a deep breath, change my mindset to professional, and text the photo to Lucas. *Lucas, I'm really sorry I gave you that impression. Yes, Alice was distraught—"* I close my eyes briefly, quailing at the memory of her sorrow—*"but she was very brave and we trucked through the crisis together. She's so happy this morning in that same tee-shirt of yours, believe it or not, and looking forward to school. It would have helped to know about the blue pyjamas. Sorry again. Hope you have a great day in that hellhole.* I delete the bit about the blue pyjamas and the hellhole and send.

"Do you?"

"Do I what, Alice?"

"Love my daddy?"

I hesitate.

"I love him this much!" She spreads her arms wide.

"That's lovely."

"How much do you love him?"

Not much, right now, although—

"How much, Lara?"

"Um, as much as this pillow here," I say.

"That's small."

"Not very small."

"Small." She stares at me, eyes big and so full of doubt she looks scared.

"I meant the bed," I say quickly. "The whole bed. In fact the whole room, even the house." Please God, no more paroxysms of angst.

"Or the whole world?"

Uh, I'm in the quicksand! "Okay."

My phone chirps. *Okay*, Lucas says.

"Yay!" Alice claps her hands and bounces on her knees on the bed.

Okay what? Okay is more of a positive word—a yes word—than a negative isn't it? Let's hope so.

"Come on." I throw back the bedding and get up. "Up we get or we'll be late."

Subject firmly changed. We get dressed, have a proper breakfast and brush teeth, during which activity Alice asks me why she hasn't got a mummy.

"Because you have a nanny." I don't know what else to say.

"We have to draw our family at school today."

"Well, you can draw Daddy and Buster and you."

"Buster isn't my mummy."

Indeed not.

"What can I draw for Mummy?"

An angel? A butterfly? A fairy? I have no idea.

"What must I draw?"

"Anything beautiful. Anything you love. That will be Mummy. Are you all ready for school now?"

"Yes. I have my backpack, and my lunch and my reading book, and my best panties."

"Always a good idea, sweetheart."

I find my way to the school without a hitch. At the end of our road I do a left and right onto Maple, cross over First and there we are. Mothers and fathers—and nannies, I presume—are taking children right inside the school. We follow suit, and Alice leads me to her classroom where Teacher Pick, round and smiling, hands folded over a pinafore covered in yellow suns and daisies, greets her charges.

"Hello, Alice dear, run along and put your things in your locker!" She looks at me and her smile fades. Hand on throat, she says, "Do we know you?"

"I'm Lara, Alice's new nanny."

Teacher Pick's chins vibrate. She purses her lips, long-suffering. "It would have been real nice of Mr. Dalton to let me know that someone else would be dropping Alice off at school this morning."

"There was a bit of a mix-up. The agency—"

"Lara loves Daddy as big as the whole world," Alice sings out, windmilling her arms and cracking my shins with her backpack in the process.

Teacher Pick's double-take is almost imperceptible, but it's there, nevertheless spectacular. The eyes of respectable parents burn holes in every part of my back.

"You run along, Alice," I say, through teeth gritted for a number of reasons. I bend to kiss her, straighten up with face aflame. I blame Lucas entirely for this embarrassment. If he materialized in front of me, teleported from that wonky old Trident…whatever it's called, I would cheerfully throttle him.

In front of the kids, his own included. Yes, I would.

"We keep a strict list of people with authorized access to our children. You *must* be listed."

"I have the relevant clearance from the child protection authorities if that's what you—"

"Those are not necessarily *our* clearances. It's highly irresponsible. We don't even know you."

I look past her into the sunny schoolyard, where Alice is tumbling about with a friend, best panties on display. "No," I say, and go back to the car, thoroughly reprimanded, passing *listed* custodians on the way. No one meets my eye with even the faintest glimmer of support or sympathy. Pick has clearly got everyone under the whip.

Before I get to the exit, I'm waylaid by a *really* big woman. I take back what I said about Pick. This one makes Pick look merely a little curvy. She's draped in robes and paisley scarves, and emerges from a door off the hallway marked Head.

"Hi," she sings, advancing, with hands outstretched like she's going to read my palm. "I'm Cherri with an I. Cherri Chandler. You must be the new nanny up at Blue Rocks."

"I'm Lara Fairmont." I stand my ground. She advances on a wave of patchouli and takes my extended right hand in both of hers.

"You are soooo welcome, honey. Would you like a cup of tea? Sure you would."

"Er, I don't want to keep you from your class."

"I do infants. They come in half an hour later." She surges around me, beads clanking, bangles ringing, earrings swinging, and spirits me into her office, which looks more like a coffee shop in Marrakech, than the ops room for an educational institution. In a second, we're in velvet armchairs doused in shawls, facing each other over a quaint, inlaid table.

Cherri talks. However, she mostly answers all the questions she asks. It goes like this:

"Did I overhear you falling foul of Ruth Pick? Don't you worry about her. Ruth's a stickler for bureaucracy. A softie at the core. Kids love her. Now why would an English person wanna work in Lobster Cove? I guess it's a nice change. Is this your first time in the US? People travel so much these days it's like the world's one country. How do you take your tea? This has been brewing awhile so it'll be pretty strong." And so on.

There's a glass teapot of hot water, stuffed with sprigs of fresh mint. Cherri lifts the pot and pours from a great height into two ruby tumblers, etched with gold. She reaches down to the side, feeling around for a tin of biscuits in a lacquered Chinese cabinet, and I fish for bits of grit and dead twig while her attention's elsewhere.

"So, Lara…" She tips the biscuits—coconut with a strong smell of rosewater—onto a plate and puts them on the table, pushing them toward me. "What do you know about Blue Rocks? It's not a bad place. Did Lukey prepare you in any way? It's not what you'd call a normal household."

"Lukey?"

She pauses, lowers her lashes and shrugs with one shoulder, coquettish. "Aw, I've known Lucas Dalton since he was a kid. I used to teach him. Of course he's Mr. Big around here these days, but—"

Really? She's known Lucas since he was a kid?

"You okay? You look like you hit a problem, honey."

I smile. "You certainly don't look like someone old enough to have *taught* Mr. Dalton."

"I don't, do I?" She leans close, the old table wobbling under her bulk. "I go to Agat, an old Abenaki woman at Emerald Lake, for my facials and some little—" she lowers her voice to a theatrical whisper— "treatments. Why not? You only live once." She waves a ruby-nailed hand, gemmed knuckledusters sparkling on each finger. "I know we're gonna be friends, so I don't mind telling." She peers at my face, too close, hunting wrinkles. I look away.

She takes the hint and sits back, though not much,

given her size. "What brings you to Maine, honey? You can tell me."

I'm English. I refuse to be set upon and made to tell everything. Besides, that invitation to confide makes me feel like I'm guilty of something. On the other hand, I bet everyone in this town is as tight as fifty sardines in a matchbox, so she's going to find out what she wants to find out without any help from me. I shrug. "Mr. Dalton offered me a good job. I needed, need, the money."

"Mr. Dalton! How formal and cute are you? I *love* that. But why Maine, honey? You're very far from home."

"It's temporary. I'll decide the way forward when Mr. Dalton gets back."

"Did he mention the *situation*?"

"Well, I know he's a widower."

"But did he tell you about—"

"He told me his wife drowned and that some people in Lobster Cove believed he murdered her. Is that what you mean?"

Cherri flinches. "Lucas is real nice in spite of what people say, and think, but things ain't the same up at Blue Rocks since Liz went."

"I gather." I pick up my glass to avoid a refill, and sip. There's definitely sand.

"Things," Cherri goes on, choosing her words with care, "would have been different if she'd been around."

"How different?"

She lowers her voice. "Liz was real refined, both his parents were. Old for parents. Married a while before kids came along. Stalwarts of our community, you know? People didn't dare question justice, such as it was, while they were here, but Lucas's standpoint was questioned again after Liz died, after Lucas's father moved to Florida."

Not fair, if you ask me. "Was there a trial?"

"There was." She nods. "Lucas got off. Insufficient evidence."

"I don't understand why people would question justice if he was innocent—"

"I didn't say he was innocent. I said he got off." Cherri watches me, teapot poised in mid-air. A sudden smile transforms her face. She looks past my shoulder. "Ah." She lowers the pot, relieved.

I turn around. A postman stands in the doorway with a sheaf of envelopes and packages in his arms, saving us both I can't help thinking. I stand up quickly, discarding my tea. "I won't hold you up. Thanks for the chat."

"You come straight back with any questions, or if you need any help. Anytime, honey. We support pupils and their carers unreservedly." She dismisses me gently by turning her smile full beam on the postman, eyebrows raised. "What have you got for us today, Frank?"

I back off, and dash out, straight through the exit, directly to the parking lot and into the Jeep without looking right or left. Sitting there, doors locked for some reason, I sort out my head. I don't want to like him...or, no, I wouldn't *mind* liking him, but...

Hell. Face it. Alice's sweet comments about love this morning got me thinking and feeling around that little niggle of excitement present in my tummy since...

Since Lucas walked out of his house in that Gothic fog and turned those desolate eyes on me, used that

63

deep voice and gave me that strong hand. But, he's no victim. He's a survivor, and that in itself is—

Listen to me! I slap the steering wheel with my palms, twist the key in the ignition and drive away from school. I'm not thinking about this again. Lucas is…he's my boss, I like him, and I don't want to piss him off. That is all.

As for Cherri's comments, I can see she's a real nice person, but she's made me indignant and that indignation seethes all the way back to Blue Rocks. When Lucas said that some people in Lobster Cove thought he had murdered his wife, I had no idea what that actually meant.

I had no idea the debate was alive and so well.

****

What should I do? Nothing, because it's not my business. Back home, on my own for the first time, I explore the house thoroughly, straightening stuff as I go, even to the extent of stripping Lucas's bed. He sleeps in a small room at the end of a narrow passage beyond Alice's room. There are other bedrooms, much bigger. None bigger than mine though. It's clearly the main bedroom where, probably, bad memories lurk.

It's a while until school comes out, but I lock up and head back to town with a copy of *The Lobster Cove Anchor* on the passenger seat. I've circled a few adverts and addresses, and have errands to run. First, I head to the Morgan Bank, the only one in town, to open an account. I'm given forms to fill out, and I'm asked to make a deposit. I take the folded cheque out of my bag and blink. Lucas *has* paid me double. I ask the accounts manager about the other cheques.

"He altered the amounts yesterday." Her smile is so

white and bright I feel the heat. Or is it shock sizzling through me at the amount of money I'm earning for what is an important—but relatively menial—task?

"He did?"

"He did." She taps away at her computer.

"Why post-dated cheques?" I ask, wondering if Lucas is regretting those generous actions, since the blue pyjamas disaster.

"Not much online banking where he goes, Miss Fairmont. He sets up everything beforehand. He prefers it this way."

After a busy fifteen minutes at her keyboard, she tells me my account will be up and running in two to five days. I thank her and leave, walking out into the sunshine, dizzy—like someone who's just won the lottery. I wander around in a daze, looking for buttons for Alice's pyjamas, and thread, and something with which to mend her sea horse and books.

Everywhere I go, wherever I look, I see lobsters. Everything is lobster in this town. There are lobsters on awnings of shops, guesthouses and restaurants—of course. You can buy loaves of bread shaped like lobsters, drink drinks out of lobster-shaped bottles and bumper-sticker your car so there's no doubt you come from Lobster Cove. Lobsters are not the prettiest creatures. I'd prefer a sea horse, for example, although I'd never eat one. However, passing by Jewels of the Sea, a pretty little jewellery boutique on Main Street—next to Shucker's Booktique where I'll take Alice on Saturday morning for story hour—thank you *The Lobster Cove Anchor*—I see a fine chain, like cobweb, made of tiny gold lobsters. It's exquisite. However, there's also a pair of small, diamond sea horse earrings, which I adore.

In the end I get thread, wool and bookbinding tape, even fat, red heart-shaped buttons for the blue pyjamas, at the grocery store, on my way to collect Alice.

Teacher Pick nails me to the doorpost of the classroom the second she sees me. "Please spend a little time with Alice and her colours."

"Her colours?"

"Most of the children in the class use blue, green, red, yellow, even purple and turquoise correctly. However Alice is some way behind." She lowers her voice. "This morning when I asked her what colour her father's eyes are, she said 'red'."

Oops. I did see a dirty whisky glass in the washing-up yesterday morning. I move swiftly to defend my new boss. "Mr. Dalton found it very hard to say goodbye, Miss Pick. I'm sure you understand that." I smile, hoping it's a that's-that kind of smile, and hoping she'll believe his eyes were red from crying.

No dice. "It's Mrs. Pick," she tells me. "Last week, Alice told me his eyes were the colour of beer. As you can see—"

I phase out. They are *exactly* the colour of beer. I'm thinking of any number of typical English pubs on the River Thames at Richmond—outside on a summer's day, where hanging baskets burst with geraniums, lobelia and begonias, and there are pints of ale on the table, in the sunlight. Homesickness stabs me so viciously I see spots in front of my eyes. Everything is wrong. I'm far from home, Lucas is far from home— and I'm worried he's still cross with me—Alice hasn't got a mother, Pick's a pain in the arse—

"—would *highly* appreciate attention to the

matter."

What matter? Oh. "Yes," I say, remembering. "Yes." I nod, smile again, in a business-like, will-do fashion and go to the car.

"What colour is the sky, Alice?" I ask, reversing out of the parking area behind the school.

"Beautiful red," she answers.

See?

We get home and go into the house. "Look at my drawing." Alice drags it out of her backpack, and holds it up for inspection. "That's me." She points. "That's Daddy." She points to a tall, wobbly stick man with a very red smile and eyelashes like two squashed black octopuses. "And that's Mummy."

At first, mummy looks like a potato, perhaps the ghost of a potato, a wavering pink-brown ovoid towering over Alice. And then I realize. It's an admirable rendition of Queenie's beautiful egg.

Chapter Seven

We settle into a routine, me and Alice. She has school every weekday morning. I drop her off and come back to Blue Rocks to make our beds, wipe down the bathroom—we share mine—and clean house.

Once the day's chores are done, and any errands completed, I walk on the beach, read on the porch, or climb the rough paths behind Blue Rocks, one of which leads me up the hill, all the way around the back of Mariner's Fish Fry, and onto Hidden Cove Drive, where the mansions of Lobster Cove hide between old trees.

Life here is utterly different, and, on the surface, I like it. I've never done anything like this before, but I'm somehow fulfilled. Do I have a suppressed urge to nest? Is that why I decide the hallway of Lucas's house needs some pepping? I drag in a round table from the never-used living room. At the bottom of the stairs, in the curve of the newel post, with flowers—a mixture of roses and hydrangeas from the thigh-deep lake of cut flowers outside Flowers in Bloom—it makes all the difference, even if I did have to buy a vase myself. Any moment now, this house will become a home. There's also a potted daisy plant from Cherri, who left it on the doorstep with a note scribbled on a paper napkin when she passed by yesterday, along with a punnet of glorious blueberries, warm from the sun. The house remains bare, but it's shining clean and the brave daisies on the kitchen dresser shout *Look at us. See how jolly we are.* I love them.

I'm not cleaning this house. Isn't that what I said to Lucas? Because I am, actually, and while I do I notice someone's spent a lot of time and brainpower on its design. Everything's spacious and practical. Is this an American thing? Am I unfairly comparing poky—all right then, *cosy*—English homes to the generous, warm, airy spaces of Blue Rocks? Yes. Simply put, it's wonderful to live in this organized way—with plentiful cupboards, bathrooms everywhere, a laundry room, pantry, storeroom, basement, wide porches, double doors and huge windows giving onto the jewelled blues of Maine, everything from pale sapphire to cobalt, and turquoise and jade. I love these colours. Compared to the restrained greys and greens of England, they are forward, honest, and pure.

I wonder if Lucas's wife designed Blue Rocks? I wonder if she died before she got around to furnishing? Or is this it: a kind of failed attempt at Shaker? Perhaps she and Lucas had big, happy plans, and the memories of those throw long shadows on his heart. Is that why he stays? And why he goes away?

So many questions, but not the sort I can ask in my daily emails to him, even though we've settled into a relaxed routine, way better than how we started out. Rather, I send short messages and pictures of Alice. I ask questions like:

Jay Sawyer says the Jeep needs new tires.

After a few days, Lucas answers, *Do it.*

Or: *Lucas, can I Hoover your studio?* There are dust bunnies the size of tumbleweeds in there.

Three days later: *Hoover*?
Vacuum, to you.
Two days later: *If you must.*
I must. I did already.
Four days later: *Don't move anything.*
Oops.

We're ten days in, Alice, Buster and me. Our routine is set. The weather's wonderful and everything's going smoothly. Life is good, although one thing's puzzling me. When I Hoovered Lucas's studio I sat in the leather chair at one of his desks and had a good read through my CV. I am a stranger to myself. I don't relate to that woman describing her life's goals, dreams if you like, on those pages. Am I trying to be something I'm not? Something I think I *should* be, rather than someone I can be, want to be? Is this a new-style Maine me, interfering with my stability? Strange, but my photo's missing. I look around for it but can't find it anywhere. Where's that gone?

****

About that new, relaxed way Lucas and I communicate around Alice? It doesn't last. My fault, I guess, hunting for answers to questions about Lucas. This is how it starts: I'm not a nervous person. However I wouldn't say I have nerves of steel either. I'm brave enough to survive general life, but I'd rather not be put to the test, so, when first I hear noises in the house I take no notice. Imagine if we all went about life jumping and screaming at every unexplained little noise, even if heard at night? But I lie in bed—in what is essentially Lucas's bed—every night and think about where I am, in this silent house on the lonely shore between dark sea and sky. Sometimes, unable to sleep, I watch through the window, like I'm waiting for something, seeing nothing except timid stars and pale surf pushing through the blackness. And then I hear the noises. You have to listen really hard or you'd think it was your imagination. There's movement, whispering, rustling, barely audible, but nonetheless there.

During daylight, the sounds are impossible to recall. When the surf's up, I hear nothing. Is it Buster, getting into the roof somehow? I reckon he'd make more of a racket.

"How does Buster get in and out of the house?" I ask Alice.

"Through the door," she says.

Figures. "Which door?"

She takes my hand and leads me into the basement. Buster has a high-tech cat flap set into the outside wall, and another in the door that leads from the basement into the house. We go outside and wander on the grass in the fresh, crystal clear air, walking all the way around the house, me looking at the roof.

"What's that?" I ask Alice, pointing at the cupola.

"Tower."

"Do you go up there?"

She looks at me like I'm crazy. "I can't go on the roof!"

"I know *that*. I mean can you get up inside that tower from inside the house?"

She shakes her head and bends to pick one of the small yellow flowers growing in the grass. She presents it to Buster who's just arrived. He sniffs politely and rolls on his back for a tummy tickle in the sunshine.

I gaze at the cupola, tiled like the rest of the house,

and neatly louvered, although one of the planks under the southern eave has slipped. What a handsome ornamental detail to place on a roof—the perfect finishing touch, like the cherry on top of a cupcake. Ornamental or not, I bet there's some way to get up there. The mermaid weathervane shifts this way and that, no more than an inch in the light breeze. Somehow she doesn't look quite so pierced-though today.

That night, the sea falls silent, so I can hear the noises properly. Not thinking about how isolated I am, not dwelling on the possibility that the house could be haunted I put my head under the duvet and resolve to buy earplugs.

The following morning, Alice and I pull up in the school car park at the same time as Cherri. "What plans have you got this fine day?" Cherri asks. I tell her I'm about to scour town for earplugs because of the noises in the roof.

"Oh, that's probably mice," she says. "They can do a lotta damage. Best get a trap from Dylan at Old Mill Veterinary. A humane trap, that is," she adds, quickly, when she sees my face. Admittedly, I had imagined a Tom and Jerry contraption with a big chunk of cheese well-placed to hide the beheading mechanism.

"Although…" she muses, "didn't I once hear something about Blue Rocks being built on a sacred site?"

No. I'm not going there. I refuse.

I kiss Alice goodbye and go straight to Old Mill Veterinary. This is the first time I meet Dylan Foster, although I've spoken to her on the phone about updating Buster's inoculations.

"So Buster not doing his job, then?" She smiles,

handing me a plastic tunnel thing, one-way entry, no exit.

"I think the job's too big," I answer. "Where should I put this?"

She hands me three more. "Best place is in the roof, if you can access safely."

"And then what happens?"

"You bring them back, and we dispose of them."

"Dispose?"

"We set the mice free in a suitable location, in the wild."

Do they *really* do that? I look deep into her kind eyes. She's not joking. Her receptionist nods, equally serious.

Okay, I believe them. I return to Blue Rocks and start looking for a trapdoor in the ceiling somewhere. I search high and low, literally. Inside and out. Eventually, I give up. I'll message Lucas and ask him how to get into the roof. I'm having one last look around on the upper floor of the house when, walking along the gallery outside the small room Lucas uses as a bedroom, I open a large, double-door cupboard for no other reason than I'm looking for something I can't find.

Hello. What's this? I push the door wide open, right back against the wall. It's no regular door, being heavy, soundproofed by the looks of it, and well-insulated around the edges. And this is no cupboard. It's more like a small hallway with—would you know?—a spiral staircase in the corner. I knew there was a way to get to the cupola! I look at the floor at the base of the stairs and, sure enough, there's a trapdoor that must open up to Lucas's studio below. How exciting. I feel like I've made a significant discovery. You know, if Lucas took these big old doors off and opened this space up to the gallery, what a fabulous feature that would be. I marvel for a moment and then go to the top of the main stairs where I've left the mousetraps.

Back in the newly discovered hallway, there's…ooh, what's that smell? Something stinks, like it's seeping in through the walls. Well, it's musty in here, surely. Whatever, I don't want that ghastly smell going through the house. There's a light switch, so I switch it on and close the door, shutting myself in. It's not claustrophobic, not at all with the light on. I balance the mousetraps in my arms and start up the stairs. Ladders are not my favourite thing—those untrustworthy rungs—and these slat-type stairs, where you can see all the way down to the floor between your feet, are the next worst thing. Come to think, this is a bit silly. I should have left these traps at the bottom and gone up, to see what's what, first. Too late now because I'm more than halfway. At the top, I pause on the small landing outside a low door, to listen. Nothing. Silence, apart from my crazy heartbeat.

Quite honestly, I'm frightened, but who else is going to do this? Should I have called someone from the sheriff's office? *For goodness sake.* Imagine calling out a law enforcement officer to deal with mice—of which you are scared—living, and/or dead. Granted, dead bodies are scary if they're human. That's when we call the sheriff, but not for mice.

"Just do it," I mutter aloud. "Do it and get out."

Here goes. I turn the knob and looking down—because determined as I am to rid the house of pests, I'd hate to squash an innocent mouse—I push open the door, giddy from climbing in the round, without breathing in the sweet stench of rot and decay. One of those mice must have passed on, because only a dead body could reek like this.

It's the worst fright I've ever had, in my entire life.

I'm looking down, so I don't see it coming. It crashes onto me, this great stinking, black, dripping *thing*, screaming, screaming, screaming. I'm screaming too! I leap backwards and crack my head on the low doorframe. Stumbling, fumbling blind, I beat off the horror, fling myself out onto the landing and slam the door. Something crunches and squeals. My hand slips off the knob and I plunge down the stairs—not far at all, because of the tight spiral. If there had been a ladder I would have gone straight to the bottom, on my head.

God! *What was that?*

Rammed against the curve of the bannister, head in hands, I'm trembling head to toes, like a leaf made of jelly. My legs have given way and, much as I'd like to flee, I can't. I also can't sit here forever halfway between bursting into tears and throwing up. I lift my head and look at the door.

Are those *fingers* pinched in the door? Blackish fingers? A cold shudder pulses through me like the shock of an ice-bucket challenge. The fingers drop to the floor, flutter, and lie still.

Not fingers, but a poor little…

Bat! Crushed by me. Next to him, lies a comrade, very dead, I fear.

Bats, that's all. I press a wobbly hand to my stressed heart, worried I've damaged it. Oh Lord. I find tissues in my pocket, reach out and wrap up the bodies, not actually touching them. Somehow I'd forgotten about the smell, but it's back, overwhelming, dead bats, live bats, and both their droppings. I get to my feet, legs as dodgy as the Trident 202's, and stagger down the spiral, clutching the bannister.

Here, at the bottom, are the remnants of the smashed mousetraps I don't remember dropping. One has fared slightly better than the rest. I slip the dead inside and take them out to the car.

Back at Old Mill Veterinary I hand the box to Dylan and tell her briefly what happened.

"I can see you've had a scare," she says. "You're quite a lot paler than you were this morning."

Granted. "Just a little."

"Ah, the legendary pluck of the Brits." She grins.

"You had to be there."

"I bet. Now tell me, how many *Chiroptera* in that colony?"

What a question, and I presume she means bats! Thousands of course, if not millions. I give it some thought. "Um, twenty. Forty at the most."

"Good. Not too large." She hands me a business card. "Call these people to remove them. It's costly but you'll have to do it. Eventually their urine and guano will damage the walls and stink out the whole house."

"I'll probably wait for Lucas to get back—"

"Don't. Do it now. That colony will only grow and it could develop into a health hazard. Some bats carry viruses that can be lethal." She says goodbye, telling me she needs to sort out those poor little bat pups.

I've no wish to find out what *sort out* means in vet-speak. I presume by pups she means babies. I'm not thinking about it. Thanking her, I dash off to fetch Alice from school. Early, I sit in the school car park and call the bat-removal people from the car.

They assure me their method is humane—before I ask—tell me their work with animals is regulated and approved by the nature conservation authority of the state of Maine, and quote me a price, which is not so humane. I can't spend this much money without agreement from Lucas, so I start typing an email. For some reason, I'm impatient. This message is too long; there's too much to say. I know, I'll call him. I might be lucky enough to catch him during downtime.

No luck. I leave a detailed message and ask him to respond ASAP.

That evening, while Alice is having supper, Lucas calls. The line is terrible. He sounds like he's racing a motorbike through a waterfall, and that's perhaps why he's yelling.

All I can make out is "Jeez, Lara!" *crackle fade beep* "Alice? Alice? Alice?" *crackle.*

"I can't hear you, Lucas—"

Crackle crackle "…wrong with her? What?"

What? "Alice is fine. One hundred percent."

"Alice?" *beep fizz clang* "…happened?"

"ALICE IS FINE. It's about bats—"

"Cats? Is it Buster?"

"Lucas! *Go somewhere where we can hear each other speak.*"

He does. He sounds like he's going down a mine on metal stairs. I wait, imagining me and Alice, tiny dots on the coast of Maine, joined to Lucas by a thin beam of light—light that shoots way up via a satellite revolving in the sparkling cosmic dust of outer space, and then back down to Lucas, a third tiny dot on his rusty flake of metal in a vast, horrendous sea, on the dark side of the world.

"Okay," he says, eventually. "What happened?"

It turns out that my message broke up—why am I surprised. All Lucas got was *Alice, lethal, virus, hazard, dangerous* and *urgent.* Of course he freaked out.

"Honestly, Lucas, would I leave a message about Alice being desperately ill. I would *never* do that."

"I know. I know. Sorry, sorry," *crackle zzzzt.* "Out here, the mind plays tricks."

I tell him about the bat situation, and he tells me to go ahead and get them removed and to get the cupola professionally cleaned and painted.

"There were supposed to be windows in that cupola." He says *coo-pohhhh-la*, with the emphasis on the middle syllable, and I say *coo-polla*, like Italians would—I think. It makes me smile.

"Shall I get someone to do that? Put windows in?"

"Why not? That was the plan. I imagined my…" *phyrr zzitz* "…up in that tower, looking at the glorious view, like a princess, and the secret staircase down to my…" *bzzzp bzzpb* "It didn't work."

No. Well.

Alice climbs on my lap, wanting to talk to her dad. It's Lara this, Lara that, and the occasional reference to Teacher Pick, and a lot about Buster. Lucas laughs and asks her questions. Seconds before they say goodbye he asks to speak to me.

"Why did you call? You could have emailed all this."

I hesitate. I could have. "I wanted to hear your voice," I say, although I don't really say—it just comes out of my mouth. "We," is what I had meant to say, "me and Alice," but I didn't.

Believe me, Lucas, out here on the wild and desolate coast of Maine, just a little too far out of Lobster Cove to be cosy, the mind also plays tricks. The mind and the heart. If I know one thing Lucas, I know this. I want to be that princess in your tower, your *coopohhhh-la*. I want it to be me.

Amy calls the second Alice falls asleep.

"I had a call from Lucas this minute," she tells me, "way out in the North Sea."

A complaint? God, I hope not. "And?"

"We didn't chat. The line was terrible, but he did manage to ask me a question."

"Oh?"

"It's personal information he's after, and I need your permission to give it. He wants to know if you're in a relationship."

Oh. "Why doesn't he ask me himself?"

"You tell me."

Obviously, I can't. I guess he doesn't want to make a fool of himself if—

"When I interviewed you, Lara, you stated 'not in a relationship', but that's not the kind of information I send to a client. I keep it confidential, for my eyes only."

My heart's skippety-hopping while my tummy does figures of eight. "Nothing's changed."

"Can I tell him?"

"I can."

"What! And bust him? No, let me."

Yes, Amy, sir. "Okay."

We chat some more, say goodbye and hang up. It's

a clear-sky night in Maine, but my head finds some clouds to shove itself into, and that's how I go around for the rest of the evening, smiling all over my face.

Chapter Eight

It's Friday. The bat squad is here, dressed in plastic suits, boots and helmets like there's a leaking chemical weapon in the house. Alice has tennis after school and I've got time on my hands. Time to be out of the house and curious. Besides, after yesterday, I could do with a break. I've heard so much about Emerald Lake. People in town refer to it all the time, like you would an attractive landmark. Today's the day. I'm going to drive up there and see it for myself.

Call me unimaginative, but Emerald Lake is more pewter than precious gem, though the vegetation's green enough. The forests spread down ravines and gullies to the water's edge, holding their old secrets. I spot a layby on the narrow shore and park there, but don't get out of the car. It's lonely, and very quiet for a city-lover like me, lately resident in the metropolis of Lobster Cove. I sit for ten, fifteen minutes, window open to the sunshine, watching the water, contemplating the sensation of being the only person in the world. I shiver, start the engine and move on, away from the grey water, up the hill, where the ground levels out and the trees stand back from the roadside.

Here's something. A small house with a sign out front that I recognize:

Agat—Abenaki—Herbaliste—Facialiste

The beautician Cherri Chandler told me about. I

slow the car to a stop. I never had time for this kind of stuff in my old life, but right now I do. I'll stop by and make an appointment. What luxury.

I park the Jeep and walk in below the little sign, squeaking on its hinge, swinging in the breeze. The path to the cabin is no more than rough stones laid in the mud. A few chickens scratch about happily in the garden, such as it is, between clumps of herbs and succulents, mulched with bark, pebbles and broken seashells. I spot beehives to the side of the house, some distance away, in the shelter of a thicket of young pine trees. Clearly, an old tree fell there and young ones are growing where it seeded. I step onto the porch by way of three shallow wooden planks, raised on bricks to make rustic stairs. Baskets of shells, pebbles, broken coloured glass and blown eggs crowd every surface. Objects hang from rusty wire hooks under the porch eaves: dream-catchers, tumbleweeds, birds' nests, bunches of dried herbs. The front door is wide open to the pitch-dark interior of the house. I ring the iron bell and wait, smelling incense. I wait a long time and am about to ring again when—

"Yes?"

I jump. Turning, I see, right there, on the porch, somehow without a sound to herald her arrival, Agat, I presume. She's brown, wiry, and white-haired. Smooth-skinned, it has to be said. She's wearing a denim ankle length shift dress and clogs. Clogs that would have scrunched up the stony mud of the path, so God knows where she's beamed herself in from. Her pale blue eyes stay on my face, challenging me to ask a question. I do.

"Hello," I say. "Are you Agat?"

"Where you from?"

"Lobster Cove. Cherri told me about you, said you offered facial treatments."

"You the new girl for Blue Rocks?"

"I'm Lara Fairmont. I work for Lucas Dalton." I offer my hand, but she doesn't reciprocate.

She spits to the left and makes a funny little circle sign in mid-air with both forefingers. "You touch that man?"

"I beg your pardon."

"You touch him? His skin, his hand? You kiss him?"

"I...well...yes, I have touched him." I shook his hand after all, and kissed him goodbye, urged by Lara. I touch my cheek like I've been stung there.

She puts her hands behind her back. "Ah, he kiss you. Go away. I don't touch you!"

"Excuse me?"

"Go. Away." She leans toward me, eyes flickering.

I drop my hand. "But—"

She brings her hands to the front of her body, presses them to her heart, and then raises a forefinger above her head like she's checking wind direction. "That man evil, evil, evil. He think nobody know, but I do. I know. I am Abenaki, a child of the Dawn Land. My ancestors are warriors, so I am not afraid. You, you must fear Dzeedzeebonda. All girls want to catch him, catch the handsome, rich man, capture his loose hair and braid it. They want, they *want* to wear his ring, but that ring will go to Alombegwinosis like the first one. Her ring went to Alombegwinosis." She holds her stomach. "They must fear him. You must fear him."

I stare at her. I have absolutely no idea what she is talking about. "Are you Agat?" I try again, smiling.

She lowers her hand and walks across the porch, putting herself between me and the open door. "Kisosen bring the sun and see everything by daylight. But even when he fold his wings and bring the night, he see. He saw him, he saw that evil man that dark night."

Right. Time to go. "Thank you," I say with the most polite expression I can manage. "I'm sorry to bother you."

She follows me to the car. "That man touch you already. He leave blackness on you. Blackness in your heart."

I drive away, not much caring that I've left her covered in dust, my black heart thumping, shaky hands sweaty on the wheel. A mile or so along the road I pass one of those signs: *Maine—the way life should be.*

Really?

****

There's no infant class at Alice's school on Fridays, so there's a good chance I'll catch Cherri at home around lunchtime. I know where she lives—along the road to Grant's Lake—because Alice points out her house each time we drive past. Besides, she said I could approach her for help. *Anytime, honey,* were her exact words. I slow down on the approach her front gate—feeling like the sheriff in his cruiser—and *bingo* there she is, peering into her post box.

I park on the roadside, get out of the car and lock it. We exchange pleasantries, and I explain why I've come. "I have questions about Lucas," I tell her.

Cherri looks at me, scarlet lips pursed. "If I don't tell you you're gonna go to the public records' office, the library, all those kinds of places and try to dig up the truth, ain't you? You're that kinda woman."

I nod.

Does it matter, though? I'm here to do a job. To look after Alice until Lucas gets home, and then to go home myself. Do I really need to know what shifts in the shadows of Lucas's life? Am I curious—is that all? Am I afraid? As long as Lucas doesn't murder me, and if he's not here, he can't do that, can he? What's this all about? I can't put my finger on the exact reason why I have to know, but I do. I must know, and I will. This is as good a place to start as any.

Cherri tips her head toward the house. "Let's go and sit in the garden out back."

Using the excuse that I have to be gone in ten minutes to pick up Alice from tennis, I refuse all offers of tea, mint or otherwise, relishing the safe warmth of Cherri's garden, billowing with crimson roses and peonies, purple petunias and sky-blue lupines. There's a marijuana plant, happy as Larry, flourishing between the mint bushes.

We sit on a wooden bench in the sun, and Cherri asks me what's up. I tell her about my visit to Emerald Lake and how I came across Agat's house, her less than friendly welcome and her weird ramblings.

"Shoot." Cherri twists her mouth. "Agat is a mad old fool. You don't wanna to listen to her."

"I had no option. Was she cursing me? She babbled on about Dzeedzee somebody…who is that?"

Cherri sits back. "Dzeedzeebonda is a monster, that's all. It's folklore. Mythology of the Abenakis."

"What sort of monster? What does he do?"

Reluctant, she tells me, with a sigh. "He's a monster so ugly he can't look at himself, apparently. I've never seen him, honey. Pay no attention. He ain't anywhere in Maine." She laughs, but I'm not convinced.

"She referred to Lucas as that monster. Why? And she spoke about other people, women wanting to catch him and *braid his hair*—what's that about?"

She takes my hand across the table. "Let me get you some tea."

"Cherri, no. Thanks. I must go in a second. Please tell me what she meant by the hair-braiding stuff."

Her eyes slide away from mine. "A young Abenaki man wears his hair long and loose until he becomes engaged to be married. Then, his woman braids his hair to show he's taken. Once married, once rings are exchanged, she shaves his head, all but the braid."

"There was something about a ring, too. She said Alombegwi…something…would take the ring. No. She said—implied—he would get the ring again, like the last one. What did she mean?"

"Alombegwinosis is no more than a fictitious imp in the folklore of the Abenaki—"

"What kind of imp?"

She leaves go my hand and sits back in her chair. "A dwarfish creature who can change his size at will."

"And what else?"

"Don't worry about it." Cherri rolls her eyes. "Gawd. The batty old crow."

"Does she know something? Did she see something?"

She narrows her eyes to amethyst slits. "Who knows what she sees and saw? She's crazy."

"Did she?"

She presses her lips together and glances at her watch. "Ain't you late, Lara?"

Well. So much for that. But I am late. I get up, grab my bag. "Your garden's gorgeous. I'm sorry to leave."

"Sorry to see you rush," she calls from the porch, waving me off. She isn't though. Her relief at my departure is palpable.

Tomorrow, I'm going to see the sheriff. He'll know what's what.

****

I'm the last at school. All the kids have gone and Pick is busy in the foyer, stacking small tennis rackets in a crate, locking up.

"Sorry I'm late," I say, annoyed that I am.

"You needn't have rushed. Alice has been collected."

"Collected?" Every drop of blood in my body freezes.

She smiles. "By her Uncle John."

Uncle John? While my blood freezes, a hot river of shock spurts through my veins. Alice has been taken by a pervert.

"Who is Uncle John?"

"Not to worry. He's an accredited relative."

Not to worry? Is this what people with children do? Let them go off with strangers? Arrive at school to find they've been picked up by some randomer? I don't think so.

"Pick, where is Alice?"

She gazes past me. "Mr. Dalton said he saw Mr. Dalton's Jeep outside Teacher Cherri's so he was going straight on over to—"

"Hi."

I whip around to see who owns the voice behind me. It's Lucas. My heart skyrockets for a second, then crashes back down, leaving me breathless. It's not Lucas. It's a brother or a cousin. He's similar, but shorter, and heavier, a little older, with different eyes.

"For God's sake!" I snap. "What do you think you're *doing*?" I'm angry. I want to cry. I squeeze my lips together to stop the wobble.

He holds up his hands. "Hey, I drove by, saw school was out, saw Lucas's Jeep parked down the road outside Cherri's, figured I'd pick up Lis and bring her over. That's it. That's all. By the time I'd parked, you were driving back up the road. You didn't see us waving. I came right back, knowing you'd be real worried."

"If you'll excuse me?" Pick thins her lemon lips, vanishes inside and locks the door.

I blink, take a breath. "Sorry." I look at his car beyond the playground fence. Alice waves at me through the window, happy as you like, finishing off an ice cream.

"I'm John, by the way. Luke's brother."

John and Luke. Biblical. We don't shake hands. Instead, he says, "Um," and puts a hand on my shoulder.

Startled, I look at the hand, and back at him. "What?"

"Luke would be real glad to know you were looking after Lis so well."

"What do you mean?" I glance at Alice, who's freed herself from the car.

"'Ticky hands." She holds them up and runs toward me. I duck away from John's hand, rinse hers under a tap in the schoolyard and scoop water onto her face.

"Dry it on your dress," says John, smiling. "Like Daddy did."

"Did?" I frown into his eyes, but he's looking at Alice.

He chuckles. "Yeah. At my wife's birthday picnic last month in Back Bay. It caused quite a stir."

"Is everything all right?" I ask John as we walk back to the cars. Alice, smitten by way of ice cream, bypasses the Jeep and climbs back into John's Corvette.

John opens the driver's door for me. I look at him, but the sun blinds me. I can't see his face properly, can't read his eyes.

"We need to talk," he says. "I'll see you back at the house."

Chapter Nine

I drive behind John and Alice, oblivious to the magnificent scenery. Don't ask me if there are wild lupines at the roadside, or sails on the silver-green mirror of the ocean, dancing like white butterflies on the breeze. Lucas is dead; I know it. That stupid corrosive, corrodible, whatever, leg of an oil rig has collapsed and everyone has fallen into the thrashing sea. Or that rusty old shit-bucket of a helicopter has crashed, killing everyone on board. One or the other. Both. For God's *sake*, what's the difference? I mustn't panic, but I do. It's my fault for being such a pushover. Lucas is a hunk, a hottie—there, I've said it—and I wanted to portray myself as a cool-headed coper to same. If I had turned around, got back in Skeet's taxi and gone back to New York, London, *anywhere*, Lucas would have had to cancel his trip. He said lives would be at risk if I left Lobster Cove. Seems like I've killed people by staying. He would be alive if it wasn't for me. Nevertheless, I blame him. It's entirely his fault I fell in love with his house, Lobster Cove and the whole of Maine apart from creepy old Agat and Pick, of course. Lucas was attractive and persuasive, and I fell for it.

Was. Oh God, I feel sick.

Force that aside for the horrible moment. There's Alice to think of. She'll have to be told. Also, I'm under contract, and I'll have to stay until I'm not needed. How terrible for Alice to lose both parents at such a tender age. How utterly, utterly ghastly. There will be two wavering ghostly potato Queenie eggs on the next school drawing—the thought literally jars me, and I almost hit the Blue Rocks gatepost as I follow John up the drive. What does it matter if I fuck up his precious Jeep? Lucas is dead.

John parks his car, and I pull up next to him. Alice clambers out, chattering away, a smudge of blueberry ice cream on her sky-blue sundress. My heart turns inside out and ties itself in a knot. She's adorable. Yes, I love her. Hot tears run down my face. I can't stop what's happening in my mind.

I don't *love* Lucas. Of course I don't. How could I possibly? I don't even know the man. Except I do. I speak to him every day. I know stuff about him. He's highly educated, talented and creative; he's got a sense of humour, an amazing high-tech job, massive responsibility, not to mention deep love and commitment to his daughter. And that's merely the start. I get out of the car, unlock the front door—that odd key rattling in my shaking hands—grip the sea horse handle and push.

Is it "love" or "loved" when a person's dead? Which is it?

"Wait here." John, hand on my arm, stops me from going inside, pointing at one of the benches on the porch. "I'll put on the TV for Lis."

Television to the rescue. Our eyes meet. "She's halfway through Winnie the Pooh," I tell him.

They go inside, and I sit on the bench. I wait ten minutes, in warm shade under the grey planking of deep eaves, mind blank, gazing up the hill at the back of the house. Is that the sound of the sea I can hear, or the hum of the wind in the pines, or my own fear pumping through my veins, or all three? Better not to think.

John returns and sits beside me. "So…"

I turn to face him. "What happened? Tell me."

"An accident."

I sink my face in my hands. Am I even breathing?

"Lucas is all right. He's alive."

"What do you mean, alive?" I lift my head and look at him. Alive does not necessarily mean good.

"He was on a rig in the North Sea, a decommissioning job."

"I know that.

"He went down on an inspection dive and something went wrong. There was a collapse. Something gave way. Some divers are still missing."

"Some?"

"Three, I think. Yes, three. Luke was lucky. The rescue crew managed to get him up fairly quickly and stabilize him through the decompression process. Real tricky with a head injury, but they did it."

I look at him, aware he is Lucas's brother and I am supposed to be the strong one. "Is it bad?" I ask, in a stranger's voice.

He thinks a moment. "No. He'll be okay. It'll take a little time. He's still under observation at the Royal Infirmary in Aberdeen."

"What do you mean under observation?"

"He's been out for a few days. It's a precaution."

"Out?"

"Concussed. Unconscious."

"But—"

"He's good. Everything is going to plan."

"*Is it*?" My voice rises to a level I don't recognize.

"As soon as he can fly," John explains, like he's talking to Alice, "he'll be coming home. Soon. I'll let you know, or he will."

"So everything's okay then?"

He stares at me, his eyes filled with uncertainty. "Yep."

"Good." I stand up. "Would you keep an eye on Alice for me, please? Just for ten minutes."

"Sure. Take your time."

I go inside, and through the hallway, glancing into the den, where Alice sits, mesmerized by a lamenting Eeyore. In the living room I open one of the sea-facing doors and go out onto the porch—the sea porch, Lucas calls it. I hear John's footsteps behind me and, pretty sure he's keeping an eye on me, I go down the stairs and walk straight across the grass, heading for the sea, eager to get away from the wide, watching windows of the house.

I'm a mess. And, yes, I overreacted, I know.

Look, it's horrible when you hear there's been an accident, before you're sure that your loved ones are alive and safe, preferably unhurt. There's that ghastly, heart-plunging moment when you know your future hangs in the balance, followed by the dizzying tide of relief like a powerful electrical charge, regenerating your faith in life.

The thing is I'm *not* in love How can I possibly be in love? I haven't spent more than a few hours with Lucas, so—

We talk about Alice mostly, but also, through that—and things like Jeep tires, vacuuming, Buster's inoculations and so on—about me and him. Us. I enjoy the contact. If he's on a really deep dive, I won't hear for a few days, but that doesn't stop me from looking at my phone for a message every ten minutes. Have I confused loving someone with feeling responsible, or sorry, for them? Am I crazy? Lonely? Delusional? Or just plain sad?

The grass gives way to a ruined border with overgrown stepping-stones leading to a gate. Lupines and daisies have seeded themselves and grow happily between the green runners of an old lawn run amok. I reach the gate and pull the bolt. It's stiff and rusty and I swear when it releases, pinching my fingers. There are three shallow, crumbling steps onto the beach and I have to watch where I put my feet. Slipping and sliding, grabbing onto scrubby dune bushes, I stumble to the bottom, dust my hands on the back of my jeans and look around. I'm in a perfect cove—the one Lucas said was out of bounds.

It's all got something to do with Agat's vitriolic reaction to my relationship with Lucas. That tipped me. And then when I first saw John, I thought Lucas was back early, or paying a surprise visit. The happy shock, followed by grim news, knocked me sideways.

I don't know why I came here. My shoes are off and my toes are cool on wet pebbles lapped by the crystal edge of a lazy, dark sea that could not look more beautiful than right now. I stare at the barely discernible distant divide between sea and sky, dragging in deep breaths of cool, salty air. Way down in my lungs, it dilutes the panic, slowing my hasty heartbeat.

What must I do?

I turn my back on the shimmer and walk up the

small beach to the steps. What I must do is carry on—calmly—doing what I'm here to do, and see what happens. There's nothing else.

"You okay?" It's John, standing at the top of the steps, Blue Rocks like a great, grey shadow behind him.

"Thanks, I'm fine." He thinks I'm mad. I can see it in his doubting eyes.

He leaves, asking me to stay in touch, asking me to let him know if there are any problems. Alice and I wave goodbye on the driveway, with Buster coiling around my calves and Alice's waist. He has feathers in his "whispers" and has clearly been up to no good.

What does John mean by *problems*?

****

Two days pass, before John rings to say there is no news about Lucas, but there's other news. Bad news. "They found the other divers," John says.

"And?"

"No survivors."

Halfway down the stairs, I sit with a thump. "That's…that's awful."

"Lucas didn't know them well. They weren't, you know, friends."

Oh. Strangely, perhaps, that doesn't make anything better. John feels the same—I can hear it in his voice. Death is death.

"I'll keep you informed," he says.

"Should I say anything to Alice?" I ask.

"Not now. Not yet. Let's see what happens. Don't tell her anything."

We ring off. Why must we see what happens? I thought everything was going to plan.

I carry on doing what I'm paid to do. I look after

Alice, take her to school, cook, keep house and drink in the beauty of Maine when I remember it's there. To be honest, I'm too tired to appreciate much. Worrying about Lucas juxtaposed with putting on a jolly face for Alice wipes me out.

Father's Day arrives. There's a big event planned in town, but Lucas isn't here.

"Bring Alice along anyway," Pick says. "You're *both* very welcome."

You know, I believe her. I'm so grateful for this crumb of acceptance from her, of all people, that we almost go. She, like Cherri, is sympathetic and concerned. The few other people in town who know what's happened to Lucas are like: *Oh*, with downcast eyes. There's a certain *what can you expect*? attitude. Is that because he has a risky job or risky reputation?

Anyway, the Friday before the event, I decide not to go, and bake a couple of trays of lemon sponge cupcakes for Alice to take to school as a peace offering. The thing is, I don't want to leave the house more than is absolutely necessary. I want to be there, as close as possible, in case Lucas comes home. I've got the only key to the sea horse door. The other is lost, so how would he get in? That's my ultra-feeble excuse to myself, anyway.

Alice doesn't mind not going, because the day dawns beautiful and I suggest it's one for the beach. Given that I'm not straying from Blue Rocks, I override Lucas's command that the cove below the house is out of bounds. To what harm could we possibly come? Besides, it's my birthday, and I'd like to spend it on the beach, that beach. Fully aware of my responsibility, I've checked the tide tables, packed a basket with swimming aids for Alice, sunblock, towels and anti-histamine ointment in case of stings. I've got sandwiches and drinking water, plus an umbrella. Alice has a bucket and spade and a small towel for Buster in case he joins us—he doesn't.

We spend the best part of the day in the cove. It's completely private, although when the trees up on the road are bare in the winter you could probably see right in here. There's no sand, only pebbles, so Alice uses her bucket to "fish" and gather treasures from the shallow rock pools exposed by the low tide. Using a book I found in the house called *Common Shore Life of Maine*, we identify starfish, one crab, a few types of seaweed and a super-cooperative cormorant that sits on a nearby rock and spreads his wings to dry. We see plovers, and oyster catchers too, but we don't need to identify those. Alice knows those already.

Last year, I had a landmark birthday. Thirty. There was a big party at Quicksilver in London, even a boyfriend, kind of, called Mark. No, Mike. Mike was his name. We petered out a week later, neither one of us particularly upset. This birthday couldn't be more different. Funny though, I'm enjoying it. I'm enjoying it more, I honestly am—if I don't think about Lucas.

Gradually, the tide turns, filling the little pools with regular waves that grow with every surge. Alice wails, standing by helpless when her favourite flat rock goes under, and small, precious flotsam and jetsam treasures wash away.

"My jews," she cries. "My shelves!" Jewels and shells, I've come to understand over the course of the day, though there are neither on this pebbly beach. The sun settles in the west, throwing the rocks of the cove into jagged shadows, stained blue-black. We pack up and go back to the house.

Later that night, once supper's been eaten and Alice is asleep, I drink a birthday glass of wine on the sea porch swing seat, browse my birthday messages, watch the moon come up over the sea, shower and go to bed early, deliciously tired, stung to a warm tingle by the summer sun. Drowsy, utterly relaxed, my thoughts turn—as they do—to Lucas.

If he would *please* come home—come home and be all right—life would be perfect.

Chapter Ten

So many questions, yes, growing in my mind, and I am going to find answers to a few. Alice has an early evening event on the main pier—to learn about night fishing—children only, no parents allowed, and no me, obviously. I ring Skeet and ask for a pickup at five p.m. He doesn't come himself but sends a driver I don't know. He drops us at the seafood market, and I confirm an eight p.m. collection. I'm not driving because I'm going to the bar.

I leave Alice and her suppertime picnic with Cherri and her troop of little ones. It's a lovely evening. Summer is coming softly to Maine. It's a privilege to be here, right now, watching late spring blend into the warm richness of July. I walk away from the water, cross Main and turn right, up Oak. Murphy's Bar is at the end of the block, on the left. Everyone talks about Murphy's. Maggie's Diner may be the facial expression of Lobster Cove with its blue and white checks and cheery welcome, but Murphy's is the heartbeat. Besides, I gather David Hu, the barman, has a reputation as the local shoulder to…well, not cry on exactly—but everyone talks about him like he's the guy who knows everything and everybody in Lobster Cove. He's the problem-solver.

Only…no, it can't be true. I walk into the bar, and it's like *men only*.

No way! This is the twenty-first century. Lobster Cove folks must surely be more tolerant and open-minded about sexist issues like this. I hesitate at the door because the barman's scowling like I've committed sacrilege.

"Are you, um, open?" I ask, with a smile.

"What does it goddamn look like?" he growls.

That could mean yes or no, but the door's open so I reckon it's a yes. I walk in, sit on a barstool and look around. Apart from the lack of smoke, this could be a downtown bar in any number of fifties' Hollywood movies. There's a jukebox, and some guys around a pool table over near the back wall. There are elements of Mo's in The Simpsons.

The barman stares, old and hostile. He could use a shave. I look him in the eye. "Good evening. I'd like a glass of white wine, please. A sauvignon blanc if you have?"

Without looking away, he reaches down, grabs something, opens it on an under-counter bottle opener and slams it onto the Formica surface in front of me. Beer. A bottle of beer, standing in a small puddle of its own self because Scary Barman bashed it down so hard.

Have I done something wrong? I cast my mind back to what little I know about American women's rights and feminism. Can men like Scary Barman still be real in a country that gave us Amelia Jenks Bloomer, Gloria Steinhem, Alice Walker, Maya Angelou, even Beyoncé? And Jane Goodall, chimpanzee hugger *and* feminist?

There's a pleasant wine bar close by, called Merlot's. I could use a little *pleasant* right now, to be frank, and I didn't order beer. I get off my stool and pick up my bag, reaching inside for cash. You know what? I'm not going to pay. I walk out.

"Hey! Excuse me?"

I turn straight back, mouth full of objections, but instead of Scary Barman I'm confronted by an altogether more agreeable person, an Asian man of around fifty, or prematurely grey in his forties, his hands spread out in apology. He's wearing a Wildflowers of Maine tea towel tucked into his belt as an improvised apron.

"Did you get it in the neck from Uncle Buck? I'm *damn* sorry."

Did I?

"He got a bullet in the wrong place in 'Nam." He guides me back to my stool, whips the beer out of sight and pours me a giant glass of chilled wine. Is there a right place to get a bullet, Vietnam or elsewhere? He hands me the wine. "On the house. Jeez, I'm sorry. You're Lara, aren't you? Lis Dalton's nanny from Blue Rocks?"

I nod. "That's me. Did I do something wrong, because your colleague—"

"Don't mind Buck. He helps out around here. Anywhere, really. Whatever he can do. This and that. He has, you know, what they call special needs."

"I'm sorry."

"He owned this place way back, but the community formed a cooperative and bought him out, so he didn't have to shut down and sell. That way he has the funds to pay for his own care. He comes across a little weird if you don't know what's what. But he wouldn't hurt a fly, honest. No need to be afraid."

"It's okay." Now that I know.

"I'm David. David Hu."

"Pleased to meet you, David." I glance down the bar. Buck's polishing glasses, grumbling to himself.

Hu follows my eyes. "We keep him away from the tourists." Big grin. "Or new folks like you."

I smile back. "It's nice that Uncle Buck has something to do, that people care for him."

"Yeah. Way back his Daddy was a real force in this town. Saved it from developers. Folks don't forget around here, so everyone looks out for Buck. Lucas is real good to him too. Gives him odd jobs up at the house, stuff like that. He'll pitch up any day soon, out of the blue, to mow the lawn."

Folks don't forget around here. Here's my gap. "I suppose you know Lucas pretty well."

"We go way back. Sure. I used to babysit him when I was a teenager. Mrs. Dalton was a pretty generous contributor to my pocket money fund. Nice kid, Lucas. Born to succeed, know what I mean? Born with looks, and now, of course, he's got the money. He's one helluva clever guy. I'm not. Not at all. I'm just the nice guy around here." He laughs—he's joking, there's no envy there. Besides, it's true.

I go for it. "Did you know his wife?"

His face closes. "Sure. We all knew Bonny, like a lotta other folks who live in this town."

"What was she like?"

He looks at me for a moment, and then comes out from behind the counter, pulling off the tea towel. He tilts his head toward a booth in the corner and picks up my wine. "Come." He sticks his head through a doorway next to the bar and yells, "Carla, come out here, willya, and bring me a Coke, ice and lemon."

I go and sit in the booth with Hu. Bonny, he tells me, was the wild one. Lucas was wild enough, but she pushed it right to the raw edge. Lucas, as a teenager, got in trouble with his teachers, had some mild brushes with the law involving fast driving, disturbing the peace, drinking, some drug use. Always a risk-taker, Bonny urged him to new heights, be it cliff-diving at Thunder Bay, swimming in the underwater caves off Skeleton Point or any number of other dangerous activities prohibited by the coastguard.

"But Lucas is bright." Hu's Coke arrives, brought by a tall woman with olive skin and black plaits streaked with silver. He thanks her and stabs the ice with a straw while he thinks what to say next, being careful. "Lucas knew—knows—when to stop. Bonny? She always egged it." He sits back. "Cruising for a bruising. That's what folks said about those two. When Bonny...when Bonny had her accident..." He looks away across the bar. "...folks kinda agreed she had it coming."

"They did?"

"Lucas was wild, but he never hurt anyone. She was different."

"How?"

"When Lis was born, Lucas quietened right down. Took his responsibility seriously, apart from that crazy-ass job he does. Bonny just carried on."

"Carried on what?"

He jabs the ice, rattling it in the glass, poking at the lemon slice. "She, uh, messed about. He went crazy."

Crazy enough to murder her?

He shakes his head like he's reading my mind. "Deep down, Lucas is a real good guy. The best.

Nothing wrong with Lucas, in spite of what people think."

"And what do people think?"

"You speak beautifully, do you know that?"

Eep. I'm losing him. "What do people think about Lucas?"

"Uh, you know." He drains his glass, probing the last dark drops trickling through the ice.

"Not really."

"Thing is, a mad old Abenaki woman saw him coming back from Emerald Lake alone, when Bonny should have been with him, the night she died."

"Agat?"

"You know her?"

"Not really, but I—"

"Hu!" A group of people come in. "Hu! Hiya, Hu."

Hu slides out of the booth. "I gotta go."

"Of course. Thanks for the wine."

"You're welcome."

He hurries off, unnecessarily fast, if you ask me, to get his hand pumped and back slapped by the new arrivals. I finish my wine and wander out into the mild evening air to wait for Alice. What, exactly, did Hu mean by *messed about*?

Does he mean what I think he means? What it universally means?

Chapter Eleven

Honestly—and perhaps it's a good thing—I haven't got much time to deliberate these issues because Pick has roped me into the end-of-term school party.

"The little lemon sponges you made for the Fathers' Day celebrations were *out of this world.* Clearly, you are a competent baker. Can we count on your assistance?"

"Yes, of course." I don't hesitate for a second; I'm that flattered.

"I'm putting you in charge of the naughty corner."

That figures. "What do you want me to do?" Offer dry crusts to those who have misbehaved?

"Ah!" She pats her stomach, covered by an apron where pairs of animals spill out of Noah's Ark pockets. "You will be responsible for the dessert section of the buffet." She hands me a list of names of mothers—and one father—who bake. I glance at it, recognizing no one.

"Great." I fold the list and shove it into a pocket. I'm not contacting any of those people, because I can do this myself.

In the end, I get all the help I need. At zero hour, two mums I barely know from school—Judy and Valerie—come over and help me while I'm finishing off a batch of cherry tarts, each with a glazed cherry and green marzipan leaf. Judy rolls pastry for chocolate cheesecake slices, while I get stuck into a sticky toffee cake, and Valerie starts on a raspberry and blueberry trifle.

Halfway through the morning, Jay Sawyer arrives to take the Jeep away for service.

"I'd forgotten," I wail. "Not today, please! I have so much to do." I spread my hands out to encompass the entire kitchen, both ovens working, pans on five of the six hotplates, microwave running and dishwasher on the third load.

"No problem." He accepts a cup of coffee and, unasked, washes the mug when he's finished, plus every item in the sink, at lightning speed, stacks it in a teetering pile on the draining board and leaves with a smile and a wave, telling me he'll make a booking for next week.

Judy chuckles over the caramel sauce she's watching on the hob. "That's Lobster Cove style for ya. Good man, Jay."

Something I've noticed: Jay's softened quite a bit since our first meeting. Is it to do with Alice's friendship with Molly? Lucas's absence? Or perhaps the presence of these members of the school gates' brigade in my kitchen, all hands willingly on deck?

By the time school's out, we're done. All I have to do is make the ice cream and the filling for the fruit flan, offered as a healthy option to those watching their weight—although you'd be kidding yourself if you ate the pastry.

In the end I buy the ice cream. I'm not a saint.

****

"You're a *saint*," Pick cries, hands clasped,

surveying the dessert display, laid out on gingham cloths on trestle tables in the school hall.

"Why, thank you, Mrs. Pick." I smile.

"Call me Ruth. And—" she clasps the hand of a man standing next to her—"meet my husband, Ronnie."

Red-headed, red-bearded Ronnie is an oyster farmer and yachtsman. He towers over Ruth, unrecognizably radiant in his presence, in her pretty yellow and white polka dot dress with flared skirt and fitted bodice—Pan Am breasts notwithstanding. Looking at her this way, she can't be much older than me.

"Lucas not here?" Ronnie asks.

"No," I say.

"When do you expect him home?"

"I-I don't really know."

He studies me for a moment while he eats a sausage roll. "Everything all right?"

"Yes. Why?"

"Seems a while since Lucas was in town." Clearly, concerning school matters, there are Chinese walls between Ruth and Ronnie. I'm grateful.

"He's delayed in Aberdeen," I say quickly, offering a bowl of cheese straws. "The weather, you know."

He nods. "Yeah, I know."

I look across to the group of small children sitting on a mat to one side of the hall, entranced by the clown hired to entertain them. I'm not telling anyone about Lucas being hurt. I have no details, and vitally, Alice knows nothing. Furthermore, John asked me not to tell her. If I spread the word, she might pick up something distressing via one of her friends. I watch her, cross-legged at the clown's feet, almost on top of the toes of his long, squeaky shoes, enthralled, laughing up at him with delighted eyes as he pulls yards and yards of knotted scarves out of his right ear.

She's too young to worry. I'll do that for her.

****

On the day school closes for the summer holidays, I get a message from Lucas. Alice has run ahead into the house to deposit her book bag and the pile of drawings she's brought home. I retrieve the message and stop, halfway through the sea horse door, one hand on the cool carvings of the metal handle.

Lucas. *Hi there.*

Hi stranger, I reply. *How are you?*

OK.

Only okay? I delete that. *Good. We've been waiting and waiting to hear something from you. Alice misses you.* I delete that, too. *We miss you. When are you coming home?*

Soon.

Can't wait. Delete. *When? Can I tell Alice?*

No.

When?

As soon as I can.

A day? A week? A month?

Tell Alice I love her.

I call John while Alice is lunching on chicken and vegetable salad, a small whole-wheat cheese sandwich, and fruit smoothie.

"He's broken two fingers," John tells me, "so it's probably a little difficult to text. I'll let you know when I hear something." I can hear he's rushing so I let him go. What else has Lucas broken? Why didn't John tell me about the fingers?

Over the next days I squeeze nothing out of Lucas. He is not communicating. He answers my texts in monosyllables. Two to be exact, in response to any question I ask: *No* and *Don't know*. It's better than nothing, isn't it? At least we know he's alive. But is he okay?

Alice stops asking about him, like he's faded out of her life.

Two broken fingers explains the radio brevity, if not silence. Except it doesn't. At breakfast one morning, with my phone on the table in front of me and Alice looking on with interest, I discover I can text or call whichever two fingers I leave out, including both thumbs.

Something's wrong.

Alice asks for more fruit smoothie, and as I get up to get the jug out of the fridge, a movement catches my eye. The tall kitchen doors are open to the sea porch and the stunning outlook of sea and sky. A brief thought occurs: I'm so worried about Lucas I can't enjoy all the sheer breathtaking beauty of what's around me. I stand and stare. On the ragged lawn, mid-way between the house and the slope to the beach, I see a familiar figure—white-haired, brown-skinned, wearing an ankle length shift and clogs. She lifts her face to the sun and holds up her arms. I can just hear her wails over the sound of the surf.

Agat.

"More smooothieeee, pleeeease."

"Coming up." I pour the last of the thick, pale liquid into Alice's glass, give it to her, and put the jug in the dishwasher.

When I look again, seconds later, the figure's gone.

I run through the house to the front door, standing wide open to the perfect afternoon.

"Hey!" I yell, expecting to see her racing down the driveway. There's nobody in sight. Anyway, she could access the front of the house from the beach, so why not leave that way? It's one of the things I love most about Lobster Cove—how people leave their doors and windows wide open, and don't bother to fence their properties. Right now, I'm not so mad about that tendency. I wait, watching and listening, until Alice comes outside and asks me what I'm doing.

"Looking for something," I say. I grasp the big sea horse handle, close the door and lock it. On the sea porch, I walk up and down, scanning the lawn and the shore to the east. There are distant figures walking on the rocks, but they could be anybody.

Alice follows me onto the grass. "Lara?" She tugs my hand.

"Mm?"

She points to the ground. "What's those?"

I look. In a semicircle around the steps leading up to the porch there are small crosses.

Crosses?

I look closer. Dozens of small crosses, maybe a hundred, hardly taller than toothpicks, each one bound at the centre with twine, stand upright in the untidy grass in a perfect semicircle around the bottom step, like…

Like what?

Like you're not supposed to go inside the house.

Voodoo. That's the word that comes to mind.

I stare at the crosses, unwilling to step back over them.

"Come, Alice." I pick her up and carry her around the side of the house, where I heave her over the porch rail well away from the scene of Agat's nonsense. I clamber after her, making her laugh.

Alice has a birthday party this afternoon. Jay Sawyer and Molly are picking her up in twenty minutes, and I know exactly what I'm going to do while Alice is away. I'm taking a drive out to Emerald Lake to have a word with Agat. It's time. Before things get worse.

Alice leaves. I'm locking up when the phone rings. John, thank God, with an update. "Everything's going real well. Lucas is making progress. He'll be home pretty soon. Nurse Nina says he's responding well to the data you send."

"The what?" Sudden thought: Is he also responding well to Nurse Nina, whoever she may be?

"Photographs of Alice, messages."

"Who is Nurse Nina?"

"My contact at the hospital."

That's not what I meant.

"Thank you, Lara, I'm sure your efforts mean a lot to him."

"My pleasure, John. Any more news on exactly when he'll be home?"

"We'll know soon," comes the habitual answer. "There's one more thing. Will you be able to hang around after Lucas gets home? Until things are back on an even keel?"

I say I will. Does he know something I don't? Probably. Definitely. We hang up. Why does John leave it so long to tell me things? He's not aware I care. Why am I so anxious?

Unsettled, I go outside to the car, triple checking that the sea horse door is locked.

Chapter Twelve

Agat is in the house; I know it. I skip the friendly-knock routine and bang on the door. Nothing. Should I walk around the back? No, I'm not comfortable doing that. For now, it's a step too far. Frustrated, annoyed, angry, a little frightened, I go back to the car, sit there for a while and think, half-hoping Agat makes a voluntary appearance, half-hoping she doesn't. Why am I even messing around here, when I should have gone straight to the sheriff?

An old blue ford truck stops beside me on the gravel road, and a man hangs an elbow out of the window. "Can I help you?"

"Not really. I'm looking for the lady who lives here, but she's not in a social mood."

"She has mood swings for sure, depending on what messages she's receiving from the spirits of her ancestors." He winks. "Agat is my mother's ant, so I know how she can be."

"Ant?"

"My grandmother's sister. Half-sister, in reality."

Aunt. "I see. Well, I'll have to come back another time."

"I'm Angelina, by the way."

Angelina? He, no, *she* leans through the window and offers her right hand for me to shake.

"I'm Lara Fairmont."

"Yeah, I know. The Blue Rocks' nanny."

We crank hands like the pistons on a steam engine. Wow, she is *strong*.

"Most people call me Angie." She drops my hand, sitting back in the cab, drumming her broad fingers on the faded paintwork of the truck's door. "You must be kinda special if Lucas Dalton lets you drive that badass Jeep of his."

I laugh. "Nothing special about me. Anything but."

She laughs too, and thumps the door panel with the flat of her hand. "Then you're my kinda gal. You got time for coffee?"

"Um—"

"You came all the way out here to see Agat, but she ain't playing ball, so you got time."

"I'm going to wait here a while, until she's in the mood to talk. It's urgent."

"Mind telling me what it's about?"

I hesitate, my mouth dry. "She, um, left some signs, little crosses, at Blue Rocks. I'd like to know what they mean."

Angie's face changes. "Shit!" She throws the truck into neutral and yanks the handbrake. Leaving the engine running, she slams out of the cab and stomps over the road, skirting the house straight to the back, like I didn't want to.

I wait a good ten minutes, guilty that I've— ridiculously—told tales like a child. The chug-a-chug of the old Ford engine and its warm, oily smell keep me company until Angie comes back, striding on chunky legs, shaking her cropped head.

"Follow me," she calls. "We'll do that coffee."

She takes off in a cloud of dust. I turn the car in

Agat's driveway. There's no movement at any of the windows, but I know she's watching. I feel her eyes like she's sitting on the dashboard, staring at me, inches away.

Following Angie, I'm aware I probably shouldn't. Are my life-preservation antennae set too low? Or am I a dumb city-dweller who is out of touch with the fundamentals of human trust? I drive after her. If her place looks dodgy, or if it's too remote, or I feel threatened in any way, I'll simply stay in the car and leave. Brave enough to seek the hostile company of Agat, I can hack this. I lock the doors and drive on, along an ever-narrowing road. The trees close in, leaving only a thread of blue sky visible between their dark points. We turn right, we turn left, and left again, and again, then right.

Will I ever get out of here?

Angie slows on the bumpy track and pulls well over to the right to let another car pass, talking to the driver as she eases by. I recognize the car, and the woman, one of the school mums I'm pretty sure. Yes, I'm right. I don't know her name, but there are the twins, Ben and Grace, in the back, waving to Angie like mad.

That's better. We drive on, past a sign that says Little Harbor and through a white, five-barred gate. Angie parks next to dark red barn conversion, with grey roof and white window frames—under a magnificent spreading tree that looks a lot like a London plane.

"Maple," Angie tells me. "We get a ton of syrup from this one." She points to a pipe and tap set into the bark.

Maple syrup from maple trees? Is she having me

on?

"Carrie says sorry she couldn't stop. The twins are mighty late for that birthday party."

"Carrie?"

"We passed her in the red car on the way in. Carrie, my partner."

"Oh, right." I see. "I've seen her at school, but we haven't met." I follow Angie to the house, stopping to admire a bank of handsome purple hydrangeas flourishing alongside the path.

"These are gorgeous!" I've never seen such beautiful plants.

Angie takes a large, leathery leaf, like she's holding the plant's hand. "I love them like my own kids. Grew them from cuttings Lucas's mom gave me years ago, back in the day when Blue Rocks had a magnificent garden."

I'm amazed. Now, the sad remnants of garden at Blue Rocks are nothing more than evidence of malnourishment and neglect, of something beautiful gone to waste.

We go up the steps onto the porch, where a row of blue Adirondack chairs stand in a row, facing the lake. Angie tells me to sit. She disappears through the front entrance, the screen door swinging shut behind her. I wait in the cool shade of the long porch, admiring the smooth sweep of lawn down to the water's edge. There's a coppice of silver birches planted on a curved finger of land to the left. I spot a weathered teak bench between the pale trunks, where there must be a glorious view across the water. To the right, echoing the curve is a semi-circular jetty which starts out at the foot of a giant willow. The birches and the jetty almost enclose a full circle of green water—the Little Harbor of Emerald Lake. I relax, soothed, revelling in exquisite birdsong. How could bad mischief be afoot amid such beauty? I'm overreacting, aren't I? Agat is obviously a local character who has episodes of—

"The little monsters finished the milk, so I hope you take it black." Angie's back, handing me a mug.

"As it comes, thanks."

She flops into the chair beside me. "So, Carrie and I have been together ten years, and we adopted the twins back in 2010. We prefer to live out here, well out of the fast lane, even though the good folks of Lobster Cove are real charitable and broad-minded."

That's good to know. "If I had a house like this, I wouldn't live in town either."

"It's a beaut, isn't it? We saved it in the nick of time. The roof was all but gone by the time the sale went through. Lucas helped us renovate. He did all the architectural and engineering work."

"He did?"

"Yeah. A real closet architect, that one."

I look around at the solid tradition in every detail—the door hinges, the porch railing, the shutters, the subtle richness of the red colouring, the white trim, all set on blue fire by the splendid hydrangeas—and marvel. Who would have thought?

She slings a thigh over an arm of the chair. "Blue Rocks is a pretty nice house. Lucas virtually rebuilt that too. You must enjoy going home there."

I laugh. "Unfortunately it's not home."

"Agat seems to think it is, for you."

"She does?" What?

Angie gazes at the lake, her eyes narrow. "Agat

isn't, y'know, psychic as such, but she's pretty damn spot-on on most things. She thinks you got feelings for Lucas."

Now I'm looking at the lake.

"She thinks," Angie goes on, "you should stay away from him. She says he's bad. That's why she's doing all this weird stuff."

I watch a small swallow, dipping low to drink, touching the surface, pushing dainty, overlapping circles of ripples over the still water. "Do you think Lucas is bad?"

"Nah. He's all right." She chuckles. "Hell, there was I time I coulda almost straightened out for a guy like Lucas, know what I mean?"

"So what's Agat got against him?"

Angie turns in the chair to face me, legs tucked under, mug held in both hands, like she's cold. "You know about Bonny, Lucas's wife?"

"I know she drowned and that some people in Lobster Cove aren't so sure it was an accident. I know there was a trial, and Lucas got off."

She nods. "Agat gave Bonny facial treatments once or twice a month, so—she claimed—she knew something of what went on. For example, the night Bonny drowned, Agat knew that Bonny and Lucas had a fishing trip planned to Phantom Creek, that side of the lake." Angie thrusts her chin out, glancing across the water to the opposite shore, and then back at me. "Emerald Lake isn't so much a lake as a complex series of saltwater inlets, and you really have to know your way around. Lucas does, and they planned to take a canoe and a tent and spend the night up there, chilling out. The creek is the most beautiful part of the lake.

You have to see it to believe it."

"What about Alice? Where was she?"

"Lucas's parents lived in Lobster Cove back then. His mother was still alive. They had Alice for the night. She was a year old. Anyhow, Bonny went to Boston for a big party, promising Lucas she'd be back in time to go camping, but she came home mighty late. Lucas's story, in court, went along the lines that they argued and he took off by himself. In the morning he came home to find Bonnie washed up on the Blue Rocks beach, dead."

"Why didn't Lucas go to the party with Bonny?"

"Who knows, but rumour had it Bonny was seeing someone in Boston. Someone at that party."

"Odd that Lucas didn't go along and keep an eye on her."

Angie shrugs. "Unfaithful is unfaithful. How's keeping an eye gonna help?"

We sit in silence for a minute, watching tiny blue-grey birds with black heads fuss about in the lower boughs of a big pine tree. "What you are seeing there," Angie points, "are black-capped chickadees, the state bird of Maine."

"They're lovely. Positively acrobatic."

She chuckles. "Sociable little things, patriotic too. The tree they're in is an eastern white pine. The cone and tassel of that tree is our state flower."

Head back, I look up to the top of the pine. "I don't think I've ever seen such a tall, straight tree."

"Those pines played a major role in the history of Maine for hundreds of years, for building houses, ships' masts and so on. Even for the Royal Navy."

"How interesting."

"You're getting a whole history lesson, right here in the garden."

We watch the chickadees until a fat mourning dove lands on a branch above and scatters the lot.

"Lucas managed to source a whole lot of old pine wood to use in this house, when we renovated. He picked it up somewhere the other side of Bangor. So, history lives on, all around us."

I nod, watching the little birds regroup in a bush closer to the water, and guide Angie back to the original conversation. "So Lucas. What happened to make people think he had killed his wife?"

Angie puts her empty coffee cup on the floor, sits back again in the chair and folds her arms. "Agat saw Lucas driving back to Blue Rocks past her house, before sunrise that morning, alone."

"But did anyone seeing him leaving Blue Rocks the previous night *with* Bonny?"

Angie shakes her head. "Not a soul. Not one. Agat claims Lucas pretended to make up with Bonny, brought her up to the lake under cover of night and romantic pretense, killed her, slung her in the boot, took her home and tossed her into the sea when he got back to Blue Rocks, unseen in the pre-dawn darkness."

"That's crazy! Why would he, anybody, do that? Why not dump her in the lake?"

"Because there were no rocks and surf to bash her head, to cover up the damage he did."

I frown. "Why didn't he kill her at Blue Rocks and have done with it?"

"He couldn't kill her inside," she says, slowly, "because that would have messed up the house and spread DNA everywhere. And he couldn't kill her down at the beach because, three years ago, when it all happened, there were younger trees along that road. You could see right over them into the cove at Blue Rocks. Anyone could see what was going on down there. Now that those trees have grown, the cove is only visible in the winter, when the leaves have dropped."

I thought so.

"Besides, she was a keen sea swimmer, and a good one, but she wouldn't set foot in a lake."

"Why?"

"She told Agat the water was too dark."

Sick, I look out over the lake, gunmetal-grey now in the afternoon sunlight, and shiver. So, wherever Lucas had killed Bonny, it made sense to have her "wash up" on the beach. That way, it looked like the most natural accident in the world.

"Agat said," Angie goes on, "that Bonny was afraid of the water creatures."

I look at Angie. "Creatures?"

"Aw." She waves a hand. "Folklore. Nasty little aquatic pinching creatures called Pimskwawagenowad. And then there's Dzeedzeebonda, a monster so hideous, he can't look at himself—"

Dzeedzeebonda?

I think back to what Cherri said, and recall how Agat spoke about Dzeedzeebonda and Lucas like they were one and the same person. Was Lucas too ugly to look at himself? Did he have that much blood on his hands, and in his heart?

"What about Alombegwi—?"

Angie cuts me off. "Alombegwinosis? He's a shape-shifter, an upsetter of canoes. To see him is to foretell a death by drowning." She dismisses that chilling statement with another flap of a hand.

"You said Lucas and Bonny took a canoe—"

"Yes. The canoe was one thing, the engagement ring another. Agat's claim that she had seen Alombegwinosis on the shore of Phantom Creek the evening before Bonny died, was yet another."

I'm sitting forward in my chair, half-turned to Angie, staring at her. "What happened to the canoe?"

"Lucas lost it. There was a big storm that night. Although he tied the canoe fast to a tree, he says, the wind ripped the rope, and the canoe was washed away. About a year ago, some guy was dredging the shore below his cabin to build a jetty, and he found it, pretty much intact. The cops dragged it off and sent it away for forensic tests, but nothing conclusive came to light. It had been in the water too long. Well hidden, some said."

My skin cools and prickles. "And the ring?"

Her ring went to Alombegwinosis.

"Yeah, the ring. A crackerjack of a diamond. It disappeared. In court, under oath, Lucas claimed Bonny always took it off when she swam, in case it slipped off her finger in the cold water. When she swam in the cove at Blue Rocks, he said, she always, without fail, attached it to a cork key ring and put it in a crevice in the rocks, always the same place. Some people she knew, folk from the local swimming club, testified to that."

"It probably got washed away."

"But the cork would have floated, so it should have washed up, storm or no, like she did. Some folks reckon Lucas took it off her finger before he killed her, not quite able to kiss that amount of money goodbye."

"That's not fair." I look into my mug, half-filled with cold coffee, as dark as midnight.

"Sure isn't, but there's no proof. Folks like proof."

"What happened then?"

"The cops searched the beach and the surrounding shore with dogs and metal detectors, you name it, but the weather didn't play ball. The storm pounded that cove for three days and charged the shape of the beaches up and down the coast. There were gales and flooding and destruction everywhere. Emergency services had their hands full and once things had got back to normal, and by the time Lucas had been dragged to court, the heat had kinda gone out of the case."

"Did Lucas have a good defence lawyer?"

"Damn right he did. The hottest shot from New York, Hank Martinez."

Hank Martinez. Yes, I've heard of him, and I don't even live on this continent. His lifeblood is the dark side of celebrity scandal, worldwide. "What then?"

"Martinez walked all over the little people of Lobster Cove, ridiculed local traditions, legends and beliefs and got the case thrown out on the first day of the trial. No evidence, no witnesses, nothing real. Said mythological drivel could not be tolerated in a court of law where a man's freedom was at stake. The town divided. Some said Lucas would be in jail if not for his wealth, that he'd bribed Martinez, that they had some sort of arrangement. Others let it go."

"What did Bonny's family think? And her friends?"

"No family. She was fostered her whole life. One family to another. No love lost. As for friends, Bonny knew everyone and everyone knew her, but no one called her a friend. Ladies had to watch their husbands around Bonny Dalton. She didn't obey the boundaries. She could be a little scary like that, to tell the truth."

I gather. And I've heard enough telling of the truth for a while. "About Agat's visit to Blue Rocks this morning," I say, standing up, "and all those little crosses—"

Angie takes my mug. "Can I reheat this? Can I get you a fresh one?"

I glance at my watch. "Thank you, but no. I must go." I look up and our eyes meet. "Is it a curse?"

"No." She shakes her head, firm. "No. It's a little, you know, token. A little sign."

"To do what?"

"To keep Lucas away, she told me. But that's hardly going to work, is it? I mean, come on."

It's working now.

"Should I tell the sheriff?" I ask.

Angie presses her lips together, shaking her head. She walks with me to the car where we say goodbye. "Pop in anytime, you hear?"

I thank her and drive off, following rustic signs pointing the way to the main road at every fork, intersection and turn.

Chapter Thirteen

The minute we get home, Alice—high on sugar, admittedly—turns clingy and whiny. She wants supper, she doesn't want supper, she's thirsty, she isn't thirsty, she doesn't want to bath, she does want to bath, she cries in the bath, she cries while I dry her. I put her to bed half an hour early. She doesn't want a story. All she wants are her blue pyjamas and her Daddy. I can only provide one of those precious items. I sit on the edge of her bed, studying her photos of Lucas, stroking her back until she falls asleep. Where is he? Why doesn't he come home?

Later, outside, I stand on the sea porch and look at Agat's little crosses. I'm actually here to clear them away, but something's stopping me. I don't want to touch them. I call the sheriff's office, and a young officer, Nate Harris, is dispatched to assist. He arrives within minutes, asks a million questions and takes copious notes. He asks if I'd like to lay a trespassing charge. I don't. All I want is for it not to happen again, and that's what I tell him. That done, he pulls on a pair of latex gloves, goes down the porch steps and removes the crosses into a plastic bag, which he seals. He doesn't touch them either, come to think of it, with his gloves and all. Why didn't I think of that? He's kind and considerate, super-polite, but I feel like an idiot who's wasted his time.

Lighting trembles in the black clouds bunched over the sea, and there's a spit of drizzle in the wind. The angry grumble of surf rolls toward me over the untidy grass. Can I muster the courage to get Uncle Buck down here to mow the lawn? Probably not. Maybe I'll call him tomorrow, depending on the weather. A squall hits the beach, driving up the shore to the house. I shut myself inside, eat supper, watch a little television, finish a heap of ironing and Skype Julie.

Julie's been on Google and come to the staggering conclusion that the sensation of overwhelming love toward one's newborn baby is not a given.

"What if I don't love this baby, Lara? What if I take one look at it and reject it outright?"

"*Of course* you'll love it! Don't be ridic—"

"Not necessarily. A high percentage of mothers feel little or no love at all in the first few hours after birth."

That figures, but I don't want to say so. "You will love her, Julie, or him. I love Alice, and she's not even mine."

"You do?"

I do. I really do, and I tell her again.

"If I don't love my baby, will you love her for me?"

For God's sake. I close my eyes and speak gently. "Yes. I will. I promise."

"You'll be back in England for the birth, won't you, Lara?"

I have no idea. At the moment I can't possibly think of leaving Lobster Cove. "Julie, you have a husband—"

"It's not the same, as you very well know. Derek

has absolutely no idea what I'm going through."

Actually, *I* have no idea. "Let's hope Mum will be back in time."

"Mum will be frozen into the Antarctic pack ice, like always. I'm going to need you, Lara. Please make sure you're here."

"I'll do my best." And I will. Also, at twenty-eight, she's three years younger than I am, and I must remember that.

The call over, I look out of the kitchen windows. The storm's passed, leaving a chill on the evening air and an untidy straggle of leaves and twigs on the sea porch. I fetch a giant outdoor broom, and pull on, over the top of my clothes, that black tee-shirt of Lucas's—the one Alice slept in that somehow has never made it back to Lucas's closet, but ended up in mine. Hair in a tight knot on top of my head, I go outside barefoot and get started on the job. Wow, hard work, and sweaty. The porch is huge and hasn't been cleaned for a while, never mind the storm. I sweep the leaves into a garbage bag—they blow straight out—and trail wet brown footprints wherever I walk. At last, the main debris out of the way, tied up in bags, I mop the planks several times over until, hours later, the water in the bucket is almost clear.

"That'll have to do," I tell the moon, rolling between windswept clouds over a broken sea. "Phew." I empty the bucket over the side of the porch railing, and the fright takes my breath away. There's a dark figure on the lawn. Cold fingers grab my heart. I push fallen-down, damp hair off my forehead with the back of my hand.

Who is that?

Chapter Fourteen

The bucket falls from my hands, into the long grass. "My God, it's you!"

"Yeah." Lucas comes out of the shadows, up the steps and into the house. He walks through the kitchen into the hallway—me on his heels—and drops his bag on the thin rug, looking around like this is the first time he's seen his own house.

"Are you okay?" I ask, breathless like I've been punched. Clearly not. His hair is shaved really short. He's ill—hollow-eyed, pale, pinched and hunched.

"Yeah." He stares at me, arms at his sides. "I tried the front door but nobody answered."

How are your fingers? Is about the lamest question I could ask right now. Also, it would be skirting a larger issue.

I clear my throat. "The sea's loud tonight, so I wouldn't have heard. I've been outside, cleaning up after the storm."

He nods, eyes on my face.

"Why didn't you call?" I ask. "I could have collected you."

"Skeet dropped me off."

"Right." We look at each other. His eyes are in shadow, hiding something—at least it seems that way, in the dim light. "I'm so sorry about your colleagues," I say. "John told me they didn't…" I swallow, with difficulty. "…didn't survive."

He puts a hand to his face, pressing his forehead hard with his fingertips. "No." His voice breaks. He rubs his eyes, squeezed shut, with forefinger and thumb.

I need to lighten this, but carefully. "How are your fingers?" My voice comes out steady, and normal.

He opens his eyes, looks down at his fingers—not the ones with the scars, the other ones—frowning like he's trying to work out what they are. "Good," he says, eventually. "Good."

"Good," I say back. "Well!" The attempt to breathe and smile at the same time turns into a nervous gulp-type laugh. "Welcome home. You certainly gave us a fright."

He steps forward, studies me up close for a few moments—no smile, nothing in his eyes whatsoever. He's merely looking. "I gave myself a fucking fright," he murmurs, and disappears up the stairs. Up in the gallery, he leans over the bannister and says, "By the way, nice shirt."

That's all he says to me for three days.

****

I'm a spare part. The next morning, Alice abandons me the second I say the magic words, "Daddy's home." I get up early anyhow, three days running, and hang around while they do stuff together. This morning is car-wash time. Jay collects the Jeep, and Lucas unlocks the garage to extract a well-hidden vintage "Mustache," Alice tells me. She has her own bucket of suds and a green rectangular sponge bigger than her head.

"I'm allowed to wash the wheels!" She calls when I bring coffee out to Lucas.

"What else have you got stashed away in that garage?" I ask Lucas, peeping in.

"Coupla things."

"Is that yours?" I point to a large motorbike, right at the back.

"My dad's Harley."

"Is the car also your dad's?"

"No."

Your mother's? Yours? John's? Fair enough, he doesn't want to talk. Lucas is, I suppose, getting back to himself, trying to repair himself. In the sinister depths of the black North Sea, he was working with people who died, and I need to remember that. To stop myself talking to myself, I go inside. Every now and again, I look out of a window to check on Alice. Maybe the car belonged to Bonny. I won't ask him. No talking about dead people. Not yet.

I'm checking on Alice, keeping an eye. This has absolutely nothing to do with the fact that the weather's warm and Lucas has his tee-shirt off.

Around noon, Lucas and Alice take off in the car. I go down into the forbidden cove with a book and sit against a sun-warmed rock, my feet in a crystal clear rock pool. I guess I deserve time off, but I feel strange, nevertheless. I didn't like to ask Lucas where he and Alice were going, but surely, common decency—elementary manners, even—dictates that he could mention where they were headed and, at least, roughly when they might be back?

After a couple of hours it's too hot, and I wander back to the house. The remains of lunch are on the table.

Pizza.

Lucas and Alice are in the den, watching football on television, arms wrapped around each other. I go upstairs, lie on my bed and read myself to sleep. My phone beeps and wakes me. Holly wants to Skype. I glance through the window and then at my watch. Late afternoon already. I get up, shower, get dressed and open my laptop.

Holly's met someone! Mere days ago, at the recycling centre, a man backed his Audi into her Mini, *somehow* getting his tow-bar stuck on her bumper—giggle. They had coffee together, straight after the incident, and he phoned her the next day to ask her out to dinner.

"Just at a pub, Jazz, but it was fun!" She tells me all about it: what she ate, what he ate. What they drank. How he kissed her very lightly on the cheek—but fairly close to the corner of her mouth—when he sent her home in a taxi—for which he paid—afterwards.

"How's your love life, Jazz?"

"Still in square one." Like it's been all year. Square one and I've yet to throw the dice. Am I even on the board?

"When are you coming home?" she asks, in the middle of our goodbyes—an afterthought, I can't help thinking.

"Soon. I'll be home in the next few days."

"Date?"

"I'll let you know." I log out and look up.

Lucas is standing in the doorway.

"Yes?" I close my laptop and push it to one side.

He hesitates. "Uh, I'm going for a run. Is that okay? Alice is downstairs, watching TV."

"Sure." I join Alice, enraptured—again—by Ariel,

star of *The Little Mermaid*, and Lucas takes off down the beach. He's been gone ten minutes when the sea horse doorbell rings. I leave Alice in the den and go see who it is.

Alex Campbell, one of the younger local doctors, stands on the doorstep and asks if Lucas is home.

"He's out for a run," I tell him.

"How long for?"

"I have no idea. Can I get him to call you when he gets back?"

"Which way did he go?"

"Come in. I'll show you." He follows me through the hall, into the kitchen and onto the sea porch. I point down the beach and show him where the steps are.

"I'll go meet him," he says. "Thanks."

"Is everything okay?"

"He missed an appointment this morning. Do you know anything about that?"

"No."

"Have you, er, noticed anything out of the ordinary? Concerning Lucas, that is?"

"I can't say, because I really don't know Lucas at all. He left the morning after the evening I arrived and, to be honest, hasn't said much to me since he got back."

He frowns, thoughtful. "Okay. I'll have a word." He turns his back and walks away.

Will he get to the bottom of Lucas's silent distance? Is Lucas suffering the after effects of a harsh wake-up call—like delayed shock? Is he depressed? Or is he feeling his way through some kind of lengthy recovery phase after a head injury? Is this normal Lucas, or Lucas the new stranger?

An hour later, they're back. They stand out on the

grass and talk for ages. Alex leaves, eventually, and Lucas goes for a shower, and to put Alice to bed and read her a story.

"Where were you," I ask, when he's back downstairs, "after the accident on the rig?"

He looks at me for a moment, eyes in shadow. "Where was I? In the Royal Infirmary in Aberdeen, then with a, um, friend in Scotland, then briefly with my dad in Florida."

So a long time in Scotland. "I didn't know. Anyway, I guess it's nice to have a friend in Scotland when you need one."

He frowns. "She wasn't really a friend."

"Oh, I thought you said—"

"Just one of the nurses who was...real kind. She went the extra mile."

I bet she did. Bloody hell! "Nurse Nina?"

He's taken aback. "How do you know?"

"John told me."

"What did he say?" Lucas's eyes are shrewd, his mouth curling into an almost-smile like there are happy memories to be had.

"Nothing."

"She had time off, and nobody to spend it with. She took me to the Highlands. We drove around the lochs, ended up in Edinburgh. Awesome. You have a beautiful country."

Hmph! "I do. However, I am not Scottish."

He grins at my peevish tone. "Ah, Great Britain, British Isles, United Kingdom, I never did get all that." He holds up his hands in apology.

"Well, I'm glad she, Nina, got you through all...all that."

"She didn't," he replies, taking his phone out of a pocket. "This is what got me through." He holds up the phone. There's my photo. The selfie I took of me and Alice when Lucas was so cross with me over the blue pyjama crisis.

"Do you want something to eat?" I ask, adventures with Nina fading to insignificance.

"Not hungry, thanks." He goes into his studio and closes the door.

After I've eaten and watched a re-run of *Goodwill Hunting*, I clean up the kitchen, put in a load of washing and go upstairs, stopping halfway. I'm the wallpaper on Lucas's phone. That's meaningful, but Alice is there too. He didn't have to use that picture. I've sent loads of Alice by herself, or with Buster.

I go back down the stairs. "Lucas?" I knock on the door and open it. He's sitting at the other desk, back turned to the window, facing me, head down, drawing in a sketchbook. Even at this distance I can see it's an excellent drawing of a house. I go closer. "That's brilliant. Is the closet architect at work?" I smile.

He closes the book. "The what?"

"Angie. She told me you're a closet architect. I've been to Little Harbor. It's beautiful."

The silence bulges. What's going on with this man?

"So," I say. "Anyway. I think, perhaps, my job here is done, Lucas. What do you think?"

He stares down at the sketchbook for a moment, picks it up and tosses it onto a pile of papers on the far side of the desk. He looks up at me, blinking, coming back from the faraway place he's been to. "What do you mean?"

"You're home now, and I should move on."

"No need. What's the rush?"

What does *he* mean? "I thought I'd stay for Alice's birthday party, and leave after that."

"Birthday party?"

"On Saturday, this Saturday, in five days' time. The day of her actual birthday. I've invited her friends—the ones who aren't away on holiday—and some of the parents are coming."

He gazes past me, totally elsewhere, not listening. "Okay."

Although I talk about the party in the following days, and even go as far as reminding him about it, he tells me two days before that he's going away.

"You can't, Lucas."

"I have to be on a rig in the Gulf by tomorrow evening."

"The Gulf?"

"Mexico."

I'm so disappointed I can't stand up any more. We're standing face to face in the hall, but I flop onto one of the window seats, close to tears. "Lucas, everything is planned. Barbecue lunch for the parents, the birthday cake, the games, *everything*. Alice has a new dress. She's so excited."

"I have to go."

"*Please*, Lucas."

"It's an emergency."

"Like last time? And look what happened? You almost died!"

"I won't be diving. Not yet. I have to pass a medical—two medicals actually—before I dive again."

Well, isn't that something? "You know, Lucas, to

135

me, sometimes the diving sounds like the safe part. Why, why on earth do you risk your bloody neck in this stupid bring-your-own-body-bag job when you have Alice and—" I look up into the double volume space above the handsome staircase—"this magnificent place to live in?"

He's looking at me, but I'm not going to look back at him.

"You have other talents," I go on, glancing at the study door. "You have it all."

"Bring-your-own-body-bag job?" The amused tone of voice, like he's about to burst out laughing, doesn't upgrade my mood.

"You told me you put on a body bag before you get into the helicopter—"

He laughs. He actually laughs. "Body bag is a nickname for the rubberized submersible suit we wear on the helicopter in case it crashes, and we all land in the water, or in case we get blown into the water when we land, or merely *fall* into the water. Without that suit, we'd freeze to death in seconds. Average surface water temps are pretty low in the North Sea, even in the summer." For the first time since his return, he sounds positively animated.

"I can't imagine anything worse!"

"Working in a shark cage is worse, even if the sharks aren't particularly hungry."

"You're not normal, do you know that? You're mad. Stark, staring mad."

He smiles. "I'll be okay." Somehow, this macabre subject has cheered him up.

"But what about Alice?"

The smile turns to a grin. "She won't miss me."

I'm so angry I can't speak.

However, come the day, Alice's birthday is a huge success in Alice's eyes, and that's what counts, what matters most. Everyone comes—not a single cancellation. I'm convinced most haven't been to Blue Rocks before. It's something about the way they look around the hallway, wide-eyed, as they come through the sea horse door. Lucas is *so not here* it's unsettling and awkward, though everyone is super polite and diplomatic.

"Some inquisitive folks in Lobster Cove," Angie murmurs out of the side of her mouth, confirming my suspicions while we dispense fruit punch in pink plastic glasses, "but you can't blame them. Lucas is unknowable and, on top of that, they can't work out whether he's tragic or heroic."

Unknowable.

Chapter Fifteen

"How are things at Blue Rocks?" Cherri asks when I drop Alice off at the beach for the Green Club holiday gathering. Today is all about whales, and Cherri has got the kids building a sperm whale sandcastle, thanks to a heap of perfect-consistency imported sand and the enthusiastic efforts of two lifeguards.

"So-so," I tell her. "Lucas got in late last night from Mexico, so he's resting up, taking it easy."

"Good. Good. You tell him we're having a good ol' wine and cheese tasting at Merlot's tomorrow night. Make him come."

"He won't." He won't. He's already said no to Alice's school play, though it's weeks away yet. I have yet to dredge the courage to impart that chestnut to Ruth Pick.

"Can I say something?" Cherri weighs her words. "Perhaps…" She pushes her blue-framed sunglasses onto her head, diamanté starfish sparkling at the hinges. "Perhaps, you know, it's time."

"For what?"

"For you to stop enabling his behaviour."

I frown. "How am I enabling his—"

"Perhaps, honey, it's time for you to go home." Head on one side, she pats my arm, smiling with kind eyes.

One of the little boys comes running, crying, with

sand in his eyes. Cherri rinses and soothes, claps her hands to assemble the group and issues a brief riot act on the rules of rock pooling. Then she sets off, crystal beads glittering, blue extra-plus sundress flapping like a tent in the breeze, the children in a cluster around her, flanked by the lifeguards, looking for all the world like a whale herself, going to a ball.

"I must go home soon," I tell Alice, on the drive back to Blue Rocks.

"Here home is!" she exclaims, pointing at the house, as we drive through the gate.

"Not my home, your home. I have to go to *my* home, in London."

"I come?"

"When you're older."

"You come back."

It's not a question. I smile. "Maybe. One day."

That evening, once Alice is tucked up in bed, I notice how quiet the house is. I make supper and watch television in the den. When the movie's over, I switch off lights and go to the kitchen to put out fresh water for Buster and nibbles for his midnight snack. There's no sign of Lucas, and he wasn't here to kiss Alice goodnight. Come to think of it, I haven't seen him all day. He must be out. I doubt he's gone to bed early. He doesn't do early nights in spite of the early mornings. Over the last few days, he's been in his studio until late, working on one of the computers, or standing at the drawing board, or bent over a desk, or making endless phone calls, just getting into the swing of things by the time I go up to bed. On my way upstairs I press my nose to the glass door of the studio, to confirm he's not there, staring into the dark room for a few minutes.

Where's he gone?

"A penny for your thoughts."

I jump. That's Lucas, right behind me.

"Isn't that what you Brits say? A penny for your thoughts? What're you looking at, thinking about, Lara Jasmine?"

Is he slurring? Yes, judging by the smell of whisky.

"Layla." Hic. "Fairmont."

I turn around. Lucas, always clean-shaven, has stubble. He's got a tumbler of whisky in one hand and the bottle, half empty, in the other.

He wags a finger at me, sloshing booze, because it's the hand holding the glass. "Hu at Murphy's says you were asking questions. About me."

"Lucas, don't."

He raises his eyebrows. "Why are you asking questions?"

"You need to get a grip because I have to go home soon."

"Home?"

"To London." Sigh of relief from me. Subject of questions forgotten, by him.

He squints at me, befuddled. "Why, Princess?"

I take a deep breath. "I'm enabling your bad behaviour by staying here."

"Huh?" He leans against the wall, next to a shallow, square niche, lit by a single spotlight, yet empty—a place where a painting should hang, or where a graceful curve of silvered driftwood should stand and be admired. He raises the bottle and places it in the niche with exaggerated care, tipping his head to the side to admire it.

"I'm going home, Lucas, and you have to clean up

your act. Do you understand?"

"Sez who?"

"Cherri suggested that—"

"Sh-Sherri, and a lotta other people in this town can fuck off, Layla." Hic.

I stare at him. "Is that so?" Clearly, I can't talk sense to him now. Also, while it might be a good idea for me to go home, it's not going to happen while he's unstable. Is this why he's been withdrawn? Has he been building up to something? Whatever, I can't leave Alice. Not yet.

"What do you think? Do you think I..." He sways. "I murdered my wife?"

Why this? Why now? "I have no idea."

"Everyone else in Lob...ster Cove has an idea. One way or the other. What does a-a sexy, intelligent, uh, beautiful person like you think, huh? Huh?"

"I don't, um, really know anything about it."

"You do, because you asked Hu. He told me."

"Lucas, I think—"

"If I tell you the truth will you stay?" Hic.

"I think you should eat something, take a cold shower, and go to bed."

"Will you stay? Will you? C'mon Layla...Jasm...ine. We could be good together. Real good."

I sigh. "*Staying*, Lucas, isn't a question of bargaining over you telling me—or not telling me— something. It's about my job, being professional, knowing when—"

"Her keys. That was the thing. Keys. And her ring. Together." He shakes his head. "They, police, said that was the clue. I hid them. They said."

141

This is exactly what Angie told me. I put out a hand. "Give me that glass."

"No." He tips back his head and throws the whisky down his throat. Most of a glass in one go.

I swoop for the bottle, get there first and rush to the guest loo to pour the rest down the drain. Will he follow me, get aggressive? I go back into the hallway. Where is he?

"Hey," he says, somewhere in the shadows. "Beautiful Lara."

I almost jump a whole floor to the gallery. "Bedtime now," I say, brisk and Pick-like, hoping he won't be smart-arsed about the concept of "bedtime" and how we may share it, by having sex.

He looms out of the darkness, coughing like he's going to be sick. It wouldn't be a train smash—there's not really much to be sick on, apart from the bare floor.

"Are you okay?" I usher him to the stairs. There's way more than half a bottle of whisky behind this state of affairs.

"No. That'sa problem. It's over."

"What?"

He taps his head. "Over." He stumbles upstairs, crashes along the gallery and slams his bedroom door.

What? I wait, listening, hoping he hasn't woken Alice. When silence settles, I go into the kitchen, put a few things in the dishwasher and turn it on. I close some of the shutters and pull a few blinds. The pantry door's open. I glance in as I close it and there—for God's sake—is a new case of whisky. Twelve bottles, assorted brands. Not on my watch. Not while Alice is mine to care for. I carry the bottles in batches of four to the sink and pour it all away, half-drunk myself from whisky fumes by the time I've finished. The empty bottles get replaced in the box that gets pushed to the back of the pantry. The recycling can wait.

Later in bed, windows open to an unusually quiet sea, I deal with things one at a time. Call me an idiot, but I like Lucas. Just not this Lucas. This Lucas shocks me with his wild, desperate eyes and unguarded talk. This Lucas is different and dangerous and out of control. Foolishly I had daydreamed about Lucas bringing that magic into my life—I'd seen us together, picnicking, swimming in the cove, brunching at Ned's Lobster Shack, in the window at Maggie's, or on the porch, waving to the sheriff as he drove by, to Skeet, the school mums and Alice's friends, even Pick, but a Pick wreathed in permanent smiles, peppered with dimples. I'd seen us slowly getting to know each other while Lucas recuperated. I'd seen us having fun, but there's no fun to be had with this Lucas.

This is not the Lucas I realized I loved when John made me think he had died. Does that even make sense? How can you love a man with whom you spent a few short hours, sorting out a stuff-up? That's how long I spent with the Lucas I liked. A few hours, followed by a void of absence, and now days and weeks with the stranger who returned in his place. The answer to these questions drifts out through the front door, now that I let it out of the storeroom of my subconscious.

The thing is, I probably don't love Lucas. I love Maine. I love the sky and the clouds and the sea, the little yachts tied up at Pier Two, the buzz of the harbour where fishing trawlers and tour boats potter, the shops and restaurants along the front, the pale grey storm-weathered gables topped with tarnished copper weather vanes of whales and moose and flying geese. I love Alice and everything about her: the school run, the extra activities, the weekly shop, even mending her little blue pyjamas, hunting down wool so I can darn her split-open sea horse and fixing her books. It's important stuff, all that, compared to luxury picnic hampers, for God's sake. Who cares about those? People love them, they don't actually *care* about them. Here at Blue Rocks, I'm working hard, earning money and making a difference. That's the difference. Picnics don't matter. This matters.

I'm in love with life in Maine and all the unique characters that contribute to its charm, down to Queenie the chicken. Add to that a Lucas-like equivalent of good standing and even temperament, and life would be bloody perfect.

Dozing, waking, I listen—the only sane person—I think—in a household that's falling apart. Was it ever on an *even keel* as John suggested? Around two in the morning, in the deep, black silence, I hear noises. I get up and hurry out of my room, along the gallery. Lucas, being violently sick. Retching and groaning so badly I want to be sick myself. I sit on the floor outside his room and lean against the wall, waiting for him to finish. Eventually, the toilet flushes and I hear the gush of a tap, turned on full. I stand up, knock on the door and push it open.

"Lucas? Are you all right?"

He's sitting on the bed, head in his hands.

"Wait there," I say, a non-essential instruction. He's not going anywhere. I fetch a big glass of water and several aspirin. "Take these," I say, holding the tablets out in the palm of my hand. He does, fumbling, spilling the water, his hands are shaking so much. "Are you okay? Will you be okay?"

He doesn't really answer that question. He says, "Fuck," falls backwards on to the bed, rolls himself up in the duvet—after a fashion—and drags a pillow over his head.

Leaving the door wide open I go back to bed, Fraught and exhausted, I sleep, on and off, still listening, worried Lucas will throw up and choke himself to death.

Chapter Sixteen

Before dawn, Alice gets into bed for a cuddle. She's delightful, warm, cute and drowsy. I wrap my arms around her and, wide-awake while she sleeps on, I think about what to do. Not for long. The next thing I know the room's full of sunlight, and Alice has jumped out of bed.

"Yay, Daddy!"

"Hey, angel," Lucas says, "Winnie-the-Pooh's on. Run downstairs, will you?"

She scampers off. I sit up, covering a yawn, pulling the bedclothes around my mostly-nakedness and pushing my hair into some sort of shape that doesn't resemble an electrocuted mop-head. "What's the time?"

Lucas, contrite, chastised and pale, is dressed, shaved and loads neater than he's been for the past while. "Nearly nine."

It can't be! I look at my watch to check it's true. It's true. "I'm sorry, I overslept."

"Don't worry about it." He's carrying a cup of something in his hand. "Tea," he says, "for you." He puts the cup and saucer down on the bedside table and sits on the bed, well away, near my feet, and studies me for a long minute or two. I wish he wouldn't. I'm a wreck after so little sleep and I bet I look it.

"I apologise for my behaviour last night," he says.

"That's okay." Hmm. White polo shirt, longish

dark blue shorts, a light distribution of dark hairs on tanned skin, that brown hand with the white scar running across the knuckles, resting on a blue, heavyweight cotton thigh...

"Can we forget about it, please? It won't happen again."

Concentrate. I sit up, pushing my hair back further, putting a hand over the giant yawn that's splitting my face. "Yes." I yawn again. "Sure. Of course."

"Did I...did I say anything really dumb or offensive to you last night?"

"Er, no."

"I'm not...I don't normally do that." He holds my eyes with his haunted, hunted ones. "What I did last night. I'm sorry."

"Sure." I sip my tea. This is the best cup of tea I have *ever* had, and I tell him.

"It is? I had to ring John's wife to ask how to make it."

We laugh, and the tension shifts—a little. "I'm touched." I am, truly. When last did a handsome man bring me tea and heartfelt apology in bed? Too long ago, and he wasn't that handsome, PS.

It's awkward. Him sitting on the bottom of my bed and me...well, me quite unable to focus on anything other than that—him, sitting on the end of my bed. Something's going on. There's a vibration in the air, like two auras touching—I read that in a book about ESP by the way, and always thought what rubbish—but now I'm not so sure...I look straight at him, but his eyes are too much, too sombre, too serious, too deep. Full of questions. I swallow and inspect my teacup. Empty.

"I failed my medical," he says.

I look up. His eyes hold mine this time, anguished and intense. "I'm sorry."

"I have a second one in a few weeks. If I pass that, I might be okay, otherwise it's over, and I guess I'll have to find another career."

How can I possibly respond to that? "You'll be fine." I nod, to convince myself.

There's a wry smile and a shrug. "I love it."

"I know." But I don't understand. Who would dive in the freezing blackness of the North Sea for a living? Or swim with sharks to earn a crust? I suppose someone's got to do it. Why does it have to be Lucas?

He looks down at his hands, running a thumb over that scar line across his knuckles. "I know that what I did last night is no way to deal with the situation. Any situation."

I nod more. Good, because I confess I was frightened last night. Lucas is big, nearly a head taller than me and super-strong. If he'd really got out of control, really wanted to harm me—

Would he actually do that? You see, I don't think he's got it in him, even when he's blind drunk. Don't ask me how I know, but there's a solid, fundamental decency to the man and he wouldn't go that far. I trust him not to.

But if he ever threatened Alice, or God forbid hurt her, I would kill him. I would.

Then we'd see who was up for murder.

"If you threaten Alice *in any way* or hurt her, I will kill you," I tell him, pleasantly enough. Yes, I am a catastrophist.

Hard to imagine, but he turns several shades paler

and looks positively ill. "I would never do that. And"—he removes the cup from my hand—"I have never threatened or hurt anyone, ever." Our eyes meet. His hold the reflection of my unswerving challenge. "Also, I did not murder my wife."

"I know."

"Are you sure?"

"Yes." Am I?

"Good." He leans forward to put the cup on the bedside table, standing up in the process. Hands in pockets he turns to the window and stares out over the ocean. What's coming next? A revelation about a missing engagement ring or lost key to the sea horse door?

No. Something altogether more sinister.

"Do you like camping?" he asks.

Er, no! On a scale of *likely* to *unlikely*, camping would score an *absolutely not*.

He stays at the window, the morning sunlight touching the front of his shirt, and looks straight ahead through the gap in the shutters. What's the view like this morning? I'd like to get up and stand next to him, perhaps a little behind, and look around his shoulder at the sea and sky, awash with a fresh, new, blue day.

"We like to go up to a place called Emerald Lake."

"Phantom Creek?" The words shoot out of my mouth before I can stop them.

He turns his head and looks at me for a long, long moment. "No," he says eventually. "I don't go there any more."

"Why?"

"Bad memories."

"Like the beautiful little cove, right here on the

doorstep of your house?"

He looks back out the window.

I've got the high road now, after last night, but I've probably said too much. Hell, the point of no return has come and gone. I go further. "If you don't face your fears, they'll hold you back all your life, and Alice too. You don't socialize, and there are a whole lot of places in town you won't go. You don't attend school functions, or Lobster Cove events, even when people reach out to you. You don't even live here. You have a job that takes you all over the world, as far away as possible."

"Had."

I'll let that go for now. "Where's it going to stop, Lucas? You need to grab hold of life and lay some good memories over the bad. Otherwise you need to get away and start over, somewhere fresh, or Alice will grow up with your hang-ups holding her back. New beginnings, Lucas, come on. You can't change the past, but you have the power to make the future bright."

He turns to face me, hands back in his pockets, eyes hard. "And how the hell am I supposed to do that?"

"By starting now. By starting over. Now. Do it for Alice if you can't do it for yourself." Okay, I've said my piece and I'm going to shut up.

His eyes don't soften. He stares me down. "Would you like to come camping with me and Alice?"

"I'm sure you and Alice would really enjoy some time alone together."

"Is that a no?"

"Yes. Thanks for inviting me, but no, thanks." It's not going to happen. Me and camping do not go together and that's never going to change.

He puts his head on one side, eyes shrewd now. "Why? Are you afraid of something?"

"Everything. The dark, the bugs, the bears, the cold, the dirt, the rain, the salient fact there's no hot shower or proper loo."

His face breaks into a grin, an instant transformation, like switching on a spotlight in a pitch-dark room. I am so dazzled I'd have fallen over if I hadn't been in bed. "The salient fact there's no hot *showah* or *propah looh*." He mimics my accent to a T, all prim.

I blush. "Stop it, Lucas. Don't tease. It's not funny."

He comes toward me, bends to level his eyes on mine. "If you don't face your fears, they'll hold you back your whole life." He raises his eyebrows. "New beginnings Lara Jasmine. New beginnings." He straightens up and goes to the door.

"No, Lucas, I'm not going—"

"I already told Alice you're coming. She's real excited."

"Well, you'll have to tell her different. I'm not—"

"Do it for Alice, if you can't do it for yourself."

I sit up, wrench a pillow from underneath me and hurl it at him with both hands and all my strength. "*No. Stop it.*"

He bats it back, and it hits me on the head. "We'll leave mid-afternoon. Pack warm stuff." That grin again. He leaves the room. "Bring along the *Hoovah* if it makes you comfortable."

I pull the duvet over my head, but I can still hear him chuckling all the way down the gallery.

I. Am. NOT. Camping. Seriously, I'd rather stick needles in my eyes.

****

Although forgiveness is in the world's best interests, Lucas will not be forgiven any time soon for dragging me out to this here lake. However—and this is the confusing part—Angie's right. Phantom Creek has got to be one of the *most* beautiful places in the world, and if I wasn't camping, I'd be missing Mother Nature, showing off in all her glory, sending the sun westward, taking the sparkle out of the water and leaving behind the softest shade of violet, like smooth, pale amethyst silk.

While I'm admiring the breathtaking vista of lake, hills and sky, Lucas swiftly pitches two tents, about twenty feet apart, on the shaggy, wild grass of the flat bank above the pebbly shore. This done, he lights a fire. Alice, tummy full of early supper, wiped out by over-excitement, is drowsily waiting on the moon.

"There's no moon tonight, sweetheart," Lucas tells her, over and over. "You go lie in your tent and I'll wake you if it comes, okay?"

In she goes and all is quiet. When I check ten minutes later, she's fast asleep, blue polka dot sleeping bag pulled up around her ears, buried in a pile of favourite teddies. I report back to Lucas, asking what I can do to help.

He flicks open a camp chair. "Sit here and keep an eye on the fire."

I sit. He goes to the truck, parked some way up the rough track, behind the tents and comes back with a fishing rod. Moving quietly, like a cat—although not one like Buster, who stomps—he goes down to the shore and onto some rocks. He casts a line. The lure drifts against the sky and lands light, shooting delicate golden ripples across the water. I hope he doesn't catch anything. On the way here, Alice was so upset at the sight of a dead duck on the road that I would hate to have to explain the ethics of fish killing. Fingers crossed nothing's biting.

The daylight slides out of the sky; the rocks, trees and Lucas turn black against the purple water. Seconds later, it's dark, and there's no moon to keep me company in this small circle of firelight. Why am I sitting alone in the flickering dark in a place called Phantom Creek? I stand up quickly, ignoring the cold prickle on the nape of my neck, and go over to Alice's tent. There's a hurricane lamp and a highly effective bug trap hanging on a branch at a safe distance. I peep in. Nothing's changed. All is peaceful. I'm not alone, not with Alice right here, even if Lucas has been swallowed by the night. I pull my head out of the tent and look around. Here he is now, coming up the beach, empty-handed, to my relief.

"Did the big one get away?"

"Sure did." He goes down on his haunches to prod the fire with a stout stick.

"Is there anything I can do?" I ask, thinking about supper.

He bestows a sudden smile. "Relax. You must be exhausted after digging in your heels so hard."

I glare, but he doesn't notice.

He sets up a little folding table and fiddles about with some plastic containers. Now he's got meat out, succulent entrecote steaks, dripping marinade. As they go onto the fire, the liquid sizzles into the flames and sends up a rich, delicious blast of herbs and oil. There's Indian corn on the cob, enormous jacket potatoes crammed with butter and a salad made of everything in the world: slow roasted tomatoes, spring onions, pine nuts, parsley, peas, semi-soft cheese, and tender leaves.

I am starving.

Oh, and now he's clearing the second table, where Alice sat for her supper earlier. Tablecloth, napkins, plates, knives and forks and wine glasses—*wine glasses*—come forth along with a mini lantern doing duty as a candle.

"Let me—"

"Sit." He waves the barbecue tongs at me. "I've got this."

I sit again, well out of the smoke, and gaze into the fire, across the vast black pool of the lake, and up to the first stars pricking the blackness. All set to *not* enjoy myself, I somehow am. This part is okay; it's fun. Also, it's a real treat not to have to cook. I feel spoilt.

During dinner, we talk loads about Alice—how much her vocabulary's increased, how much she loves books, how she's shooting up, all general stuff. After that, he tells me about the food; how much he loves to cook outdoors, how he's been camping out ever since he was Alice's age. The fire dies, he makes me coffee and we discuss the stars. He points out some of the constellations, Ursa Minor and Ursa Major, and Pegasus, over in the east.

"We never see those in England," I say. "It's always overcast." It is, a lot of the time, but somehow I haven't found time to search the heavens for stars. Perhaps you need a special person to help you find them.

I brush my teeth, wash my face with extremely cold water, and head for my tent.

"Are you joining me?" Lucas asks.

"What?"

"That's my tent. Yours is over there." He points.

"I thought I was sleeping with Alice."

"I am. That's your tent opposite. I thought you could use a little privacy." He hands me a spade and torch and points to where the "toilet" is. The fun stops here. Through the dark bushes, into the night, in Phantom Creek? I'm not going. I'll hold it in until morning.

In my private, tiny tent, torch balanced upright in one of my shoes, I scramble out of my clothing, and dig around in my bag for a pair of winter pyjamas. Sitting—because that's all I can do—I put these on, plus some thick socks, and find a bulky long-sleeved tee-shirt to pull on over the lot. The night is cool—not freezing, but by no means warm. I fold my clothes, place them on my bag and slither into the sleeping bag. It's brand new. Did Lucas buy it especially for me? I'm touched if that's the case. I even have a mattress and pillow—something I wouldn't associate with camping, had I ever given it a moment's thought. I switch off the torch and listen to the silence come roaring in.

Maine—the way life should be: you know, I'm starting to believe that. I turn over. I'll never sleep, in spite of the comfort of my bed, I'll never sleep, I'll never...

I do, because I wake up, in pain. My left leg's trapped, the one closest to the outside of the tent. In an instant, I'm wide awake. What's going on?

What's happened?

Chapter Seventeen

The possibilities are few. Is it a boulder that's rolled off the mountain and come to rest on top of me? But what mountain? There are some low, forested hills behind us, through which a boulder could not roll. I shift, and pull, and then kick.

"Lucas!" I yell. The boulder, which is very hot, I might add (is it volcanic?) moves, I swear. I freeze, and listen. There are noises: loud squidgy, bubbly sounds like a tummy rumbling. A huge tummy.

A huge tummy? A huge tummy of a giant, warm, moving thing?

What…?

No. Oh. My. God. Ohmygod! OHMYGOD.

It's a bear.

I should not have shouted! I've disturbed it, but at least it's moved and my leg is free. I move away, all the way—a full twelve inches—to the other side of the tent.

Startled, sleepy—I hope—grunt from the bear.

I wait, terrified, ears straining, as quiet as the dead person I might soon be. The bear settles again, rolling inward. Very slowly, I reach for the flap that covers the little window in the front of the tent, and lift it. I see black. Lucas doused the fire when we went to bed, and he doused it well, but its remains are somewhere to the left. His tent is opposite mine, I'm sure, not more than twenty feet away. How do I warn him? How do we get away? Dare I switch on the torch? The bear snorts, shooting my heartbeat right off the scale. Can it hear my heart beating? Can it smell me? What do I know about bears that will help me survive this situation? Over the years I've seen loads of American movies starring bears, yet I only know two things about them: one, they all look the same, and two, they are always, but *always*, pissed off.

Right. Make a plan or die. My plan is this: to silently unzip my tent, flash a beam of torchlight toward Lucas's tent, run for it, wake him, and listen to instructions. On my knees now, I pick up the torch with difficulty, my hands are shaking that much. Nose to the ground I find the zip. Holding my breath, I ease it up a few inches and push the torch out.

The bear farts. Imagine—when you're seconds away from a heart attack anyway—a short, sharp burst of ten trumpets in a cupboard under the stairs, only…trumpets don't stink. I know what's coming, but I can't hold my breath any longer. The stench almost knocks me out. Is this even normal? What is *wrong* with this bear? He settles, spreading himself, squashing me, tipping the tent, bending the frame. I have to get out. I hope to hell I can run fast enough. The torch is on and I'm out of there like a Usain Bolt of lightning, only twice as fast.

I duck behind Lucas's tent, heart thundering. "Lucas!" I hiss, "Lucas, Lucas, wake up!"

"Wha—" Startled, sleepy grunt from Lucas. Too loud.

"Shhhh."

"Who's that?" he asks in a low voice, wide awake.

"It's Lara. There's a bear."

A second later, he's upright in front of me, Alice in his arms. "In the car. Quick. Don't make a noise."

Luckily he's wearing white shorts. I follow those at speed, up the track, silent, because our lives depend on it.

Lucas opens the Jeep, slides Alice onto the backseat and pushes me into the driver's seat. "Strap her in," he says. "If there's trouble, go for help." He switches on the ignition, halfway, so the lights come on.

"I'm not going anywhere without—"

"You'll get a mobile signal on the main road, a mile or so past the turnoff to Little Harbor."

Is that so? "Get in the car, Lucas."

"Relax."

Relax? I grab his arm. "Please can we leave? Let's go. Who cares about a bit of camping equipment?"

"It's not a bear. No one's seen a bear around here for a long, long time. They were shot to oblivion over a hundred years ago."

That's too bad, but right now I don't feel sorry for bears. The less the merrier, as I see it. "Lucas—"

He's gone. I lean forward over the steering wheel, eyes popping to see beyond the beam of the headlights where he's stepped into the dark. I wait, tensed solid, expecting the bear to emerge any second, dangling Lucas's blood-stained head in his claws. Wait, I hear something! I lean out of the car window.

"Shoo. Shoo. Off you go now. Good boy." Followed by some gentle hand clapping.

What the hell is that about? Is Lucas a bear-whisperer?

He comes back to the Jeep, smiling. "Take it easy," he tells me. "That's no bear, it's a moose."

"A *moose*?"

"Yeah." He grins. "He's a beaut. One of the biggest I've seen around here."

I think of the antlers mounted in the hallway back at Blue Rocks. "Are they dangerous?"

"Not really."

Not being a total idiot, I'd choose survival over death any day, but somehow I feel stupid having been lain on by a non-dangerous animal. "He was bloody heavy!"

Lucas's face is over-straight. "Sure."

"Why would he want to lie on me?"

"Something attracted him."

"Like what?"

He shrugs. "Perhaps he was lonely, looking for company or warmth. Perhaps he liked your smell."

I smell like a lady moose? This is not something I'd add to my online dating profile, if I had one—unless I stay in Maine. Also, the way Lucas is standing there, looking at me through the window of the Jeep, mouth curved up, amusement kindling in his eyes, he might as well be laughing out loud in my face. There's no difference.

"Not funny," I warn, but smiling because I can't help myself. Besides, I've made him laugh and that's lovely to see.

"No," he says, and, unable to control himself, bursts out laughing, properly, moving away from the car so he doesn't wake Alice. I open the door and tumble out of the driver's seat, laughing with him.

"Shhh! Shhh!" we urge one another between outbursts, which makes everything funnier. I laugh until I'm weak. Weak and brave, because I *desperately* need the loo. I fetch the torch and the spade and go up the path a little way from the camp. Along with the retreat of adrenaline, the relief is exquisite.

That done, I find my way back to Lucas, who's surveying the remains of my tent without much hope in his attitude. He thinks a moment, goes down on his haunches and gathers my bedding.

"I'll stick it in the back of the Jeep," he tells me. "You can sleep there."

"Um…" There's no cover on the back of the Jeep. Lucas took off the roof thingy, to load up back home, and then covered everything with a neat tarpaulin, which is now folded away in the darkness somewhere.

He strides off, chucks my stuff over the side of the truck, and points a thumb in the general direction. "In you get."

I obey. What must I do now? The obvious. I pull my bedding straight, separating mattress from sleeping bag from pillow, and rearrange everything into a bed. Cold, not thinking *at all* about what lies beyond the headlights this time—correction, what lies beyond the darkness because Lucas has switched off the headlights—I snuggle down quickly and shut my eyes: it's lighter and brighter that way. Pray God the one hundred year bear absence continues because I feel like the last sardine laid out on a tapas tray. Imagining—or is it dreaming?—a bear at a cocktail party, with red lipstick and bright red nail varnish, paw hovering over the salmon blinis, the sudden jolt nearly shoots me over the side.

I die of fright, scream, use the F-word, sit bolt upright all at the same time. It's Lucas, chucking his stuff into the truck and jumping in after it. Alice stirs—

hardly surprising—inside the cab and he reaches through the back window to soothe her.

Lying back, eyes shocked wide open, I stare at the sky—black velvet encrusted with diamonds—while my poor heart hammers its way down the scale of terror, to normal, not for the first time this evening.

Lucas, with much fidgeting, sorts out his bed, making it up, getting in, getting out, getting in again, while I pretend to be asleep. The truck rocks on its advanced, multi-something suspension and I roll from side to side in my snug cocoon. Eventually he settles, like a dog that's turned around and around on a chosen spot. All is absolute silence, and darkness.

"Hey?" he whispers.

Hey what? More rustling, and—my but he's deft!—he slides down the zip of my sleeping bag and takes my hand, clasping it in his, fingers laced. Right. After much accidental touching, and that silly goodbye kiss Alice forced on us, we are *deliberately touching*. A touch for touch's sake, rather than the long way around to something else.

Well.

"You okay?" he asks.

"Mm." Fake sleepy, but wider-awake than daytime itself. To be honest, it's nice having a large, strong mountain man sleeping by my side. I'm no camper. That's it. That's all.

"You're a born camper," he says.

"Am not," I whisper, after a suitable interval.

"You did everything right. Even when you fully believed there was a bear lying on you, you didn't flinch."

The American meaning of *flinch* is possibly

161

different to ours.

"You remained calm and followed instructions. You're a born survivor."

He's just being nice, but I like the smile in his voice. "Even the light show was perfect," he says.

"What's a light show?"

How sexy is that soft laugh, coming at me through the blackness? "It's what happens if you go into a tent, switch on a flashlight and take off all your clothes."

That explanation takes a moment or two to sink in.

"And," he goes on, "when picking a spot for ablutions, go behind a really *thick* bush and switch off the flashlight."

"Oh," I say. "I see."

And so did he, obviously.

"Hmh," he murmurs, and that's it. His hand goes slack and his breathing deepens and steadies.

I stare into the dark, confused. As a romantic, first-kiss venue, this location has advantages: delicious meal, wine, handsome brave man, stars; and disadvantages: back of truck, toddler sleeping eighteen inches from my head, no actual kiss. Why am I thinking about this? The cocktail-party bear would be a safer train of thought. Anyway…

I'm warm, comfortable, safe, wanted—*wanted*, Lucas wanted me to come, and being wanted is a brilliant feeling, so surely he… No, I'm leaving next week…in a couple of days, going back to London. No way can Lucas…and me.

Asleep.

Chapter Eighteen

Everything's back to normal. Lucas is happy, Alice is happy, and I...

My work's done. Time to go. My flight's booked, my bags packed and loaded in the Jeep. Lucas insists on driving me to the airport while Alice stays with a babysitter.

Saying goodbye to Alice is the hardest thing I've ever had to do. We sit on the bench outside the sea horse door, her on my lap, and hug each other.

"Be a good girl. Look after Daddy, see?"

"And Buster."

"Buster too."

"You come back."

"I'm going home now, sweetheart."

"I miss you. You come back."

I swallow. "I'd like that."

She presses her face to mine. "I love you."

"I love you too, darling."

I unwind her arms from my neck and hand her to the sitter, and then navigate toward Lucas and the Jeep by staring at my feet, one in front of the other, through blurry eyes. He opens the passenger door, guides me in with a hand on my shoulder, pulls out the seatbelt and shuts me in. He gets in the drivers' side and off we go, me waving and Alice waving back.

"You come back!" She waves. We blow kisses. I

can't see her any more. We're through the gates and on the road. I clamp a hand over my mouth, but it's an inadequate floodgate. By the time we pass Jay's Automotive at the bottom of the road, my heart's broken, and I'm howling.

Lucas doesn't say a word. I'm in a bubble of grief, worlds away from him. Although, there is one sad connection—this is how he must feel *every time* he says goodbye to Alice. How can he bear it? Why does he do it? Whatever, it's none of my concern now. That last fact inspires me to cry more and harder. I cry and Lucas drives, and this is how we eventually get to the airport.

"Thanks," I manage, when we approach the terminal buildings. "Please, drop me off—" Oh. He's in the parking garage already, swinging the Jeep into one of the few available spaces.

I release the seatbelt and reach for the door, but he puts out a hand to stop me. "Just a minute."

The interior of the car is quiet, but for the panic-attack intensity of my heartbeat. I glance at Lucas, who's taken something out of his pocket.

"Thank you for everything you've done for me and Alice." He hands over a small carrier bag printed all over with turquoise and silver wavelets. I peep inside. There's a small, flat box, a little bigger than a matchbox, wrapped in the same paper, tied with a silver chiffon bow.

"You've been incredibly generous to me as it is, Lucas. You really don't have to—"

"Open it."

"Now?"

"You have time."

I do as he says.

Oh!

Two small diamond sea horses. Those ones. The earrings I lust after each time I pass Jewels of the Sea.

Open-mouthed, I turn in my seat to face him. "How did you know?"

"Alice took me straight there. The day we washed the Mustache."

"But Lucas, I-I can't accept these." I thrust the box back into the bag and hold it out. "They're diamonds, and...and..."

"And what?"

"Um, they're expensive."

"You'd have preferred moose-shaped ones, wouldn't you?"

I have to smile, though I'm awash in tears. "Or maybe lobsters."

He smiles too, closes a hand over mine and pushes the bag back to me. "I want, Alice wants, you to have these."

"They're too expens—"

He shuts me up by leaning close and touching my cheek. "You deserve them. At the very least."

"No, Lucas, I—"

"You were, are, the best. You earned them. Does that sound better?"

"No. You paid me for what I did. You *over-paid* me. They're too much." I give them back. If he thinks diamonds will dry my tears, he's very wrong. With fingertips pressed to my eyes and tears leaking everywhere, I crouch in the seat, utterly baffled by my despair and confusion. Quite apart from anything else, I'm an idiot for being so out of control of my emotions. It's embarrassing. Lucas must be dying to get rid of me.

He drops his hand and moves back, holding the pretty little box loosely on his thigh. His chest heaves, up and down, in a mighty, silent sigh. "I can only do it this way, don't you see?" Silence again for a heavy quarter of a minute, then he goes on. "I have," he says, carefully, "money. And, most important of all, I have Alice. That is what I have. Everything else is…" He looks down at his hand, holding the box.

Is what?

"Is *lost*. Broken. Do you understand?"

The seconds tick away. It's not appropriate to look at my watch, so I don't. Another thing: right now, I don't care if I miss my plane.

"I'm…I'm not sure I do, really."

After a while he says, "It's all to do with Bonny. Her death. All that.

We sit for a bit until I say, "I have to go."

He doesn't stop me. Is he relieved? He takes my hand, puts the box in it and closes my fingers around it, his hand covering mine. I look at the thin scars running across all four knuckles. "Either way," I say, "yours is a pretty dangerous job for fingers." He laughs, a brave attempt at normalcy. Our eyes meet, hold for a moment, and then we both move to get out of the car.

He gets my luggage from the boot and gives me a big ol' hug, like he's hugging his best mate. We exchange overly smackish cheek kisses.

I pick up my cabin bag, extend the handle of my case, and make ready to wheel it off. "Thanks for everything, Lucas, and—" swallow hard—"goodbye. Look after Alice, whatever you do."

"Of course." He nods, stands still and watches me walk away.

Before I get to the lifts, I turn around. "Remember," I call, "if it's lost, you can find it."

"You suppose?"

"I guess."

"Maybe."

"Keep looking."

"I do." He raises a hand in farewell. "Enjoy your time back on the mothership."

The lift arrives, the doors open, I get in, turn around and see him, standing there, staring after me, eyes dark. The doors close on my jolly little wave and that's that. Seconds later the lift lurches upward and spews me out in the departure hall. I go straight to the ladies loo, to the basin at the very end of the long washroom and take the earrings out of my bag. I cry some more and put them away. I can't wear them now. It's all too much. Besides—and I don't have to look in the mirror to confirm swollen eyes and red nose—my face is not worthy of diamonds.

I'm not sure life with Lucas would, or wouldn't, have worked out. Either way, I'd like to have known, and now I never will. Whatever happens, I will never forget this man.

Chapter Nineteen

The queue is long and wide. I lose myself in the forest of trolleys, mountains of luggage, and gabbled snatch of words from every language in the world. At last, at long last, it's my turn at the front. I've been called forward because my connection to London is already boarding.

"Well, if it isn't your lucky day, ma'am," Miss American Airlines exclaims, bright as a sunbeam.

I heave my case onto the scale. It's way overweight but there's no reaction from Miss AA. Perhaps she won't notice. Maybe it *is* my lucky day. I hand over my passport and wait.

"You," she says, tapping her keyboard, "have been upgraded to First—" she looks up with a movie-star smile—"by Mr. Lucas Dalton. Isn't that the best idea?"

"I have a better one." There's a deep voice in my right ear. Someone's standing very close, a hand on my suitcase, lifting it off the scale. Have I breached security? Am I being robbed?

I look to the side. "Excuse me! What are you—"

Lucas.

"What are you doing?" The simple sight of him brings tears to the surface.

He grips my upper arm, turns me to face him. "Let's go home."

"I am. I am going home."

"No."

"No?"

"I, er, there are things I need to talk to you about."

"What, now?" I look at Miss AA, whose eyes are ready to launch from their sockets, and then back at Lucas. "The flight's boarding. I'm late already."

"To hell with that." He steps up to the counter. "This passenger, Miss Lara Fairmont, will not be travelling today."

I pull him back. "No, Lucas. I *am* travelling. I'm going home."

Miss AA looks from me to him to me, wild-eyed, smile fixed.

Lucas smiles back. "Miss Fairmont won't be travelling."

"Lucas, stop it!" I push in front of him. I want to agree with him, but I must be careful. I have so much to lose.

"Listen to me," he says, blocking access to the counter. "This is not right. You leaving. Me letting you go. How can we be sure—" he waves a hand about, mixing air—"if we're apart?"

It's all too much. "*Why are you telling me now?*"

"Because I didn't realize until you walked away." Hands in pockets, eyes sharp with hope, willing me to agree, he looks right at me, holding my glare.

"Realize what?"

A voice pipes up behind me, sarcastic and loud, so everyone can benefit from her wisdom. "Wouldn't it be kinda nice if folks could settle their disputes outta the queue so we could all get where we wanna go?"

Miss AA's smile slips. She catches the eye of a man standing near the front of the neighbouring queue, and gives a little nod. He strolls over and hovers. I glance at his name badge: Kyle Smith, Security.

"Realize exactly *what*?" I hiss, when I want to shout. I don't mean to snap, but I'm not getting my hopes up for nothing. Also, I don't want to get arrested by Kyle under the Loud And Aggressive At The Airport Act. Kyle Smith, Security, takes the hint, and arranges for another counter to open up.

"Excuse me?" Miss AA peeps around Lucas. "Miss Fairmont? Would you be able to confirm without further delay whether you will be trav—"

"That I like you," Lucas says, straightforward and sure, like he's telling me the time.

I hesitate. Is this enough to go on? I take the plunge. "Are you sure?"

"Yeah."

I stare at him, watch the rare smile start in his eyes, though his mouth hasn't moved yet. "Oh," I say, because I haven't got anything else.

Miss AA waves Kyle over. He ropes us off from the rest while she and Lucas deal with the admin, giving me far too much time to reflect on what I've done. Am I making a massive mistake?

I like you.

Like is important. More important than *love*, many would say. I like Lucas, too. I do. I like him back.

****

On the way back to Blue Rocks—on the way "home"—Lucas asks a pile of questions about me. He's unstoppable. Why now? I field the barrage and wonder if this intense cross-questioning is something that should have happened before I did the airport turnaround. He remembers each and every detail on my

CV and asks questions around those, and manipulates the conversation so it's impossible to hold anything back. I tell him everything about my childhood, my education, my business, my business disaster, my parents, Julie, and even touch on my sad dating history, briefly, because I'm not a victim, or a loser. I'm living life to the best of my ability, aren't I? And that's what I'd like him to think, because that's what I believe.

Lucas pulls over at a petrol station at Ellsworth. While he's filling the car—and I'm wondering if I've been astonishingly weak for being so easily persuaded to return to Blue Rocks—a woman leans out of a car alongside and asks if she and her husband, fresh in from Chicago, are heading in the right direction for Lobster Cove. Lucas assures her she's on the right track and asks where she's staying.

"Sea Crest Inn, close to the spot we honeymooned thirty years ago. Bob and I met at a beach party near there when we were teenagers." She lowers her voice. "I wanted to surprise Bob with a romantic sunset picnic on the beach tomorrow. Sea Crest Inn doesn't fix picnics, though. Someone told me Mariner's Fish Fry does bag lunches, but I want something more special than that. D'you by any chance know someone who'll do something real special for us?"

"Sure do." Lucas makes a note of her name—Beryl Streep, no kidding—on his phone, tells her it'll cost one hundred and fifty dollars, and asks what time she'd like the picnic delivered.

"I'll meet you in the car park at five p.m.," she whispers, glancing though the windscreen, furtive, because Bob, presumably, is ambling back to the car. She and Lucas exchange phone numbers and conspiratorial smiles. "Shall I pay you now?"

"Tomorrow. Safe journey now." He waves them off.

"What are you doing?" I ask, when he's paid for his fuel and is back in the car.

"Giving you a reason, maybe, to stay in Lobster Cove."

Clever. I like that.

We get to the outskirts of town and drive on through to Blue Rocks. "What now?" I ask, as we turn between the gateposts.

"Right now? We go inside the house, fix a drink and go sit on the sea porch, on that swing seat, together, and wait on the moon."

But we don't. The sitter greets us at the door, anxious. Alice has been restless and fractious all evening. We go upstairs to find her temperature has spiked to one hundred and five, and spend the rest of the night with her, in the emergency room at the Lobster Cove Hospital.

Home in the small hours, Alice cool and hydrated after a rogue twenty-four hour virus "doing the rounds" we all fall into bed and sleep. I set my alarm for seven, for I have a picnic to worry about. Moving like a zombie, I make lists and drive to town as soon as the shops open for a basket, napkins, food, ribbons, card, and a million other things to make Bob and Beryl's picnic special. I totally blow the budget, but who cares? This is an investment in my future, maybe, and I'll damn well give it everything.

In the Blue Rocks' kitchen, I scrub up like a surgeon and pull on latex gloves. Yuk, but God double-forbid that I transfer one molecule of rogue virus to Bob and Beryl on their thirtieth wedding anniversary. I disinfect the kitchen countertops and the disposable containers I've bought, even the champagne glasses and bottle. I'm taking no health and safety risks; who knows if what I'm doing is even legal in the state of Maine.

And I'm nervous. It's only a picnic, for God's sake, but my confidence is lower than zero. Am I hiding from reality behind the high walls of Blue Rocks, behind that sea horse door?

Alice sleeps most of the day. She comes into the kitchen when I get back from the Sea Crest Inn stunned, basking in Beryl's effusive gratitude, though a little rattled to come across Agat walking on the road. I slowed down, to offer her a lift, but she marched on, eyes forward and unblinking, ignoring me. I drove on, rebuffed, a little shiver tickling my spine. Could Agat have had something to do with Alice's sudden fever?

No. No, that's impossible.

"How did it go?" Lucas asks. Alice stands next to him, an arm around his leg.

"She was deeply impressed."

"Of course."

"I feel amazing."

He grins, one hand stroking Alice's hair. "Great."

"Thanks, Lucas."

"Daddy?" Alice says, looking up at him.

"Yes, sweetheart?"

"Lara back, Daddy? Lara come back."

"She did, yes. I brought her back."

"Why?"

He looks down at her. "She was leaking. I had to bring her home to fix her."

Alice runs to me and we hug. "Yay," she cries.

"Yay!"

I couldn't express it better myself.

Chapter Twenty

So, if I dated Lucas—say I met him on a dating site, through work, or via one of my friends—would I want to *take it further* as the saying goes? Do I know him well enough not to scare him off?

Why did he ask me to stay? Why did I? Because I was hopeful? Now, I'm puzzled.

This morning, I scanned one of the English newspapers online, coming across an article on human attraction. Recent studies were undertaken at the University of York, around first impressions. Apparently, deciding someone's character takes only one tenth of a second. Eyes indicate attractiveness, while mouth shape is linked to approachability. Masculinity divulges itself via *structural features*— made me laugh!—or *attractive skin, e.g., tanned.*

Who knew, huh?

In conclusion, your brain requires a glimpse of one hundred milliseconds, or less, to warn you the pheromones are limbering up. The article went on to quote other studies that proved women seemed attracted to the strongest, and not necessarily the best-looking, males in a random group. Imagine doing research for a job like that? Watching line-up after line-up of strong, handsome men and pondering their attractiveness with regard to procreation. Are bespoke picnics the way forward for mankind, I ask myself? Man-studying seems mighty beneficial to the planet, although I do recycle as much picnic packaging as possible, without being disgusting.

What I'm getting at, the long way around, is: nothing's happened. I'm living a type of hi-honey-I'm-home life, without the sex. Alice is better, the school term has started, and Lucas is away, seeing a Saudi Arabian client in Dharan about a new rig in the Safaniya oil field. Julie is still sniffy about my non-return to London in her time of need; I need to remember she is the first woman in the world to have a baby, but since she extracted a promise from me to be there or die no later than the end of the first week of December, she's let up a little. My parents are coming home too, from the Antarctic freeze to the tropical climes of a London winter, already predicted to be one of the coldest *since records began* as the newsreaders are so fond of saying.

And Holly? Her head's in the clouds of paradise with Recycling Centre Man, whose name is really Alan, and has no need of proximity to anyone else right now. As for other friends, and far-flung cousins—including busy-busy-busy Lauren in New York—we keep in touch on Facebook. It's like I've never been away.

All that said, and getting back to Lucas, there *has* been a slight shift in our relationship, though it's hard to define. It's different. Like we're starting over, but from another place. He's still paying me, which on one hand is weird, but on the other is amazing because I *am* working for it, that's what we agreed, and I'm throwing chunks of money at my bank debt and, very soon, I'll be back in control. It's a good feeling.

Furthermore, news just in: Seacrest Inn has

requested two picnics for later in the week, and one for today, following Beryl's ecstatic reviews. It seems my picnic has fortified that marriage for the next thirty years at least, and it's fun to be part of that. Picnics, after all, do matter.

On the way back from the inn, today's picnic delivered, I'm cruising along in the Jeep on my way into town, minding my own business when a long, low, black car overtakes me on the blind corner. I tread on the brake as he cuts in front of me, missing an oncoming car by inches.

"Ooh!" Alice shouts, from her child seat behind me. "Ooh, very fast. I love fast."

"That's too fast, darling," I tell her, flashing the headlights in anger as the car roars around the next curve. How *dare* he, when I've got Alice in the car! Coming into town, I pass the garage and see the same car, crouching on the forecourt next to one of the fuel pumps.

Pulling up alongside, nose to tail, I roll down the window and observe. He's a fat man—with a tattoo of barbed wire around one thick wrist and heavy, silver skull-and-crossbones rings—slotting his credit card into his wallet, car full, bill already paid. "I suppose you use a lot of petrol, driving like that," I say.

He looks up at me, chewing on a huge blob of gum like a moron. "Sure do, lil' lady." He grins, showing over-white teeth. As far as *structural features* go, he scores a neat zero. "We call it gas."

"People in Lobster Cove don't drive like that. Besides, I have a child in the car. Please take care."

He laughs. "You kiddin' me? You ain't from this hick town now, are ya, Queenie? Hey. I'm here for a coupla days. Maybe I'll see ya around!"

I bristle, looking down on him, grateful that the Jeep is higher than the car he's driving.

"Queenie?" Alice says. "Can we visit Queen—"

Her words are obliterated by Mr. Manners firing up his missile. He revs the engine to screaming point, and then rockets off onto the road, burning a trail of hot rubber on screeching tires.

"What *is* it?" Alice asks.

"A subhuman creature," I tell her, smiling at Jay who's come out of the workshop to see what's going on.

"One born every minute," he says. "Ya looking for an egg, Alice?"

We go home to Blue Rocks, Alice holding her egg with customary care and attention. While I'm preparing supper, it occurs to me that somehow, in spite of all the unknowns, in spite of my recent encounter with the King of Rude, I've never been this happy in my whole life. It's a strong happiness; something I can build on.

I'm so happy.

At least until the following day, until Alice and I are playing with her dolls' house up in her bedroom.

Chapter Twenty-One

It's windy out. I start to teach Alice how to play French cricket on the grass in front of the house—even though there are only two of us—but the wind steals the plastic ball, tossing it into the battered shrubbery along the front of the house.

"Come on, let's go inside," I say. In her bedroom, I brush the tangles from her hair and replace her hairband.

"Look at my doll's house." She points.

"I have. It's lovely."

"Can we play?"

We take cushions from the bed and settle down in front of the house. It's new, white, tall and narrow, and opens by way of a façade of double doors with windows cut into them. There's a kitchen on the ground floor, a living room on the second, a bedroom on the third, a bathroom and children's room on the fourth and a room in the roof under the gable. I'm guessing an expensive present from Daddy, because the house is well-furnished, a little old for Alice, nevertheless beautiful.

"You be this doll." Alice points to a man doll, sitting on a sofa in the living room, reading a tiny newspaper. "He is Mr. Lady. I will be Mrs. Lady." She points to Mrs. Lady, flat on her back in the kitchen, pots and pans awry.

"I tell you what, Alice." I pick up Mrs. Lady and walk her up the stairs. "Mrs. Lady needs a rest while Mr. Lady cooks the dinner."

Alice tweaks the newspaper out of his little hands and puts him upright at the stove. Mrs. Lady has her rest and Mr. Lady feeds and bathes the kids—a baby and a toddler I found in the roof—and puts them to bed. Mrs. Lady comes downstairs, they have *diner à deux* and go to bed. At this stage Alice closes the front of the house and makes me lie on the floor with her, on the cushions, so we can sleep too.

Within two minutes, it's morning in the Lady house.

"The children must go to school," Alice says.

"What about the baby?"

"The baby must stay at home."

"With the mummy?"

"No," Alice replies. "With the daddy."

"Oh. Does the mummy work?"

"If she wants."

Guilty that I've been too harsh on poor Mr. Lady, I help him get breakfast and dress the kids. There's a chest of drawers in the children's bedroom, the drawers of which are stuck closed.

"It doesn't open," Alice tells me.

"But there's stuff inside." I shake the chest to illustrate my point.

She shakes her head, and walks Mrs. Lady off to work across the bedroom floor.

I fiddle and prise, and end up forcing the little drawer with a pair of Alice's blunt-tipped scissors to satisfy my…

Hold on a minute. *What's this?*

I look closer at the drawer, open now. There's a coin, a large green bead, a miniature teacup and…

And a ring. An adult's ring that looks very much like a valuable, solitaire diamond set in platinum.

Can it be—*of course not*. It's a toy! I put the drawer back and it slides freely Had someone glued it shut? What a stupid place to hide something like this.

A hundred questions fly around my head, and none of the answers are pleasant.

"Alice?"

She turns to face me, on her knees.

"Is this yours?" I hold up the ring.

She nods.

"Are you sure?" I ask.

"No," comes the answer, and she carries on with what she's doing.

Is it real? Alice tells me to hurry up and get the Lady child to school. I do, popping him into the "car"—the abandoned plastic lid of something—along with his dad and androgynous sibling, and sending them on their way.

I should tell Lucas about this ring. I look at it from every angle, unable to tell if it's real. Why wouldn't it be real? But, if it's real, why hide it here? Is it Bonny's lost ring? I shiver. Why would she do that? Or him? Or maybe Alice? It's utterly beautiful. I'm no expert, obviously, but I bet the stone's flawless.

Texting Lucas, I change my mind. I'd rather do this face to face, but why? So I can see his reaction? Why must I see his reaction? Don't I trust him?

"School's finished," Alice cries. "Mrs. Lady is coming home."

I fetch the children from school, under the bed, and

turf them out at the house, reaching all sorts of conclusions about Lucas. If that ring is real, there are going to be ugly problems. If the ring is a fake— something out of a classy Christmas cracker, maybe?— there's probably nothing to worry about, but I need to know.

Mr. and Mrs. Lady share evening chores and put their children to bed.

"Alice, how about we drive to town for an ice-cream once Mr. and Mrs. Lady are in bed?"

She's enthusiastic, and the Ladys get an early night.

"We'll drive down to Bar Harbor," I say. "Would you like that?"

"Yes!"

We'll go to Bar Harbor because I can't very well take the ring to a local jeweller, can I? Not in a town as small as Lobster Cove. Who knows how well the staff at Jewels of the Sea know Lucas, or the piece of jewellery in question? I touch the diamond sea horses in my earlobes. They sure wouldn't forget him in a hurry after he bought these earrings. Even if he bought nothing, even if they didn't know him, they would remember him. He's like that. Impossible to forget. I stand on the threshold of the house, one hand on the sea horse handle.

I hope everything's going to be all right.

"Come, I want ice-cream!" Alice is already at the car. I strap her into the child seat, check the ring is in my shirt pocket, get behind the wheel and we're on our way.

At the end of the drive, I look left and right, and—

Why is that police car there? It's that pleasant

young officer, Nate Harris, who dismantled Agat's mini-cross display, and one other, parked outside the Blue Rocks' gate.

Are they waiting for me? I look, again, for approaching traffic on the deserted road, make sure my indicator's on and turn toward town. Driving slowly and checking my mirrors I see the blue and white car sway onto the road behind me. Am I being followed? Why?

At the end of the road I turn left down Main and the police car follows. Are they going to tail me all the way to Bar Harbor? Because guess what? I'm not going there any more. I cruise down Main, check my mirrors again and see the car swing a right onto Maple. Phew. I touch my pocket where that ring, for some reason, is burning a hole. Why do I feel so guilty? I haven't *stolen* it, have I? Am I being watched? Absolutely not. Nate Harris, parked outside Blue Rocks in that big cruiser is the least subtle method on the planet of "watching" somebody.

And, yes, I feel guilty because I'm doing something really silly! I turn right onto Oak and right again onto First.

"Why are we going back?" Alice asks.

"To buy ice-cream at the grocery mart."

"But this is not Far Harbor!"

"Maybe, just maybe, the ice-cream is better here in Lobster Cove."

She's not convinced. Oh, and there's Nate Harris again, parked outside the grocery mart, leaning against the car, impassive behind his Ray-Bans.

I park right next to him. I mean, what else can I do?

"Hello," I say, getting out of the car, smiling. "Is it just me, or does everyone feel they've done something wrong when a police officer follows them?"

He greets me, smiles back, polite. "Sometimes, seeing a police officer in the vicinity makes folks think twice about breaking the law."

What does he mean by that? "Well, I'm *sure* glad I haven't done that," I say firmly, getting Alice out of the car. Why am talking like an American?

"We had a call this morning from one of caretakers up on Hidden Cove Drive about a pedigree shih tzu that had escaped the perimeter fence."

"That's a dog, right?"

"Sure is, and a real pretty one too." He grins.

I shrug, backing off. "Never a dull moment!"

"You have a nice day, now."

The relief is exquisite, and it rinses me clean. I have no idea why. On the trip back to Blue Rocks, I think about it. I'm not guilty about having the ring, not at all, but rather about sneaking around behind Lucas's back. It's not right.

"I love my blue ice cream," Alice tells me, from the back seat.

"Actually it's red, Alice. Raspberry. A kind of pinky-red. Does daddy let you eat ice cream in the car?"

"No."

Whoops. "Don't mess then, see?"

"I won't."

She won't. There's not a molecule of that ice-cream going to waste.

I smile. "What colour is the sea, Alice?"

"Green." She's not far off.

"And the sky?" I glance at her in the rear view mirror. She's gazing up through the car window, smiling.

After a while, she says, "It's bluetiful."

Even Ruth Pick couldn't argue with that.

Chapter Twenty-Two

At home, I do what I should have done all along. I take a photo of the ring and send it to Lucas: *Lucas, I found this in Alice's room. Can she play with it, or should I keep it somewhere safe? L.*

That covers all the bases. I look at the message for a few moments, and add an X. Nothing ventured, nothing gained.

Lucas gets back to me: *Sure she can play with it.*

Hm. *Okay thanks X.* Enough now.

The next morning, seconds before I leave the school car park after delivering Alice, I get a message from Lucas: *2nd thought better not. Pse keep ring safe.*

I drive to Blue Rocks, fetch the ring and go straight to Bar Harbor.

"I'd like to know what the stone is, please." I ask the clerk in the first jewellery store I see. He calls the jeweller—a qualified gemmologist no less, lucky me—and the jeweller takes the ring into a little lab at the back of the shop. He looks at it for a long time before he comes back.

"It's an artificial diamond. An excellent replica of, I would say, a Tiffany design."

"Thank you. That's exactly what I wanted to hear."

He gives me an odd look, speculating.

There's no charge, but I'm feeling expansive so I buy a black leather ring box with a gold mermaid stamped onto the lid. That'll keep it safe.

****

There, nothing's changed. Although, something *has* changed. It's a small change, but I actually get a message from Lucas telling me when he'll be back from the Middle East. Cryptic communication, but still: *Back Tues night late L X.* At least I know. And there's an X, oh yes there is. That's new. Venturing from both sides, then.

He's not late: he's early. The sea horse doorbell chimes around nine. When I open up I see, not Lucas, but Nate Harris.

My heart stands still.

Harris fills the doorway, but when he turns to the side, to acknowledge the person with him, I see that it's Lucas, and I can breathe again. "Hello," I say. "Is there a problem?"

Lucas is drunk, and angry. I'd go as far as to say his eyes are murderous. He pushes past me into the house, colliding with the single piece of furniture in the hallway—the table near the bottom of the stairs—leaving me to face Nate who's got an expression like a depressed undertaker.

"What happened?" I step outside onto the porch, glancing behind me, hoping Lucas doesn't lock me out of the house.

"Some guy from out of town cast aspersions on the good folk of Lobster Cove."

"How?"

He lets that go. "Hu tells me Lucas shoved him around sooner rather than later. He should have let it go."

I'm alarmed. "Has this happened before?"

"No. And while the out-of-town gentleman in question is not—"

"Gentleman?"

"—is not the sort of person we'd like to encourage in Lobster Cove, Lucas cannot take the law into his own hands." He glares at me, eyes cold and hard as coffin nails.

"Yes, Officer."

"Lucas needs to put a lid on that temper of his, before things get outta hand."

"He doesn't have a temper, but it's a difficult time—"

"Keep an eye on him, d'you hear?"

"Yes, Officer."

He drives off, and I feel like the mother of a delinquent teenager, berated by a teenager.

Inside, the house is quiet. Alice is fast asleep and Lucas must have gone to bed. I stand in the hall, not sure what to do. Lucas needs help, and I know of only one person who's capable of giving it. I hope. It's not too late, so I call Lucas's brother, John. He's on voicemail. I leave a message for him to call me in the morning.

I switch off lights, catch up on emails in my bedroom and go to bed myself. Lights off, I crack open the shutters and look out onto the sea. There's a bright silver sickle moon—and a figure on the lawn, cold in the sharp cut of the early autumn night, hands in pockets, shoulders hunched, standing by the gate at the top of the steps to the cove. It has to be Lucas and, to make sure, I go down the passage to his room. The door's open, and it's empty. I go back to my bedroom and stand at the window again. He's still there, gazing at the sea. What's he thinking?

Are Lucas and I actually friends? The reason I'm wondering is because I'm unsure what to do. Do I go outside and talk to him? What do I talk about? I can imagine the conversation. This is exactly how it would go:

"Lucas, do you want to talk?"

"No."

Does he need company? Comfort? To be left alone? I'm no good at fixing broken wings; I'm not sure it works. Has Lucas got broken wings, or is he soldiering on through a trauma, taking forever to get to the other side? The thing is, he asked me to stay; he started this new phase of my life. He came after me, at the airport, after we'd said goodbye, cancelled my flight and brought me back to Blue Rocks—not because I'm this amazing child-minder, but because…

Because what? There's a herd of elephants in the room that need to be ring-fenced and airlifted somewhere else, and the queen of them all is Bonny. She stands between us in a way that she might as well be physically present. Is Lucas aware of that? Does he feel that? I have to talk to him about her, but when? He's drunk right now, but not very. Not like last time. If I put this off, keep putting it off, will there ever be a right time?

Do I go outside, or do I go to bed and lie awake for hours waiting to see what happens next?

I go outside.

"Lucas?" Standing next to him in the cold, I hold his arm. Motionless, he stares at the dark beach, where the pale surf breaks like torn lace across the pebbles. The tide is high, and the water close, too close. Waves must surely break right up here, on the grass, during the fierce winter storms about which I've heard so much. I stand alongside Lucas and stare too, because I don't know what else to do. After a while, he turns his back on the water and folds his arms around me.

"Forgive me." I think that's what he says, murmuring into my hair.

A second later, we're kissing. How did that happen? It just did. Slow, delicious kisses of discovery, so tender, so *perfect*, I forget how cold my bare feet are on the dew-soaked grass.

Excitement heats my nerves, driven by the pressure of Lucas's hands on my body, his lips on my mouth, his closeness, the smell of his warm skin.

"I could work in London," he says.

All sensation vanishes like air whooshing out of a balloon. I tense in his arms, startled. "Why?"

His grip tightens. "So we could see each other."

"See each other how?"

"Like we do now."

I leave go of him, an unbidden image flashing through my mind of that Jeep, parked in a narrow London street, of Alice waving at me through a window streaming with incessant, cold, grey rain. What about Buster? What would happen to him? Head down, I whisper, "It wouldn't work." But I don't think Lucas hears over the sound of the sea.

We go back to the house, holding hands. It's chummy, and awkward.

"Time for bed," I say, taking care to keep my tone neutral. Taking care, so it doesn't come out as: "Time for bed?"

"Sleep tight." He disappears into the studio, and I

tramp upstairs on cold feet.

It's a start. Or is it?

****

John calls, first thing in the morning. I scuttle upstairs and shut myself in the bedroom. "Can you come and see me? It's about Lucas. There's something I'd like to discuss."

"Is he all right?"

"I think so…it's just…"

Just what exactly? "I-I thought you might like to come over for a visit."

"Not now. Rayna is showing signs of early labour. I can't leave her. Can you guys come here?"

"I…no. Don't worry." John's hands are full, and what was I going to tell him anyway? Lucas was very drunk one night and slightly drunk yesterday? That's lame. I can handle this. "Never mind, really."

"You sure?"

"Sure. Call me when Rayna, um, improves."

"Will do." He hangs up.

"Who's Rayna?" I ask Alice, at breakfast.

"Uncle John's labradog," she tells me.

I think for a moment. "And who's Rayna's mummy?"

"My Aunty Debra. She has a baby in her tummy."

I'm not sure I'll be getting much help, let alone a visit, from John any time soon.

****

After dropping Alice at school, I go into town to do some shopping and here's David Hu coming out of the grocery store, the exact man I want to see, though I would have happily put it off.

"Good morning, David."

"Hi." He lowers his voice. "Everything okay at Blue Rocks this morning?"

"Er, yes."

"Lucas okay?"

I seize the moment. "What happened last night?"

David Hu sets down his shopping bag and looks around. "Lucas came into Murphy's for a drink and a chat on his way home. Said you had told him to get out more."

"I did, but not so as to get into trouble."

"Not his fault. Some guy, a real oddball, came in and started making comments about you."

"Me?"

"He told the assembled company you'd challenged his driving. He used real bad words. Lucas got pretty pissed off. So did a few other people."

"I see."

Back home, I peer through the glass door panes of the studio. Lucas, head down has two laptops open on either side of his desktop and rivers of paperwork flowing in every direction. I go to the kitchen, make coffee and carry it in to him.

"David told me what happened last night at Murphy's," I say.

He doesn't look up. "Yeah, well, some prick took it on himself—"

"David told me. Why let a low-life get under your skin, Lucas?"

"I didn't like what he had to say."

"Like what?"

"You don't want to know." His head comes up, his eyes, fully focussed on me, are the colour of a fine single-malt whisky and equally dangerous, this time of the morning.

"What did he say?" I sit on the edge of his desk, arms folded, determined.

His eyes darken. "That you were a sexy little hellcat, cute as fuck, with an accent like a princess and great tits."

I'm so taken aback I laugh.

He frowns. "What's funny?"

"That. That comment."

"It's true."

I raise my eyebrows. "So, now, you agree with the low-life? How did you come to argue?"

"Jeez!" He's on his feet. He's got me by the waist, lifting me up in one quick, strong movement so my legs are around his waist. I have to hang on, arms around his neck, or crash through the window.

"*Lucas.*"

He strides to the end of the room where, opposite the last tall window, next to the man-stuff cupboard, he more or less chucks me onto a sofa. He straddles my body, pinning me with his thighs to the leather cushion, leaning on his elbows, his forehead resting on mine.

"Quit messing about," he growls, but smiling—his eyes filled with laughter like I have never seen them before. I'm fascinated.

"Only if you get some barbed-wire tattoos around your wrists!" I wriggle, but he holds me tight.

"You on contraception?"

"No."

He shoves a hand in his pocket and slaps the obligatory condom packet onto the back of the sofa.

"Quite the boy scout," I remark, lifting my head to see what else has come out of his pocket. My photo.

The one that was missing off my CV. I guess that condom has been waiting for me and I say as much.

"Who else?" Lucas, voice gruff, won't look at me now. Businesslike, he's taking off my clothes.

"Hey, not fair! You've still got all your clothes on, and I'm completely—"

His sudden grin drives a hot tremor the length of my body. "Then quit lying on your sexy little ass, doing nothing."

There's some laughing and little wrestling by me, which is quite pointless because Lucas, way stronger, is making a point he's in charge and, moreover, he's on top, and he's hungry.

"Anything you don't like doing?" he asks, eyes on my naked breasts.

"No." You only live once. Ooh, there go my jeans. And the rest.

Lucas, kneeling over me, eyes loaded, merely unbuckles his belt, unzips his jeans, and lowers himself. Do I imagine that I'm at some disadvantage here? All I've done is open the top two buttons of his shirt, fancying some shirt-wrangling over and off a set of big shoulders. That, alone, would be mega-arousing—but I should have worked faster, should have leaped to and stripped him bare before he…

Okay, I'm going to stop with the shirt now because…because Lucas is running those large warm hands up and down the outside of my thighs and I might well ignite—ooooh, and the inside—or erupt, or both, any second, ruining the impression of a languid, experienced, utterly-in-control seductress.

Hands on my waist now. His breathing is turning me on. His *breathing*.

Now, a quick, hmm, highly efficient tearing of foil.

Here he is, all of him. Wow, that's fast. And that's the end of me, because, at the same time, he is a neat, effective kisser with perfect timing. Hands on my bum, pulling me up so he can go deep, gentle kisses on my eyelids and nose, then gentle tongue in my mouth.

I go from starved to saturated in that split second before take-off.

Flashpoint.

Sensational.

"Mm, mm, mm," I say, swallowing the urge to grind out loud, unladylike grunts of pleasure, like an ecstatic pig on a mountain of clover—with flowers.

He's smiling against my cheek; I can feel the crinkle of the skin near his eyes. Those fabulous sexy lines that spring up high on his cheekbones to signal the start of that scarce grin. Does he know I'm thinking about pigs?

I want Lucas to like this, I do. I wind my legs around his waist, pull my weight from under him so we land up half on our sides, facing each other, him still mostly on top and me wedged against the back of this obliging sofa, smooth and cool on the skin of my bare back. During all this movement Lucas keeps his hands on my breasts, looking at me. I settle, and hold his face. It's my turn to kiss. His eyes are wide open, blank, but also somehow seeing way deep inside me, seeing things even I didn't know were there. He's glazed, but there's a world of ideas revolving there.

Oh right. Here it comes, and we're flying, shooting past that exquisite point of no return. I wind my arms around his neck, pull him in with my legs, as far as he can possible go, and then some. Lucas is not ladylike whatsoever. Not so much the grunts of a happy pig but the shouts of a boxer taking heavy body blows from a sturdy opponent.

He comes with such intensity, like it's the last thing left in the world to do, like he's going to die, I'm not kidding. It's a first for me. Sexy in retrospect, I later decide, but frightening right now, to be honest. I'm concerned.

"Lucas, are you okay?"

"Yeah." But he's out of breath, chest heaving like he's busy with a heart attack.

"Open your eyes and look at me!"

He does, and laughs. "Man!" He throws his head back, laughs again, drops his head and looks at me. "You," he says.

"Me?"

"Yes, you. You are fucking awesome!"

I am? "Thank you. You're not bad yourself."

"Ah, Lara Jasmine Layla, are all Englishwomen this sexy?"

"Absolutely, yes."

"Absolutely, yes." He mimics, his accent perfect, his facial expression not so.

"I hope I don't look like that when I—"

He's kissing me again. "You're cold. This is like eating ice cream." Kiss.

"I am cold. I have nothing on." Nothing bar a pair of small, diamond sea horse earrings.

"You have earrings," he says. Kiss.

I touch them, a fingertip on each. "I love them."

"I love you." Kiss.

What?

Silence.

Silence for a full five seconds and then the sea horse doorbell shrieks like someone has bashed a dinner gong over our heads.

Lucas turns his head in the direction of the door. "Who the hell—"

Any number of people. "Get off, Lucas. Get *off* me. Someone's here." It can't be Alice. Why would it be Alice? She's at school until I collect her. It could be the receptionist from Sea Crest Inn who said she'd pop by with a few orders and a cheque, or Ronnie Pick with the basket of plums he promised me, or Angie, or Jay, collecting Molly's pullover she left here the day before yesterday. What if it's John? Maybe our call this morning bothered him, and he's whizzed up from Boston at the speed of light? It could even be Agat, delivering a dolly stuck full of pins.

Lucas takes his time over a last, long, slow kiss. A sweet full-stop on a weekday morning. I close my eyes, tasting my future there.

"I'll go." He gets up, kneeing me in the ribs.

"Ooph! Thanks, because I *am* naked."

"My pleasure." He grins and takes off his shirt, handing it to me. "Here." It's all gorgeous: the smile, eyes, shoulders, hair on chest, arms, hands, six-pack, everything.

"Do up your jeans." I avert my eyes, take the shirt and put it on. It's huge and warm and smells of Lucas.

And me.

Us.

****

Who's the unwelcome guest with such inappropriate timing? I wait, hiding in Lucas's studio until he comes back, pulling on a tee-shirt. "Got any

197

cash?" he asks.

"Sure."

"Lend me fifty. It's for Uncle Buck. He needs an advance."

"Advance for what?"

"He'll come and mow the lawn next week."

"When next week?" I make a mental note to be off the property on that day.

"Who knows? Maybe he comes the week after. Maybe he doesn't come at all."

In the kitchen, I get my purse out of my handbag and hand fifty dollars to the Bank of Lucas. "I hope he pays you back."

"You." He winks. "He will. Always does, one way or another." Off he goes. A minute later he's back, opening the fridge. "I don't mind helping him out. He had a rough time in Vietnam, back in the seventies. I reckon he's paid his dues." I glance through the kitchen window and see Buck's ancient pickup clattering away down the drive.

Lucas, fridge door wide open, gazes at the contents.

"What are you looking for?" I ask.

"Food. Sex always makes me hungry."

Always? Like a daily occurrence? "There's pancake batter." I point to a sealed plastic container on the middle shelf.

"Oh boy." He takes out the bowl. "Want some?"

"I'm going up to have a shower."

His eyes light up. "Need some help?"

I laugh, going upstairs, coming down showered and changed twenty minutes later to the sound of the doorbell, again. It's the postman this time with a letter for which someone needs to sign, followed quickly by Cherri, bearing several jars of home-made blueberry jam.

"A peace offering, if you like," she tells me.

"Why a peace offering?"

"You know, after what I said about you enabling Lucas to carry on so irresponsibly. Ruth said it was too harsh. I was real sorry to hear you'd left."

I have no idea what to say. "Thanks," will have to do.

She puts her head on one side. "But you came back? Something must have changed your mind."

I give it to her straight. "Lucas asked me to stay."

"For how long?"

"Um, a bit. Then we'll—I'll...see."

She watches me for a moment, and says, "Those earrings are real pretty."

"Yes."

She leans closer to inspect. "Classics. Suitable for every occasion. Beautiful. If you're wearing those, you don't need anything else, do you?"

Indeed not.

"Lucas is here," I say. "Would you like a cup of coffee or something?"

"Gotta dash. You too. School's almost out."

She leaves, and I go back to the kitchen where Lucas is busy constructing a giant mountain of pancakes, dripping with butter and syrup.

Chapter Twenty-Three

Lucas claims he's never eaten scones. We're lying in bed early on Saturday morning, before Alice is awake, nose-to-nose, sharing a pillow, discussing food. Buster stomps along the passage to Alice's room, to jump on her bed and knead her awake.

"It'd be real nice to formalize this arrangement," Lucas whispers, as I sneak out of his bed before Alice comes in, "and then we won't have to creep about like thieves in the night."

"I do the creeping," I remind him. Lucas never comes into the main bedroom if he can help it. "And what do you mean by formalize?"

"You tell me."

There's only one way to formalize when there's a four-year-old in the mix, and that's to get married. Is Lucas testing me for a reaction?

He gets up to go for a run, followed by a swim—possibly the last of the season. The mornings and evenings are cool and crisp now that it's October, the nights cold. Although the leaves on the trees in town, along the road to Bar Harbor and up at Emerald Lake are tinged with gold, the midday skies are blue and the sun glorious.

At breakfast Lucas reads yesterday's paper while eating his way through the freshly baked dozen scones made by Alice and me, first thing. I've helped her make one shaped like a sea horse.

"You can have it, Daddy, but you can't eat it."

"What?" Lucas, hand spread on heart, makes a show of being distraught. "But I like the ones you made *best*. I like them more than Lara's ones." He smiles at me across the table.

"I'll look after it, Daddy. I'll keep it with my shelves and jews."

She wraps the sea horse scene in a table napkin and puts it beside her plate.

"What are shelves and jews?" Lucas asks.

"Shelves and jews," Alice replies.

I laugh. "Shells and jewels. Stuff she finds on the beach."

"Ah." His right hand hovers over the table, between the honey and the blueberry jam. "Which beach is this, Alice?"

"This beach, Daddy. The bidden cove."

Shit. Well, it had to happen.

Alice jumps down from the table and runs out into the sunshine on the porch. I can see her through the window, on the porch swing, covering Buster with a pink and white crocheted dolly blanket.

"More coffee?" I ask.

"I thought I told you the cove was out of bounds." Lucas has lost all interest in his food. Cutlery down, he stares at me like a stranger. "What the f—are you playing at?" He mutes the word with difficulty, furious.

I'm not playing at anything, but this is something I haven't thought through. Somehow, the more Alice and I went to the cove, the less I thought he'd mind; the more okay I thought it would be, but it's not like that. He's mad.

201

"It's not out of bounds to me. And it's beautiful. Alice begs to go, regularly, so I take her. She adores it." I tell the truth because I cannot dodge the bullet.

Alice runs back into the room, following put-upon Buster, slinking along, tail down, with the blanket draped over his back.

Lucas glances at her, then glares at me. "It's where her *mother died* for God's sake," he hisses.

"Daddy! Teacher Pick says it is very rude to whisker in public." She follows Buster up the stairs.

"I've said it before. How many people in Maine— in the world—have got their own private beach? Why live here, Lucas, in this gorgeous house, in this perfect spot, and not go to your own beach?"

He's up now, walking around the kitchen, opening the fridge for no reason, picking up stuff and putting it down. "I think you know why."

"Then why not move away from here? Go somewhere where there aren't any memories?" I almost tell him to go and live somewhere he's not afraid to be. Because that's why he has that job that takes him away from home for weeks at a time—so he doesn't have to be here at Blue Rocks with the ghost of Bonny reflected in every window. I know I'm right. This is where the desperate comment about living in London has been growing roots.

He doesn't answer. Alice is back. "Come, Daddy, come and see my jews. We go to the beach." She pulls him toward the door, but he resists.

"No, Alice. We're not going there."

"Please! Come. Come."

"No!" His aggressive roar slaps Alice out of her joyful mood. Her eyes fill, her mouth turns down and she bursts into tears.

"Look what you've done!" I'm horrified, half-crying myself, scared of what *I've* done. I pick Alice up. "Why do you have to speak to her like that?"

"I *won't* show you my jews, Daddy. I *won't* show you my diamond."

"Diamond?" Lucas, standing very still, stares at Alice. "What diamond?" He's utterly calm, like he's had nothing to do with the perfect storm of distress thrashing in my arms.

"In the table rock," she cries. "You. Can't. See. It. You not allowed!"

He turns his eyes on me, so dark I can't see his thoughts. "Does she mean the Cocktail Rock?"

"I have no idea." Alice flings her arms around my neck, cracking me across the nose. "Ow! There's a rock she loves lying on, very flat, about a yard square that's exposed at low tide. It's got a deep fissure running diagonally—"

He's gone. "Lucas!" I shout at his back as he runs down the sea porch steps and sprints across the grass. "I don't think Alice means an *actual* diamond—" On the other hand, Alice is obsessed with that crack in the rock.

Oh my God. What are the chances?

Could it be? Could it be Bonny's diamond? How many times, while we've been on that little beach has Alice implored me to look at her jews? "Mm," I say, vaguely peering into the crack in the rock, my eyes so full of sunlight I can see nothing in the dark split, wet with seawater, fringed with a little green weed, smelling of cool salt.

"You can't have my diamond, Daddy," Alice

screams, bawling her eyes out.

I sit on the porch swing with Alice in my lap, my hands, my knees, everything, shaking.

"Alice," I say, after a while, "if you stop crying, we'll go to the beach, see?" She shuts up immediately. It's a brave effort, punctuated by mighty hiccoughs. She wipes her eyes with the back of her hands, but it's not enough and allows me to stall for time. We go inside and wash and dry her face. To be honest, I'm not too keen to see what Lucas is getting up to on the beach. Perhaps Alice will forget that I said we'd go there.

No chance. Nose blown, face clean, she tugs my hand. "Want to go to the beach. Want Daddy."

We go. Lucas, sitting on the wet pebbles next to the flat rock, ignores our approach. He stares out to sea, his empty eyes telling me all I need to know. He found nothing. Alice runs to him and, absentminded, he draws her into his arms, sitting her on his lap, kissing the top of her head. I hang back, leaving them to it. I'm a spare part in this, and I wouldn't know where to start, what to say—but I'm not leaving. I don't want to leave Alice and Lucas alone here, where the autumn shadows are damp, the sea cold and the sorrow deep.

Sorrow? Angie said Lucas and Bonny's marriage was over. Did he, does he, believe that? It's hard to think so, looking at him now, huddled on the wet stones with his daughter. The wind, fresh off the sea, freezes me to the rock on which I've perched. Alice has short sleeves, and I'm worried she'll get cold, and ill. Pulling courage from where it's retreated to hide from my foolishness, I stand up and go toward them, putting a hand on Lucas's shoulder.

"Lucas?"

I might as well not have spoken. Arms around Alice, he stares across the waves.

"Please, get up and come with me, or the tide might cut us off."

Eventually—because I don't want to frighten her with scary talk—my desperation registers with Alice. She gets off Lucas and, taking one of his hands in both of hers, tries to pull him to his feet. "Come, Daddy, come *at once*. Lara says." She puts her little back into the job, slipping on the pebbles. "Help me, Lara, help me."

Lucas stands, picks up Alice and walks across the beach to the steps. Today, the cove isn't the way I know and love it: a peaceful, private suntrap, lined with warm pebbles and fringed by the blue beauty of the sea. Today, it's a sad, cold reminder of love gone deeply and dangerously bad. I climb the path, wondering what to say. I've been such an idiot. Lucas asked—told—me not to come here, and I disobeyed orders. Apart from ugly memories, it's a dangerous place with that swift tide, the wind and currents. With the awful reminder it holds for him, it's lethal.

"Oh," cries Alice, pointing, as we go into the house via the sea porch. "Buster! Look at his whispers!"

Buster slips past with remarkable speed for such a large animal, his whiskers coated in glossy butter and dotted with crumbs, his eyes fixed on the exit, and, bad news, the lower half of Alice's sea horse scone clamped in his jaws. I give chase, but he boosts himself down the steps, streaking across the grass to hide in the straggle of scrubby bushes on the far side.

That bloody cat.

I march into the house, flustered and frustrated.

"Honestly, Lucas, that cat is too much. It's time somebody trained him to—"

The table is virtually bare. Buster has eaten the scones, the butter, even the jam, and I bet my life he stuck his fat head into the milk jug and had most of that while he was at it. Honey paw prints on the table top tell the rest of the story. Alice surveys the devastation and bursts into fresh tears. Buster's ravaging of the breakfast table is the absolute last straw, but at least it takes the spotlight off the awkward happenings in the cove.

"We'll make more sea horse scones," I tell Alice. "Lots. Stop crying and take Daddy to fetch a pen and some cardboard."

She stops crying. "Why?"

"Daddy's going to draw a lovely sea horse to use as a template."

"What's a temp—what did you say?"

"A template. A shape to trace around."

Lucas raises his eyebrows. "I am?"

"Yes." I fill the dishwasher with everything Buster has, or might have, licked, sweep crumbs into the bin, wipe the table and start over. "I need a sea horse. Just the outline to cut out and use as a baking shape."

"I'm sorry," Lucas says.

"*I'm* sorry," I say. "I should never have taken Alice to the…I shouldn't have taken her there. You asked, told, me not to."

"I can't stop hoping," he says. "I can't stop myself. I don't know what to—"

"Come, Daddy, get crayons." Alice takes his hand and pulls him out of the kitchen.

Alice called it the *bidden* cove. Entirely the

opposite word to *forbidden*. Somehow, that gives me hope.

Suffice it to say, Lucas doesn't come lightly to drawing. He and Alice disappear for a while into the studio and come back laden with sheets of cardboard, pens, rulers, T-squares, and a large and small pair of compasses. He also brings along something called a French curve, and a *spline*, which is a strip of rubber with a bendy metal wire inside—both for drawing curves. I hand over *Common Shore Life of Maine*, in case Lucas needs inspiration, and get busy with a new batch of scone dough.

Clearly, inspiration is unnecessary. In minutes, Lucas creates a stunning sea horse on a sheet of cardboard. Not a sketch, but more of a diagram. Correction, a highly accurate technical drawing, complete with parallel lines, circles, notes, symbols.

"Wow, that's incredible. Leonardo da Vinci's Vitruvian Man comes to mind," I say, leaning over him to gauge progress before I add eggs to the dry scone ingredients.

"Have you seen it?" he asks.

"The Vitruvian Man? I have."

"In Venice?"

"Yes."

"Lucky." He hands over the drawing. "There's your sea horse."

I hold the card in my hands and marvel at the exquisite delicacy of the pen lines. There's no multiple meaning here, no subjective interpretation required. Here is an image with one intended meaning. It's the beautifully executed, working drawing of a sea horse.

"I'm not cutting this up," I say, holding it to my

chest. "Can you do another one? Just the outline?"

"That one is too *hard*, Daddy," Alice says. "Draw a nice one, like mine."

At last, a smile. Lucas looks at the picture Alice is holding up: a cross between a purple kite and a green fish skeleton with wings.

"That's beautiful darling," he says. "Can I have it?"

"You can keep it forever." She jumps off the chair, scattering high-tech pens, and runs outside to where Buster sits on the top step of the sea porch, casting me filthy looks for spoiling his fun.

"I will," he calls, drawing another sea horse, freehand this time. It takes him ten seconds.

"That's perfect," I tell him, brandishing the kitchen scissors. He stares at the sketch for a moment, then lays it back on the table and adds unnecessary detail to the fins.

"May I take you to dinner tonight?" he asks, not looking at me, giving the sea horse an eye, plus lashes and an eyebrow.

I hesitate. This is a surprise. "Thank you."

"Anywhere you'd like to go?"

"Mariner's."

His eyebrows go up. "Really?"

Mariner's Fish Fry is at the end of Hidden Cove Drive, above Sea Crest Inn. I've passed it often on my walks. There's a squat lighthouse with a deck around the second floor, and a glorious view of the bay. It's bedecked with lobster buoys and traps giving the place a working harbour feel, although it shouts romance and adventure to me. "Yes. Yes, please."

He looks up. "Done. I'll make a reservation."

"Alice mustn't be up too late."

He's giving the sea horse earrings and a necklace. "I'll get a sitter for Alice."

Oh. A date, then. We're sleeping together, but we haven't been on a date. How ridiculous is that, and why does it feel so awkward?

He gives me the sea horse. I cut it out and transfer the outline to my dough. Half an hour later we have a dozen fat, golden sea horses and life regains a tenuous equilibrium.

Chapter Twenty-Four

"There's only one thing to eat at Mariner's," Lucas says, pulling out my chair. "Fresh lobster."

Lobster doesn't cut it for me. I'm not having any. I wouldn't know where to start. "I'm, er, not a big fan."

"Trust me."

"No."

He sits down opposite me. "Any particular reason why you wouldn't?"

This is a fathomless question! However, I'm going to stick to the realms of lobster. "I'm concerned lobster hunting is bad for the environment."

"Lobster hunting, huh?"

I nod.

"Don't worry about it. The environment is fine. If you did a job like mine you'd know what seriously impacts the environment. Lobsters aren't even on the scale. What seriously affects the environment in these parts is climate change. The sea is warming up. Local lobstermen find black sea bass in their traps in ever-increasing numbers. It used to be too cold for them this far north, but not any more."

"I don't mean that lobsters *damage* the environment." Is he laughing at me? "I mean *we* damage the environment by yanking them out of the sea. We shouldn't eat them. We should leave them where they belong, to fulfil their role in the delicate balance of the marine ecosystem."

His eyes level with mine. "You're not serious. In that case we shouldn't be eating anything."

He has a point, and I've lost the argument—weak to start with. I concede with a polite smile and turn my attention to the view. Lucas has booked the best table up next to the windows, looking out across the deck. Although there's the bright buzz of a popular restaurant on one side of us, there's the navy blue sea on the other, trickling the liquid gold shimmer of boat lanterns.

The evening doesn't get off to the best start. Lucas remains consumed by the possibility of what might have been, no matter how slim the chances. At Blue Rocks this morning, I glimpsed a man who was almost set free—until he raced off to the cove to hunt for his innocence, finding nothing. That man is not here tonight. When conversation stalls, he thanks me for what I've done for Alice, tells me how much he appreciates my input, and praises me for my hit and miss child-rearing *wisdom* as he calls it. We discuss the view, he tells me what I'm looking at—Lobster Cove, essentially, from the north, all the way past Pine Island to the Martin Lighthouse across the bay—and we study the menu. But, all the while, lurking behind the smiles and the chat, there's a shit-storm of unbearable despair in his eyes.

After half an hour of this, and not very much wine—my glass of Chablis has somehow evaporated—I put a hand over one of his.

"Hey, we can go home. Honestly, we don't have to do this. Why don't we go back to Blue Rocks and get a take-away? We can sit on the porch and—" And what? Anything but this. He's making himself do this; it's not what he wants, or what I want.

He's staring at my hand. When he looks up I can see he wants to go home, badly. He pulls away from me, sits back, pulls in a deep breath. "No. I'm going to do this." He picks up the menu. "What do you feel like?"

"Um…"

"C'mon, try a little lobster. You haven't lived until you have. I'll order, shall I?"

Baptism by fire, then. "Okay, but be kind. To me and the lobster."

He pours more wine and a waitress comes over. There's a lengthy discussion—in Lobster-ese—of what's on offer and how it's prepared. Lucas thinks, deliberates, considers, and eventually orders something for both of us. I shudder to think. Out of control of the situation, I sit back and enjoy the lovely aromas around me. The air is warm with the buzz of garlic and herbs frying in a little butter, cooled by the tang of lemon juice and salt on a sharing platter of oysters going past, borne aloft by a fast-moving waiter.

Our food arrives. Several lobsters embracing on an enormous plate, with rice, salads, sauces and lemon wedges tucked in all around. We are given bibs. I am afraid, very afraid. The waitresses withdraw and, panicked, I say—firmly—to Lucas, "I'm not…I'm not getting involved with that. It's pretty, but I'm not going in."

He grins. "Bear with me. It'll be all right."

Oh God, what is he doing? He has plier things, nutcracker and tong things, *eating tools.* What is wrong with him? He laughs at my expression of horror. That sexy, warm laugh I adore. Why doesn't he laugh more often? No. Thank heaven he doesn't. I'd go mad. I cover my eyes.

"You Americans are barbaric, you know that?"

"*Bah*-baric?"

"You say *lobstah*."

"You say lob-*staaaaah*."

I peek through my fingers. "That's correct. I speak English properly."

He shouts with laughter, turning heads. People stare. "Wrong. The Pilgrim Fathers removed themselves from England and, in isolation in a new land, preserved the English language in its purest form. *I* speak proper English, unlike you, influenced as you are by all that European aristocracy."

I lean forward, hand still half over my eyes. "You're a savage," I say, in an undertone. "You savage the language as you are savaging that lobster."

He objects, laughing. "I am, we Americans are, extremely humane. We don't hunt, shoot, and fish any more than the Brits, and if, when, we do, we do it properly."

"Is that so?" I have to smile. The smell, no, fragrance, of that lobster is—it must be said—unlike anything I have ever experienced before. Lucas swiftly cracks, pulls and cuts, piling the meat into a separate bowl, tossing coral pink shells into yet another. In spite of heavy reservations, my mouth waters.

"Come." He dips a chunk of meat into a dish of melted butter and holds it out to me. "Open mouth."

I come out of hiding and do. Oh, *heavenly*. "Mmmmmm!" Wow. *Oh.*

Lucas watches me, those excellent hands poised over his work, fingers spread, juice and melted butter running between them. He's genuinely delighted. "Do I have a convert?" The smile is slow, but it spreads.

"Maybe."

He gives me more, and some more, until I tell him to stop, and feed himself. He hands over the bowl and I Hoover it along with the rice, the tomato salad with chives, and the cucumber and avocado in a creamy lemon dressing. He piles my plate with more lobster and orders a second bottle of wine, asking the waitress to call Skeet, because we're going to need a ride home.

"Or we could walk," I suggest, splattering warm butter on my bib.

"Sure could. It's downhill all the way."

"You don't say."

The second bottle's open, and the tone of the evening has changed. Is it merely because I'm eating lobster and thereby cheering up Lucas? He's twisting and breaking stuff, splitting and crushing, juices running everywhere, working hard to get the last of the meat, the little I've left him.

"How come you're so clean?" I ask, looking down at my bib. "Apart from your hands."

"Years of experience."

"You've been coming here for years?"

"Until Bonny got pregnant. Then she went off lobster, among other things."

Okay, Bonny's back and I'm running with it. Thank you, wine. "What other things?"

"Me." He spends a long time rinsing his hands in a bowl of water with lemon slices floating on top. Eyes down, he dries them, finger by finger, on a special little towel brought by a waitress. She gathers plates, clears and wipes and, in spite of protests, leaves us with the pudding menu.

"Why?"

He looks me in the eye. "We had problems."

A man approaches our table, with purpose, so I've timed it wrong. "Nice to see you out, Lucas, how's things?" Lucas introduces me to Claude Bennis, head chef. For a few minutes we chat about lobster, and the glorious fall weather, and touch on the local restaurant business, and then Claude moves on to greet people at other tables.

"What sort of problems?" I'm about to say, but the waitress comes back and, somehow, I order something called Maineberry sorbet. Where am I going to put that?

"You'll have to help me, Lucas."

"No way," he says, as a double helping of blueberry cheesecake arrives, compliments of Claude, "this is going to kill me."

Both helpings are huge and we can only laugh. Much better this way, laughing over giant puddings in this cosy, lamp-lit space, with the black water hidden behind the bright reflections on the window glass, and the gloom of premature death forced down into dark corners.

"You look great, by the way," he says, as I'm lifting a spoon of delight to my lips. My hand jerks and most of the sorbet slips onto my chin.

"I do?" I scoop, lick and wipe. Not smiling—I've got purple ice cream all over my teeth, haven't I?

"Yeah." He's looking at me, unfortunately, as he would be. After all, you don't pay a woman a compliment like that while gazing out to sea. His eyes are soft, a little heavy. "You've lost weight and gotten tanned. You look—"

"American? Are my teeth whiter?" I stretch my lips, baring my teeth, happy that the sorbet's gone. He's right about my weight. Without the constant worry over Hampers, coupled with Alice's healthy diet, I am thinner. No, better than that: I am thin.

He laughs. "A little."

"Why, thank you." We're back on track.

Eyes wide as a bush baby after strong coffee urged by Claude to help the digestion—I know why, because we're going to be awake all night jumping about, stoked on caffeine and sugar—we stagger home. The midnight air is chilly, and we puff vapour as we walk. Lucas gives me his jacket, puts an arm around me and guides me home.

"Bonny," he says, eventually, while we walk beneath the dripping trees, "had affairs. That's how the kinder folk of Lobster Cove referred to her…her preference for variety. In reality, she got drunk and slept around."

"I'm sorry."

"She never wanted kids, I suspect. 'Not yet, not yet' she always used to say. If Alice hadn't come along, there would be, like, nobody."

Of all the responses that exist in the world, there isn't one for that. We walk, into the mist that curls down on us, thicker and thicker, saying nothing. My stomach hurts. This trek to Blue Rocks will either do me the world of good or kill me. At least I've got that to think about.

Back at the house, Lucas pays the babysitter and she disappears in her little car, swallowed by fog before she's reached the gates. Upstairs in the silent house, Lucas checks on Alice, tucks her in, and joins me in the bathroom. We shower together—a fairly functional event, although there is one scrumptious kiss under the downpour of hot water that should go in the record books.

Later, breathless and shivery after flawless sex, Lucas heavy and sleepy against my side, arms around each other, legs tangled together, I lie wide-awake in the dark. The foghorn wails over the muffled, incessant thump of the surf. Cosy and entwined in darkness, Lucas and I could be the only people in the world.

Except, he's not present. Like last time, and the time before, and all the times before that, something's missing. It's high time I faced up to that. Something stands between us, stops me from telling him I love him. And I do. I love him with all my heart, and he loves me. He said so.

He's not mine.

Chapter Twenty-Five

"You will be happy," says the day. Out on the sea porch I look at the view. Blueness all around; so beautiful, my eyes ache. All is paint box bright, dipped in golden sunlight.

"Did I imagine that clammy mist last night?" I ask Lucas who, bearing coffee, comes out of the house to sit beside me on the porch swing.

"No."

"It's like the whole world has been washed clean."

"Sure is."

"I don't think I've ever seen anything more beautiful."

"That's Maine for you!"

I gaze at the gilded sky. "However many times I see this view, it's not enough. I could look at it forever."

"Nothing stopping you."

I turn my head sharpish to face him. "Isn't there?"

Resolute, he stares back. "No."

I think we both know there is.

Maine—the way life should be. Yes, true, great, but is it the way *my* life should be?

Lucas blows on his coffee and sips carefully for a minute or two. "I've got something for you." He leans down to put his coffee on the floor, like you're not supposed to, on a porch swing.

"What is it?" I hold my mug up and away, prepared for slopping. He hands me a business card: *Jolivette French, Frenchman Bay B&B.*

"Is that Gigi's mother? Gigi who babysits Alice sometimes?" I ask.

"Sure. I saw her this morning, on my run. She wants to know if you'll supply a couple of picnics for a group coming into town next week." He sits back, half-turned to me, right leg bent, up on the seat, left foot on the floor, rocking the swing.

"I suppose I could."

"Call her. She heard about you from someone at Sea Crest Inn. Your fame is spreading. Soon you'll be part of Lobster Cove folklore."

"You think?"

"See? You're even starting to sound like an American. A Lobster Covian, at that."

I laugh. "Is that a compliment?"

He leans across and kisses me. "You should start a business. Right here, you know that?"

Imagine a deli like Hampers in Lobster Cove. Could it work? Maybe it's only me, but this place sings *picnic*, never more so than on a day like today. Add to that the sandy beach at Sea Crest Inn, the secret coves, the magical islands and hidden inlets, the hills behind us, laced with lakes and draped in forest. Could I develop a successful business here? Hope fills me. I look away from Lucas's eyes, back at the glittering sea. He watches my face. I look down. I've exposed myself. He knows what I'm thinking. He understands.

I'm not going there. It's a wild dream. Fun, but entirely impractical.

"Well?" He takes my empty mug and stands up.

"No." I smile up at him. "I doubt my temporary work visa would stretch to that."

"It can be changed. You could immigrate and apply for a green card."

"I suppose."

"Or you could marry an American guy."

"I could."

"Would you do that?"

I hesitate. "It would depend on the actual guy."

He throws his head back and laughs. "Nice. Nice one, Lara Jasmine." Whatever that means.

"What about you?" I ask, brave. "Will you marry again?"

He lowers his head, smile gone, and looks at me under his eyebrows. "No."

I sidestep the dour thrust of disappointment. Serves me right for asking the question, for pushing him where he's not ready to go. And, PS, that includes the forbidden cove—forbidden for a clear-cut reason, although…

"Something's got to happen before I do that. *If* I ever do that," he says, quietly determined.

You know what I should do on this glorious gift of a day? Assemble a perfect picnic, drag it, and Lucas, plus some rugs and cushions, down to the forbidden cove and *fuck Lucas's brains out. On that goddamn flat rock.* Bonny used that rock for cocktails. I'll use it for something else! I'll change the name of that rock and etch it into the folklore of Lobster bloody Cove. That'll do it. That'll banish the ghosts, take care of that *something.*

Reckless and desperate, that's me.

"What are you doing today?" I ask.

Leaning on the porch rail, holding the mugs in one hand, he looks at his watch. "I have a load of work. Feedback for the Saudi Arabians. And you?"

I lift a bundle of matted blue wool off the seat beside me. "I have this."

He frowns. "What is it?"

"Alice's knitting project. A bunny in a blue dress."

"That's a bunny?"

"It will be. However, I have to undo most of what she's done while she's at school and re-knit it all."

"Isn't that cheating?"

"I want to encourage her, not put her off. She's enthusiastic, and should be supported. She's getting better every day, honest." I begin the process, undoing the stitches, thinking of Alice, later this evening, every feature of her little face utterly focussed on her masterpiece.

"Hmm," is all Lucas says, going inside.

Ten minutes later, he's out again. "You know, it's a shame to waste a day like this."

"Meaning?" By no means a knitter, I pick up a dropped stitch but somehow it looks back to front.

"Why don't we take one of those famous picnics of yours and go to the beach?"

Yesssssssssssss! I abandon the knitting. "What a lovely idea."

We go to the forbidden cove. My suggestion, and Lucas's reaction is strangely neutral. The tide's in so we sit high up on the shore in the sun and eat antipasto and grilled lemony chicken between thick, toasted slices of Italian bread, followed by fat green grapes that taste like cool honey. No flat rock. Today will not be the day the Cocktail Rock becomes the—

Never mind. It was a stupid idea.

Replete, again, considering last night's meal, we lie side-by-side on a thick rug, and bask.

"Shelves and jews," he murmurs, after a moment. "Christ. For a moment I was convinced."

"Convinced of what?"

He doesn't say anything for a while, and then, when I think he's dozed off, he says. "Bonny used to take her engagement ring off when she swam. It was a loose, and she was afraid it would slip off. She had a special little hook on a key ring made from the first champagne cork to pop at our wedding. People reckoned that if her death had been an accident, the cork and the ring would have been found there, on the beach. The lawyer for Bonny's defence suggested I had removed the ring because it was too valuable to let go."

"It could have washed out to sea."

"It would have floated, they said, because of the cork. It would have turned up."

"Not necessarily."

"It happens. That's the way the tides and currents work around here. Ask any of the lobstermen, or yachtsmen. What the ocean gives back, is part of the folklore in these parts." Another lengthy silence. "Hardly a day goes by when I don't think about that fucking ring. I searched for it, but the weather was terrible. Big storms, huge tides."

"Tell me about the ring I found in Alice's dollhouse."

"A replica. Bonny wore it when she travelled."

"You gave it to Alice to play with?"

"I don't really remember."

There's a bit of a silence. "Well, you found Bonny.

That's…that's…" That's what? Important? Amazing? Essential? "That's the main thing. Finding the real ring wouldn't prove anything, would it?"

"It would to me."

Maybe the real ring wasn't insured? Is that what he's been fretting about down the years? I'm sure I know Lucas well enough to say I'd be surprised if that were the case.

"Think about it," he says, like he's talking to himself, "would a woman, about to kill herself, bother to take off her ring? Would she take a set of keys to the beach?"

Suicide? I hadn't thought about that. Clearly Lucas has, a lot. "I suppose," I say, "she must have had them with her, otherwise where else would they be?"

"I need to know for sure."

Wouldn't she have left a note if she'd killed herself? I've never pondered the vital importance of a suicide note until now. The *clink* of a falling pebble distracts me. I glance in the direction of the sound. Is there someone on the steps? Are we being watched?

"She was so brittle I couldn't hold her together. She fell apart in my care."

"What about the man she was seeing at the time? Did you know him?"

Silence sprouts and fills the cove, muffling the surf and chasing the seagulls away. Clouds thicken out to sea. I'm cold. I reach into a basket for my pullover.

"Sure I know who it was. It was Hank Martinez."

I frown. "But wasn't he your defence lawyer?"

Lucas nods.

"But why would you use Hank Martinez to defend you when he was—"

"Because I knew about Bonny and Hank. Mrs. Hank Martinez didn't, and doesn't. Neither do their teenage children. No one else in that outwardly perfect family knows apart from me and Hank. God knows how because Bonny was less than discreet."

I recall seeing a photo of the Martinezes in the *Hello* magazine, at some charity gala event in London. They are a handsome, happy couple. In a movie, they'd be played by George Clooney and Cameron Diaz. "What are you saying? You made a deal with him? He got you off in exchange for your silence?"

Lucas sits up. "Yeah, I guess."

I stare at him. "I don't understand."

"Bonny forced Hank into making a mistake. I know she did. She was one of those women. If she wanted something, she went for it until she got it. When she didn't want it anymore, she broke it, and moved on."

"Is that what she did to you?"

He looks at me for a few moments. "Martinez was lucky. Bonny hadn't got that far with him. My silence saved his marriage. His expertize kept me out of jail. Fair deal."

Fair deal? I'm not so sure, and I say so. Martinez gets off free as a seagull to progress his hotshot, flashy, New York life, and Lucas is dumped with a thundercloud of doubt hanging over him, unable to enjoy life in a town split over his innocence—in spite of Alice, beautiful Blue Rocks, his exciting career, anything, *everything*.

"I kind of feel I deserve it," Lucas says, "because—" he turns his head to look at me, his eyes unreadable—"I was glad Bonny died. Happy."

Those words punch me in the gut. "*Lucas*. How can you say that?"

"It's the truth." He frowns, like he's confused himself by realizing a significant fact. "I cannot begin to describe the relief that flooded me, after the original shock and horror of finding her. That's why I feel so guilty. That's why I have to know she didn't kill herself. I have to know, even though she was so hard to love."

I'm that shocked I'm breathless. If he found it difficult to feel and *show* grief after Bonny's death, is it any wonder Lobster Cove is divided?

Next thing, he reads my mind. "Another truth about…all this is that I don't much care what Lobster Cove folk think about me. I care what *I* think about me." He prods his chest with a thumb. "And I care about Alice. She's the world to me." He stares at me, his eyes hard. "Have I shocked you?"

I stop gawping and shut my mouth. "Um."

"That's it," he says, voice flat. "That all. Now you know everything about me. There's nothing else."

"I'm sure you did everything you could." I think about Alice, skipping off to school this morning, full of the joys of the world, particularly excited to show Ruth Pick a fallen chunk of wasps' nest—thoroughly inspected by me, for emptiness—found by Lucas this morning.

"I didn't. I should have tried harder."

"Maybe she should have tried harder too."

"She couldn't. She wasn't that sort of person."

Enough. "Great!" I yank on my pullover, angry now. "You tried, she didn't have to, and now everybody, you, Alice, and…and *me*, we all have to live under the burden of your *guilt*, because *bloody Bonny* couldn't *bloody* behave herself!" I stand up and start throwing stuff into the picnic basket. The little bowl of grapes overturns. Grapes tumble onto the pebbles like fat, green tears and something inside me breaks. "She's between us all the time, Lucas, isn't she? Isn't she? Like a horrible dark shadow on all our lives, making everyone miserable!" Bursting into fat tears of my own, I turn my back and stamp up the beach to the steps. Not my most Zen-like moment.

Approaching the house, my anger fades to remorse. This isn't about me. It's about Lucas. And it's about Alice and, yes, like it or not, Bonny too. If Lucas is the One for me, but I'm not the One for him—for whatever reason—that's bad, and that's too bad. Am I going to hang around waiting for him to love me the way I want him to?

No. I'm ashamed of myself for even thinking that! I'm ashamed of myself, period. How *could* I have spoken to Lucas like that?

My phone rings. Julie, wanting to discuss baby-led weaning, whatever that is, this minute.

"Can we do it later?" I say. "I'm busy."

"Why?" Her hurt tone is the last straw. "I have to leave for the spa in ten minutes—"

"Don't be so needy," I snap. "Be *havvy,* for God's sake!"

"Lara?" she squeaks.

"Pull yourself together. Grow up. I'll call you back *later*. Goodbye."

I ring off, not before I hear her shout, "You're *jealous*—"

Am I? Would I rather be Julie, who doesn't have,

need, or want to work, who's adored and worshipped by wealthy, devoted Derek, who doesn't have a thought in her head beyond her own comfort and happiness? Or would I rather be me?

I'm really busy. Sorry. Dealing with something awkward. Love you X, I message, quickly, blinking back new tears. Am I staying in Maine because I can't compete with Julie?

I stop walking, ankle deep in scratchy grass and look at the house, at the simple solidity of the architecture, somehow restrained and majestic all at once. I've grown to love it. To me, this house is the heart of Maine. A few days ago I felt I could change my life to live here forever, but now? Lucas aside, could I move my life to Maine?

No. Because Lucas is not *aside*, and I'd always be waiting, wouldn't I? Waiting to see what happens? Waiting for some spark to ignite in him, to burn up those dark memories and fling their ashes into the blue-grey salt of the Atlantic Ocean. I could wait forever. What sort of life is that?

Blue Rocks—what a hard, cold name for such a beautiful house. A house that could be a home if someone loved it enough. Walking toward the porch, I half turn back. I shouldn't have abandoned Lucas like that, never mind the scene. I'll go back, apologise, tell him I love him—because I do, don't I?—and we'll discuss our way through this, support each other, get help, whatever it takes.

But I don't go back, because there's no point. Whatever happened to Bonny, Lucas feels guilty. No, Lucas *is* guilty. That's the way he sees it, and that's the crux of the problem. I can do nothing about that, and neither can Lucas. The only person who can ease the nightmare by telling the truth is Bonny: a dead woman.

Reminding myself that I tried to leave Lucas, Alice, Blue Rocks, Maine, everything, mere weeks ago, I wonder if I shouldn't give it another go. Try harder. Stay away. Walking on, I get to the house, approaching the porch with a wary eye, glancing, like I always do now, at the ground, to see if Agat's been back.

Nothing.

Nothing, until I'm up the steps and across the porch, standing in front of the swing. I look down to where I was sitting. Someone watched us leave the house. Someone did this while we were in the cove. I retreat into the deep shade against the house like it can protect me. With my back against the wooden cladding, my heart crashing against my ribs, I stand dead still and scan the garden.

****

Lucas comes back. I watch him approach, picnic basket in one hand, rugs rolled up under the other arm.

"Lucas," I blurt, when he's at the top of the steps.

"*Jeez.* What are you doing? You scared the shit out of me!"

His reaction alarms me. "Why? Why did I scare the shit out of you, Lucas? Did you see something?"

He shakes his head. "What are doing hiding back there in the shadows?"

"Look." I point. "Look on the porch swing."

He stares at me for a full ten seconds—and I swear he gets paler with every passing one—puts down the stuff he's carrying, and goes over to the swing. He looks at it for a minute, and then looks at me. "What?"

"Someone's finished the bunny."

"The what?"

"The blue bunny Alice and I were knitting. We weren't even halfway through. Someone's finished it."

"For crying out. I was expecting Buster, disembowelled, at the very least!"

Oh God. Don't say that. "*Don't touch it.*"

Too late. Lucas picks up the bunny, looks at it, turning it over in his fingers, looks at me, looks at the bunny. "What's the problem?"

Hand over my mouth, sick and trembly, I turn my eyes on the garden again. The clouds have gone, pushed by the wind to the horizon, and the coastline basks in the mellow, early afternoon sunshine. I shudder. Somehow, everything about the scene is sinister. Dragging my eyes away, I watch Lucas, willing him not to come closer, willing him to put that thing down.

He doesn't. He brings it to me, holding it out. "Looks like someone did you and Alice a favour."

I shriek, stopping him. "Take it away!"

He props the bunny on a windowsill, shoves his hands in his pockets and looks at me under his eyebrows. "Lara? What's up?"

I don't know. Why is he speaking softly like that? Is he looking at me funny? What's going on? "It's Agat, isn't it? Isn't it?"

He's taken aback. "Agat?" His eyes shift. He strolls to the edge of the porch and looks down the distant shore, across the grass and out to sea, and to the east where the pebble beach ends in a jagged tumble of rocks.

"Yes. She hangs around. Does stuff."

He comes back to me and stands a few yards off, like he doesn't want to come near me. "What do you mean?"

I tell him how I first ran into Agat outside her house and how I found out about Alombegwinosis, Dzeedzeebonda and Kisosen, the watcher in the night. How I learned about the stealer of rings, the shape-shifter, the upsetter of canoes, and the young, handsome Abenaki man, possessed by his woman, his head shaved. "And Agat planted horrible little crosses here," I point to the grass, "to keep you away, from me, because she said you were evil, that you had blackened my heart!"

"To keep me away?"

"Yes! After you were hurt, diving. You stayed away. You didn't contact me for ages at a time, you—"

"Agat wouldn't hurt you. It's nothing."

Nothing? "Oh really?" My voice goes squeaky. "What about hurting *you*? What about Alice?"

"She loves Alice. She's protective."

"But not you. She tried to keep you away by planting those stupid little crosses—" I choke on a gasp. Everything I've pondered over the last weeks falls into place with an explosive crash. "Did Agat kill Bonny and blame it on you?"

He stares at me for a few seconds, impassive. "No."

"She's a troublemaker, Lucas. She's got it in for you."

"I am aware of that. But she loves Alice and was always nice to Bonny when no one else was."

"She doesn't believe you're innocent."

"Maybe I'm not."

All my muscles freeze. I'm so frightened I can't move my mouth around the words. "What do you mean?"

He comes a few steps closer. "If Bonny killed herself, it was my fault. If she killed herself, I murdered her. It's all the same, don't you see?"

I shake my head. "No. No it's not. Not to me."

"It's all the same to me," he says, softly. "To me. And it will be to Alice, when she's old enough to ask questions about her mother."

He stands in front of me, blocking the sunlight, hands in pockets head down, while I'm still firmly jammed up against the back wall of the porch. We're inches apart, but Bonny's there, making sure we don't touch.

Something's got to happen before I do that, Lucas said, earlier today, and this is it. Bonny is what has to happen.

She has to go. Or I do.

Chapter Twenty-Six

Fetching Alice from school brings me back to reality. Waiting at the school gate in the autumn sunshine is the most normal thing in the world. Lucas is right. Agat is nothing more than a harmless old woman with—maybe—a sixth sense. How ridiculous to be spooked by her. She's vibrant local colour, nothing more. Part of that famous Lobster Cove folklore. Go along with it, Lara; get with it!

Here comes Alice with Molly, who's coming over for a play date this afternoon. They climb into the car laden with carrier bags of craft paper, coloured pens, stickers, glitter and glue, brimming with ideas for the class party Halloween poster.

At home, Alice is thrilled with the completed blue bunny—yes, I inspected it for pins—who sits central on the black poster card while she and Molly draw wonky spiders in fluorescent marker pen.

"You see?" Lucas murmurs in my ear, when he comes into the kitchen drawn out of his studio by the smell of baking. "The bunny is a big success."

"I know, I feel stupid." I touch his arm. "I shouldn't have spoken to you the way I did earlier. I'm sorry."

"I understand." His lips brush my temple. "I understand."

"I should thank Agat, really, for letting me off the

hook. I'm a lousy knitter."

"Do that. She's a good person to have on your side, especially at Halloween." He steps away, surveying my handiwork for the Halloween bake sale—rows of orange pumpkin cookies with smiley faces, black witches' hats iced with green hatbands, black cats with yellow eyes, squares with chocolate spider webs across one corner, ghosts with BOO and EEK written large on their robes. "Wow," he says. "Which one should I try?"

"No, Daddy, don't eat them all," Alice cries. "They're for school!"

"Just one little biscuit?" Lucas puts a whole ghost in his mouth.

"What's a biscuit?" Molly asks.

"A cookie," Alice replies. "Lara's word for cookie is biscuit. Daddy likes to copy her."

"That's funny!"

They giggle, scribbling away at the poster. Lucas picks up a pen and adds some pink Leonardo da Vinci bats. He changes pens to send bright green spiders scuttling to every corner, helps himself to a black cat and goes back to his studio, laughing.

A perfect domestic scene. Everyone happy. Normalcy at its height.

Jay collects Molly at six. I make supper and the three of us sit together at the kitchen table to eat.

"Will tricksters and treatsters come to our house on Halloween?" Alice asks.

Lucas glances at her. "No."

"Why, Daddy?"

"Because we're too far out of town."

Is that the real reason?

I wonder.

****

The next morning, under a hot, hard shower, I reflect that many things are not normal at all. The sex is, always, astonishing, fabulous, amazing, but Lucas is distant. We're not intimate. That's the only way I can describe it. I haven't slept with oodles of men—far from it—but Lucas is way, way better than any of them in bed. He's knees, waist, head and shoulders beyond the lot of them stacked together.

But…and it's a big but, there's that same old barrier, or perhaps it's a void. Lucas doesn't give himself—his *whole* self—to me in those intense intimate moments in the big bed upstairs, wrapped in the moonlit darkness. Either he's holding something back, or there's someplace I can't reach. Make no mistake, sex with Lucas is brilliant—*perfect*—but it's a bit like this:

"I'd like some astounding sex please, Lucas."

"Yes, ma'am."

That's it. There's something between us, something he can't, or won't, give.

He's told me he loves me.

I love him back, but I can't say the words.

You know, Lucas is still paying me. That's weird, and maybe that's the problem. Perhaps I'm the problem.

"Lucas," I say, once I'm home from taking Alice to school. "I feel uncomfortable that you're still paying me and we're…we're sleeping together. It doesn't feel right."

He's in the studio, sitting at one of his computers. I'm standing behind him, my hands stroking his hair, ears, neck, shoulders. He reaches up and runs his fingers over my forearms causing riots in many parts of my body.

"If I stop paying you, you might leave."

"I might anyway, Lucas. Perhaps I should."

He grips my arms, but says nothing until I try to pull away and then he lets me go and stands up, turning, pushing the chair away and catching me in his arms. The movement is so quick I'm unprepared. He holds me tight. I can't move or breathe. "I love you," he growls. I can hear the words resonate in his chest, through my squashed ear. "So no more talk about leaving, okay? Stop talking about leaving."

"We *need* to talk about it."

"We just did."

We stand, fused together until he releases me in a sudden movement. I stagger back, looking away from those potent eyes. "Lucas, there's something—"

His phone rings. He glances at the screen. "I have to take this. It's going to be a long one." He answers the call, and I slip out of the room and go onto the sea porch, gasping for air like a beached fish.

Later that day, Lucas hears that he's failed his second medical. I keep watch, looking for signs of stubble and empty whisky bottles, but he hangs together.

"Is that it?" I ask. "I mean, can you not do *any* sort of diving ever again, as long as you live?"

"Alex Campbell says I'm only good for honeymoon diving from now on in."

"Honeymoon diving?"

"Diving in two feet of warm, crystal clear water to look at pretty fish."

"That sounds rather nice."

He grins. "It does?"

"As long as there are no sharks."

"I could probably swim with dolphins."

"Alice would enjoy that."

"Yes." He goes out, and I don't ask him where.

He comes back after midnight and gets into bed with me.

"I'm so sorry," I say, cheek pressed to his chest. "I wish I could help."

"You do," he says—I think—kissing the top of my head and falling asleep.

I raise my head and sniff. Toothpaste, that's all.

Chapter Twenty-Seven

The last weekday of October already. I collect Alice from school, and we drive out to Emerald Lake to see Agat. I've got a tin of cookies for her; they're a mix of cheerful pumpkins and brightly coloured spider webs. I thought it better to leave off the witches and ghosts. I'm trying to thank her, not make a point. Alice is tremendously excited. All along the way we pass gateways decorated with all the trappings of Halloween—barrows piled with pumpkins, witches, wizards and warlocks hovering in trees, and black cats sneaking and creeping along and over walls. On fire with fall foliage and redolent with the rich smell of wood smoke, it couldn't be more festive. Christmas must be amazing in Maine. I wonder what I'll be doing at Christmas? Where will I be?

Agat has jolly jack o' lanterns along the front of her porch, and some not so jolly ones. "Unhappy." Alice points to one with a hideous grin and plus signs for eyes.

"Evil," Agat says, opening the front door.

"What's evil?" Alice asks.

"Naughty," I say quickly. "What do you say to Agat?"

"Hello, and thank you for knitting my bunny!" she sings, like I've told her to.

"You like it?" There's no denial. Agat's voice is

soft. I wouldn't say she smiles, but she moves her mouth into an expression of acceptance. She reaches out to touch Alice's hair. "Precious Lis," she murmurs.

"Lara made you *biscuits,* Aunty Agat. They are cookies, but she says *biscuits* and Daddy loves them."

Agat raises her eyes to mine. "Good," she says.

"He also says *biscuit* now. Molly thinks it's funny!"

I hold out the container. Agat won't take it, but steps aside and points to a space on the old tabletop at the back of the porch. I gather I have to put it there, that she doesn't want to touch it while I am. That's okay, so long as there's no spitting and finger wagging. The cookies get placed between a jar of seagull feathers and a chipped, white enamel bowl containing a lifetime's collection of seaglass.

"Wait," Agat says, going inside. Alice fiddles about, touching everything, while I look out at the trees, leaves rustling in the smoky wind, falling like coloured rain.

A few minutes later, Agat's back with a small plastic bag of something frozen. "Wild duck for Buster," she tells Alice, placing it on the table. "Take. Check for bones before you give it."

"Thank you," I say. "Come, Alice, we must go."

Alice picks up the little bag. We leave. Agat watches us until we're in the car, and then goes inside and shuts the door.

Back at Blue Rocks, Lucas has put out huge happy-carved pumpkins on either side of the gate. There are more merry pumpkins on the porch flickering in the dusk.

"Who's going to see those?" I ask, when he comes

to open the sea horse door for us.

"We are."

Lucas has colonized the kitchen to make chilli. There's music on, wine open—and a cheery pile of carved pumpkin debris, used pots, dishes and chopping boards on every surface, reminding me of that evening back in June when I first walked in here.

"How did it go with Agat?" he asks, on the point of going upstairs to supervise Alice's bath time.

"Not bad. We're not big mates, but she was okay with Alice. She gave us wild duck for Buster."

"Great." He chases Alice upstairs with such spooky wails, that even Buster pays attention. He looks up from extensive tail-grooming in the middle of the kitchen doorway, his yellow eyes shining with the thrill of the hunt.

"For a black cat on Halloween, you sure are laid-back," I tell him, "and very indoor-orientated. Shouldn't you be out and about scaring people?"

Buster watches the stairs for a minute and then carries on licking, ignoring me. I'm not sure I'll give him the wild duck. I know he's a naturally large cat, but he's a teensy overweight in my opinion. Perhaps rich, fatty treats aren't the best idea Also, call *me* mad, but what if Agat's poisoned it? Lucas's Buster-disembowelling comment sticks in my mind. I'll ask Lucas what he thinks. Meanwhile, I won't put it in the freezer because we might forget it. Someone might eat it by mistake, months hence. I'll put it away, somewhere high up in the pantry, discuss with Lucas, and either debone it for consumption tomorrow morning or chuck it out. I put the duck in a recycled, sealed plastic container and stash it on the top shelf, closing the door. I help myself to a glass of wine, take one sip and change my mind. Sod it, I'm going to chuck the duck. Why take risks?

Retrieving the container, I hover at the kitchen bin. Not good enough, because I know that cat. I go out through the sea horse door, checking from habit that the key's in my pocket—where it mostly lives—and put the duck, container and all, in the outside bin behind the garage. The wind's picked up, driving sharp arrows of drizzle into my face. I run back to the house, where the pumpkin lanterns gutter in the porch and the open door throws a long rectangle of yellow light. I crunch over stray leaves on the threshold and quickly shut myself inside.

"Where were you?" Lucas comes down the stairs with Alice in his arms, wrapped in a towel.

"Outside." I shiver.

"Why?" Alice asks.

"To check I'd locked the car." I see no problem telling a small white lie if it keeps someone safe, even Buster. I glance at him. He's in exactly the same place, only stretched out on his side, fast asleep.

Lucas carries Alice into the den and puts her on the sofa. He lights a fire and closes the shutters against the throb of sudden, heavy rain on the windows. I dry Alice and help her into her pyjamas. We turn down the lights, light candles and watch Halloween cartoons suitable for a four-year-old until Alice's bedtime. Before he takes her upstairs, Lucas reads aloud two *Winnie* stories and then carries Alice out onto the sea porch to look for witches. The rain's cleared, the air's crisp and still and the moon's beautiful, burning a track of white fire on the dark sea.

Once Alice is asleep, we eat chilli and drink red wine in front of the fire. That done, we watch a movie called *Haunted October*—Lucas laughs and I scream. We go to bed at midnight, the very height of the witching hour, Buster—Blue Rocks' own living Halloween symbol—following us to Alice's room, where he curls up on her feet like a plump, furry cushion.

Chapter Twenty-Eight

"There's good news," Lucas tells Alice and me at breakfast, once we've made it through the most haunted night of the year, unscathed. "John called. Rayna had her pups in the night, and he wants us to go down to Boston and see them."

Alice is wide-eyed with wonder. "Can we have a puppy, Daddy, can we? Molly's got a puppy, so I *must* have a puppy!"

Lucas smiles at her. "Not this time, sweetheart."

"Why? Why?"

"We have Buster," Lucas says.

When Alice has left the room I ask Lucas why Alice can't have a puppy, although I shudder to think what Buster might do to a puppy.

"Most of the professional child-minders who look after Alice won't accept the additional responsibility of a dog. A dog would make it more difficult to appoint the best person, it's that simple."

Simple, and bleak.

Lucas's phone rings. He answers it, heading for the studio, leaving me standing in front of the sink, staring out the window. What he said flattened me, emptied me out, drained the colour from the world. I must decide what to do because he's presuming I'm moving on.

Later, Lucas asks me if I'd like to go to Boston with him and Alice to visit John, Debra, Rayna and her puppies. "It'll be our last chance to visit Debra before the baby's born," he adds, "and a good time for you to meet the rest of the family, dogs included. We'll drive down this afternoon, spend a night or two, come back."

I hesitate. A good idea and a natural progression, I guess, but something's not right. "No. No, thanks, Lucas. I won't come, if you don't mind."

He does mind, and I see it on his face. "Can I, you know, tell John about us?"

"Maybe not yet." What about us, anyway?

"Why don't you want to come?"

I smile right into his eyes and shake my head. "It's not that I don't want to, it's that I strongly feel I shouldn't. Don't ask me why."

He doesn't. He disappears to crash about in the pantry. A minute later, "Lara!"

"What?"

"Where's that case of whisky?"

I join him in the pantry. "Whisky?"

"There was a case of whisky in here. Right there." He points to the floor, beneath the bottom shelf, right at the back of the room.

"Oh that," I say. "I threw it away.

He frowns. "Threw it away? Where?"

"I poured it down the sink."

"You—"

"That night you were drunk, Lucas. I was really worried about you, Alice, everything. I poured it down the sink and recycled the bottles."

"Ha, hahaha! Funny, Lara, real funny. That whisky's for John. I've been collecting it for four years, at auctions, all over the world."

"Four years?"

"Yeah. He gave me a case of vintage champagne when Lis was born. It's a real treasure, kept in a vault at the Morgan Bank. I've done the same for him, with whisky. With the baby due, I'd like to take it with me to Boston this afternoon."

My heart slides downward. "Well, perhaps you should have kept John's whisky there too."

"Lara?"

"I threw it away, Lucas."

"We're talking upward of five thousand dollars here."

"I'm deeply sorry. I threw it away." *Five thousand dollars.*

Lucas faces me head on, and head lowered, like he's about to charge. "Didn't you notice the bottles were unusual? All different shapes?"

"I know nothing about whisky." Even my voice is frightened by what I've done, and will do no more than whisper.

"Clearly not!" Lucas glares and there's a terrible silence that could go either way. Minutes pass. I dare not move until Lucas throws his hands up in frustration and shouts "Fuck!" at the ceiling. He marches out of the room and slams himself into the studio.

Standing on the driveway that afternoon, saying goodbye to Alice and Lucas, I'm desolate. Lucas is mad, and I'm frightened he'll stay mad.

"Get in the Mustache, Lis," he says.

"But why Lara not come? Why?"

"Don't ask me again, sweetheart." There's nothing sweet in the way he says that.

"Lucas," I murmur, "Don't be a-n-g-r-y with her, please. It's nothing to do with her, it's fully my fault."

He has the grace to look chastised. "It's my fault, actually. See you day after tomorrow."

If our relationship can survive this, I suppose it could survive anything, but it's too soon to make that suggestion.

"Are you going to tell John what happened to his whisky?"

He glances at me. "Probably not. Alice, in the car."

"I should do that, shouldn't I?"

"Come with us then."

"No. It wouldn't be right—"

"Oh, look, Daddy and Lara." Alice points to the ground. "Pretty!"

We look. Behind the car, on the side away from the house, there's a bright circle of fallen maple leaves, about four feet across, arranged in yellow, orange and red rings, with a centre of red rosehips. Each ring is perfectly constructed, each leaf perfectly overlapping the next, every stalk pointing to the centre of the circle, each apex outward, like a giant flower.

"Who did that?" I say, knowing the answer, full well.

"Agat's been," Lucas says.

"What is it?"

Lucas walks around the circle, studying it. "I'm not sure, but it's a real work of art."

"It's beautiful. Do you thinks it's like a…a truce of some sort?"

Lucas nods. "I suspect it is."

"That's good."

"Sure is." He picks up Alice, and puts her in the car seat, strapping her in. I hug and kiss her, and shut the door.

"You take care now, Lara." He kisses me.

"Lucas, I'm *sorry*."

He strokes my hair. "It's okay."

Is it?

They leave, waving, me calling out to Lucas to drive safely. It's a long way to Boston. I stand in the porch, touching the handle of the sea horse door until the sound of the engine fades. About to go inside, I change my mind. Taking my phone out of my pocket, I go out onto the driveway and take a photo of the flower of leaves Agat made for us.

To give Buster credit, he ambles outside to join me, and rubs his head on my ankle. I know it's his suppertime, but it's comforting anyway.

That evening I Google Abenaki symbols and there's not much. All I can find are some Native American symbols that are similar—concentric circles that represent fire, which is a bit worrisome. In some tribal cultures, smoke was used to purify sacred items, while fire was the symbol of the heart of the people. Smoke also carried prayers to the Great Spirit. Generally, fire symbols appear to represent cleansing and renewal, because out of the ashes of the fire comes regeneration, etcetera. Generally, it's positive. Blue Rocks, I reckon, will not be struck by lightning or spontaneously combust.

There's nothing to worry about.

There's *really* nothing to worry about, I'm sure. However, in the morning I decide to drive out to Agat's, bearing a fresh-baked batch of giant blueberry and white chocolate muffins. The day is clear and cold; so cold, I'm driving over ice-crusted puddles, so clear, I could be looking at the world through a sheet of polished ice. Perhaps I could pop in and see Angie, to get her angle on the fire-flower on the driveway, although *popping in* isn't my forte. Popping in can be highly inconvenient: refer Uncle Buck's ill-timed visit to Blue Rocks to cadge fifty bucks off Lucas. I wouldn't have put it past him to stomp around to the sea porch doors, grumbling. If he'd peered through the windows he could have caught me and Lucas in the act. Maybe I should ring Angie; see if it's convenient to have a quick word.

In the end, I don't have to. I get to Agat's little house and see Angie on the porch watering plants. I stop the Jeep and get out.

"Beautiful morning," she says, putting down the watering can.

"Perfect," I answer. The windows of the house are closed, the blinds drawn. Angie's locking the door while we speak.

"Is Agat away?" I ask.

"She's not well. She's in the hospital."

"I'm sorry to hear that. I brought her a little something to thank her." I hand the box of muffins to Angie. "She left a beautiful pattern of leaves on our driveway yesterday. Pretty impressive. Alice loved it."

Angie pockets the key and turns to face me, frowning. "You sure?"

"I can't imagine who else would have done that."

"What did it look like?"

I take out my phone, pull up the photo and show Angie. She studies it at length, a forefinger tapping her lips. "It looks like fire."

"Do you think it's a-a message of some sort?"

She stares at the phone a moment longer, and

hands it back. "Nah. And even if it were, she won't be able to do anything about it."

"Meaning?"

"She was admitted to hospital last night with an intense headache. So intense they had to sedate her. CT scans this morning revealed a tumour on the brain."

"Do you mean cancer?" I step forward, putting my hand on Angie's arm.

Angie sighs, raising her eyebrows. "Strangely enough, no. Just a big ol' benign thing, growing away in her head."

"That's terrible. I'm so sorry."

"We think it may have caused her to, y'know, imagine stuff, behave strange."

I nod. "Can…can anything be done?"

"They can operate, but Agat's well into her eighties. It's real risky."

"Her eighties! I can hardly believe that."

"All those magic lotions and potions she uses. Maybe I should try them, whaddaya think?" She smiles.

"If you do, I will."

Angie cracks open the muffin box to take a peek. "Thanks, Lara. Agat'll love these. I look forward to helping her eat them."

We say goodbye and I get back in the Jeep.

"And," Angie calls after me, "don't worry about that leaf stuff."

"I won't."

"Did Buster enjoy the duck?"

"The—"

"Agat told me she gave Alice wild duck for Buster. Did he enjoy it? She was real keen to know."

"Er, no, it's still in the freezer. Agat said to debone

it first."

All the way home I think about Agat, wild duck and fiery leaves. However, no need to feel guilty about the duck because when I pull up in front of Blue Rocks, I see that Buster—possibly somebody else, though Buster springs firmly to mind—has helped himself. The fallen garbage bin lies on its side, strewing rubbish across the driveway. I park the Jeep, get out and clean up. There's no sign of the duck, merely the empty plastic container, prised open with claws and teeth, and no sign of Buster.

Inside, I make a cup of tea. The view draws me through the house onto the sea porch. The sea is mercury silver, the sky a chilled duck-egg blue. I put on a pullover, pick up a rug and ensconce myself on the porch swing, so cleverly placed in the full sun, well-protected from the wind. It's *just* warm enough, perfect if I ignore the frozen tip of my nose. I drink tea and gaze at the beauty. Seagulls glide on ice-white wings, way out to sea, like snowflakes in a summer sky, their distant ringing cries and the soft boom of low surf the only sounds. Only, it's not summer any more. I put down my cup and snuggle under the rug, pulling it up to my eyes. I didn't sleep that well last night, worrying about leaves and signs. Besides, the weather forecast has already predicted a swift end to this fragile state of affairs, so I might as well enjoy myself while it lasts. My eyelids are heavy; I'm toasty-warm.

Mmmmm, glorious…

Life is perfect now—right now—in this exquisite moment, curled up on the porch swing in the sun with Lucas, floating in the dark gold of his eyes. Is his heart still in lockdown? I think not because there's a deep connection now, a glimpse of forever. Am I wrong to want so much? Am I greedy or—God forbid—needy? I love him. Sunk in the lace-trimmed cushions—where did they come from?—with Lucas half on top of me, one long leg pushed between mine, his arms wound around my shoulders, his mouth against my hair, murmuring…

What's that he's saying?
What?

Chapter Twenty-Nine

There's a terrible noise. Did Luca belch? That's not sexy! I snap open my eyes, sit up, dragging the rug around me. I'm alone, an empty teacup beside me, and…that noise. What *is* that?

"Lucas?" I actually say his name, blinking, putting my hand on the hard bench where there's not a lace-trimmed cushion to be seen. Lucas?

Bleaagh.

Is it a bird? I look out to sea, across the lawn. Can I can really see the curvature of the earth, or is it an optical illusion—

Bleaagh.

—and if it is, why doesn't it bend the other way, like a wide, shallow, blue bowl? There are white sails in the bay, spinnakers out like balloons—blue, red and yellow.

Bleaagh.

I wonder if I could learn to sail? This would be as good a place as any. The best. How amazing to feel the sails fill with fast-moving air, to be powered by the wind like the ancient explorers—

Bleaagh. Bleaagh. Bleaaaaaagh.

I throw the rug aside and get up. Leaning over the porch rail I see the cause of the commotion.

"Buster! What are you doing?"

He's crouched to the side of the steps, in long

grass, head extended, convulsing. He's choking. He's choking on Agat's duck! I creep down the steps without much of a plan in my head. All I know is, one, Buster needs to be okay by the time Alice gets home and, two, *Agat will not get the better of me*. Not even now, when she is, apparently, beyond capable of stalking this family. I will pick Buster up quickly and hold him tight, because he's bound to struggle. I'll rush him inside, close the doors to confine him, call the vet on her emergency number, and race to the clinic. That's the only thing to do, so that's what's going to happen.

"For God's sake, Buster, work with me," I plead, under my breath. He glances at me, terror in his yellow eyes, and chokes again. "Nice kitty, beautiful kitty, clever kitty, Buster," I say, soothing him. "Who's the handsomest kitty in the world? Who? Good kitty, shhhh."

Buster relaxes a little. Here's my chance. I bend, taking care not to make any quick movements, and stretching out my hands, slowly, I grip him around his middle. He's going to bolt; I know it.

A head-splitting uproar rips the air. The explosion of an erupting volcano, a bomb blast, eight trucks colliding with an express train, a chainsaw, a jackhammer, and washing machine full of tin cans. Buster ejects my grasp, leaving a trail of lacerated flesh—mine!—and turbo-boosts to the far side of the garden.

I race after him. A glance in the direction of the din reveals Buck, pushing an ancient lawnmower on a mighty steel roller over the stony ground to the side of the house.

"Buster!" I yell. "Buster, *come here*." He's not

going to, is he? He's in self-preservation mode and terrified. What cat ever hung out around a lawnmower? "Shut the fuck up!" I scream at Buck, waving my arms like a madwoman. Buster dives into thick bush, squeezing between the gnarled and twisted stems of plants bowed over by decades of easterly gales, and disappears. I go after him.

"Fuck you, Buster," I mutter, taking care not to scream, but what's the point? Nothing will placate a cat choking to death while scared to death!

I'm in, pushing my way through the tightly woven undergrowth, thick with rotten leaves, going after him on hands and knees. I can't let Buster die. I can't heal Lucas, I can't protect Alice forever, but I can stop Buster dying, or die trying myself. My pullover hooks on a branch and I have to pull my arm out of the sleeve to free myself. It doesn't work. Now my arm's stuck *and* my head. I squirm free, leaving the pullover behind, knotted in the branches, reminding myself that I am a cat person, I *am*. Just not today.

For a moment, I stop scrambling about in the undergrowth, to listen. A mournful yowl drives me on. Please God, let Buster be stuck, so I can reach him. I jam myself between sticks and stalks, and solid, old, uncooperative deadwood. My jeans rip and the offending sharp, splintery point rams my thigh. I crawl on, knees mashed by old broken shells and salty grit, breaking nails, eyes stinging with sand and slapping twigs. I lose a clump of hair on one of a million protruding branches and bash my knees on rocks. Covered in muck, eyes streaming, I barely register the shredding of my shirt.

I pause. "Buster? Buster, kitty?"

No lawnmower at least, only the loud grunt of the nearby surf, and a shrieking seagull. I'm stuck. That saying *dragged through a bush backwards*—it's the same forwards, trust me. I'm up against a wall of vegetation and there's one thing to do: force my way. I push, grunting, and the wood bends, only to bend back and hit me in the face. I can't let Buster die. I can't go through another blue-pyjamas cataclysm. The blue pyjamas aren't even alive, for crying out.

"Buster!" I'm desperate, breathless, panting, so panicked that I don't hear it at first. I barely see it; it's that stealthy.

What—?

Oh God, an alligator! I swallow my heart. No, it's not an alligator. Like the bear wasn't a bear, but merely a moose out and about in the wilds of Maine. Dead still, sensible and calm, I swivel my eyes.

An alligator.

A long, wide, brown thing, a stealthy killing machine, slithering on its fat belly three yards to my left. Buster's dead for sure because this mean beast has his eyes straight ahead. Please, please, please, I pray, take Buster. Eyes squeezed shut, I offer Buster, *will him to be eaten* instead of me.

But alligators are restricted to Florida, aren't they? Or haven't I concentrated properly on the National Geographic Channel that forms the greater part of my knowledge bank of the Great Outdoors? Maine is not swampy right here on the coast. How come there's an alligator? Didn't I hear they've existed on planet earth for ninety million years? Or is that sharks? Or crocodiles? Aren't alligators and crocodiles fundamentally one and the same? Cold blooded killing machines, perfectly honed for survival? Whatever, there's one in the underbrush, here and now.

And me? I lick my sandy lips. What if he smells me? Perhaps if I freeze he'll keep going and pass me by. I stay completely still and the alligator slides past. On my stomach, head down on my arms, nose full of sand I wait for the alligator to smell me, and turn. I wait to die.

"Fuck," the alligator says.

I lift my head, blinking. In front of me, wreathed about with leaves, two feet ahead of my nose I see the worn soles of a pair of size twenty boots. "Buck?"

"Shaddap you." He crawls forward on his elbows, hardly making a sound. I stay where I am, spent. Buster must choose now. Life or death. He might well choose death with Buck looming, the peak of his battered, brown baseball cap penetrating the vegetation like the muzzle of some prehistoric reptile. I wait for Buster to die of fright while I try not to do the same. There's more creeping from Buck, some waiting, leopard crawling, and then a pounce, "*Goddamn,*" and a scuffle. I drag myself upright, pushing upward through the bushes, to see Buck dragging Buster out of the thicket in some kind of sack. I reverse, scrabble, trip and stumble back to the entry point, but it's no good. I have to go back the way I came, crawling. On the ground again, in the composted slushy sand that's never seen the light of day, all the twigs and branches I've pushed forward, snap back and scratch and tear me, like I'm not scratched and torn enough. A big branch jumps back and knocks me sideways. Eew! My hand's on something cold. Is it a glob of cat sick? I'm not looking.

Clink.

I look. To be frank, there's not much space in the dingly dell to look, but I twist my head sideways and see, out of the corner of my eye that it's a key. Here's a bit of luck, to find something you didn't even know you'd lost. It's *my* key, the sea horse-shaped one Lucas told me never to lose! OMG, close call. I grab the key and reach behind me—more scratches—to shove everything into the torn pocket of my jeans. Determined, eyes squeezed shut against the whip of the retaliating branches, I reverse the way I came, surprised, actually to see how little progress I made. Whatever. In my memory, this misadventure will lodge as ten miles' worth of hacking through the barbed and stinging plants of the Amazon jungle, at its impenetrable heart.

Buck and I emerge from the jungle in different places. He sets off immediately across the lawn, gripping the thrashing fur bomb in a bag that is Buster. I chase them around the side of the house.

"In the truck," Buck barks. "Quick!"

I jump in and grapple for the seatbelt, somehow knowing we're in for a wild ride. There's no seatbelt, only a terse "Hold tight!" instruction from Buck, who wrangles the reluctant ignition with gritted teeth, rams the truck into gear, spinning the wheels as we rocket down the drive. By the time we get to Jay's Automotive, Buck is driving foot flat, and talking on the phone. Somehow, he also has a hand on the horn, due—I suppose—to the lack of hazard lights on this rusting wreck.

"Tell Doc Foster to stand by," Buck roars over the noise of the engine. "*Operation Black Cat Down.* I'm on my way with Buster Dalton. He's in a bad way."

We're gunning down Main, when we're stopped by a tour group crossing the road to the fish market. There's too much of a crowd for Buck—even Buck—to take a gap. Nate Harris pulls up alongside and eyeballs me through the open window.

"Excuse me, Uncle Buck, sir." He leans forward to speak to Buck. "Would you pull over, please, so we can—"

"Nah! This here ain't a tea party. This here is an emergency situation. Buster ain't breathin'. I need an escort to Old Mill Veterinary, boy, not a friggin' tail. Get your fancy ass out in front of me and step on it. We'll talk after."

Now there's traffic. Nate eases the police car forward, siren on and blue lights flashing. Buck lurches into his slipstream, and we scream off. I close my eyes, waiting for the smash.

As for Buster, he's completely limp. I'm terrified he's dead.

Chapter Thirty

"Well, well, well. What have we here?" Dylan Foster strides out of the surgery into the reception area, taking Buster, still bagged, out of Buck's arms. "Buster Dalton, what's up this time?" With a quick word to the receptionist, she puts the waiting room—full of patients from goldfish to golden retriever, their owners wide-eyed in silent wonder—on hold. "Walk with me," she says. "Tell me what happened,"

Stupid as it sounds, I think I'm in shock. "Buck," I gasp, "can you...can you?" Spots jiggle in front of my eyes. I grab his arm.

"Nah, c'mon!" he says, arm firmly around my waist, supporting and propelling me, so all I must do is move my feet forward, one at a time. "We need to work with the doc now, ya hear? Coupla deep breaths is all ya need."

I suck oxygen that smells of squashed vegetation, tobacco, old lawnmower oil, veterinary disinfectant, and dog. "He's choked on a duck bone he got out of the rubbish, or something. Or maybe he's been poisoned."

We're in the surgery where a nurse awaits, masked and gloved. Dylan puts Buster on the operating table, cuts off the sack, scrubs up and pulls on gloves. Buster is nothing but a huge pile of motionless fur. The nurse locates one of his front legs and shaves a small patch so she can insert a drip.

"I can't look," I say to Buck, knees shivering.

He swings a chair to face the wall. "Sit," he says, and goes across to a water cooler to fetch me a cup of water.

"All done," Dylan says, "and there are no symptoms of poisoning as far as I can see.

"What?" I reply through chattering teeth, water slopping on my shirt. I look down at myself.

Oh. Not much clothing. No pullover, ripped shirt, camisole hanging by one strap revealing whole of left breast, admittedly in bra, though mud-encrusted. Unwittingly, I have invented a fashion leader in my spare time: shredded jeans. One of my shoes is missing. My earrings! My hands fly to my earlobes, sending the cup spinning across the floor. I'm so relieved they're both in place I start to cry. Cherri's right: *classics for every occasion,* indeed.

"Duck bone all right," Dylan says.

I turn around. She holds up a pair of narrow tongs, displaying the cause of Buster's near-death experience. "Lucas sure will be grateful. This fella means everything to Alice."

"Is he alive?" The bone is surprisingly small. I had imagined a giraffe's femur, at least.

"Oh yes," the nurse says, eyes down, hand stroking Buster's side. "Shall we move him to a cage?"

Dylan and the nurse carry Buster between them to a roomy mesh-walled compartment in the next room. I get up and follow. "Can I take him home?"

"We'll keep him overnight for observation. He'll be fine tomorrow, sure thing."

Buck joins me. "I called Lucas."

"He's in Boston," I say, staring at Buster, willing

him to move.

"He's back. Jus' pullin' into Lobster Cove this minute."

The nurse brings me a chair, a blanket that smells of shampooed dog to wrap around my shivering self, and a cup of tea. No way is it as good as Lucas's tea, but it's hot, strong and sweet, and exactly what I need this moment.

Buster opens heavy-lidded eyes, aims a couple of weak licks at his chest fur and falls asleep again twitching his whiskers. Thank God for that.

Ten minutes later, Lucas arrives while I'm sitting in front of the cage, keeping watch. He talks to Dylan in the next room, quickly, and next minute, he's on his haunches in front of me, one hand on my shoulder, the other arm around Alice, who's gazing at me speechless, eyes round.

"Buster's all right, Alice darling," I tell her. "Did Daddy explain?"

She nods, finger in her mouth. I grip Lucas's arm, drawing strength. "You came back early."

"Alice was really keen to get back, from the minute we arrived. In fact, before we arrived."

I frown into his eyes. "Why?"

"Once she'd seen the puppies she begged to come home. We spent the night and left early this morning to drive back."

I glance at Alice, who's pulled away from Lucas to go and sit cross-legged at Buster's cage, one small hand through the mesh, tickling his neck. "Thank God she wasn't here." Buster's in a deep sleep, and it's hard to believe it's not permanent.

"Buck told me what happened. Are you okay?"

Lucas asks, his voice low, eyes anxious.

"Of course."

"Because you don't look okay. I think we should take you down to the emergency room at the hospital."

We stand up together. "Don't be ridiculous," I say. He kisses me, and it stings.

Moments later, in the clinic bathroom, I see why he's concerned. Torn clothing aside, my face, chest and arms are scratched and bloody, my knees grazed. There are twigs in my hair and splinters in my hands. A sight to behold. But, it's nothing serious. I wash up as best I can, pat myself dry with paper towel and go out into the parking lot where Lucas and Alice, already in the Mustache, are waiting for me.

"Where's Buck?" I ask.

"Gone back to Blue Rocks to finish the mowing. He's real sorry for causing the incident."

"He wasn't to know."

"He said you were incredible. Says you should join the Navy SEALs."

"Really? Why on earth?"

"You're a real fighter. 'Warrior' was the word he used. You honoured the motto 'Leave no man behind.' He's impressed."

I laugh. "All's well that ends well, in that case."

We get in the car. "I left the sea porch doors open," I say, as we turn right onto First and head home. "I hope nobody's wandered in and cleaned out the house."

"Not much to clean out." There's a grin in Lucas's voice. "Besides, who would do such a thing?"

"Agat, for one."

"Uh, we need to talk about her."

I turn to look at him. "What about her?"

He glances at Alice in the rear view mirror, and then stares ahead. "Later" is all he says.

The beautiful day has turned ugly, as forecast. We drive up to Blue Rocks in swirling sleet, the sharp-edged wind ripping the trees, layering the road with slippery, fallen leaves. Lucas parks close to the front porch. I reach into the back to release Alice from her car seat, and we run for it, the howling wind snatching our clothes, blowing our hair upright, chilling my already frozen body.

Agat's circles of fiery leaves are nowhere to be seen.

"Keys please." Lucas holds out a hand.

Hair in my eyes, I dig in my back pocket and hand them over. They rattle into the lock and Lucas pushes open the sea horse door. We go inside, I scrape my hair out of my eyes and look at my watch. Nearly suppertime for Alice. Don't ask me where the time's gone.

Lucas goes straight to the kitchen, finds a tube of antiseptic gel, gives it to me and shoos me upstairs. "Go lie in a hot bath. Sort yourself out. I'll do Alice."

****

In the bathroom, I run hot water into the bathtub and undress, inspecting my naked, battered body in the full-length mirror. Blue bruises bloom on my shins and forearms and I'm criss-crossed with sand-filled cuts and scratches. I throw my clothes in the laundry basket and kick my crumpled jeans across the floor to the door. They're beyond saving. I'll throw them in the big kitchen bin when I go downstairs.

Forty minutes later I'm clean and warm in the baggiest clothes I can find in Lucas's closet—I went in there to borrow a pair of thick socks and kept going. Going downstairs, I meet Alice coming up with Lucas, to bath.

"You look amazing," Lucas says.

"I hope you don't mind?"

"Why would I? I mean, would you mind if I came downstairs dressed in your clothes without having asked if I could borrow them?"

"It's not the same."

He grins. "If you say so."

Together, we bath Alice and then take her, wrapped in a towel, to her bedroom.

"Alice, where are all your bunnies and teddies?" I survey her bed while helping her into her pyjamas. It's bare. There's no sea horse or blue knitted bunny either. All her *Winnie* books are gone.

"In Daddy bed," she says. "Come and see." She pulls me along the gallery to Lucas's room, and there's everyone, higgledy-piggledy, tucked into Lucas's bed, *Winnie* books—and others—spread everywhere.

"What's this, Alice?" I ask.

"It's for you. You must get in Daddy bed."

"Why?"

"When I am sad, I get in Daddy bed."

"I'm not sad."

"But you have ows and blood. Get in." She pulls back the covers, toys and books tumbling everywhere. "You sleep here now."

Lucas, leaning against the doorframe, chuckles. "Looks like the arrangement's been formalized."

Alice climbs in next to me and Lucas reads us a story, followed by another, by which time Alice is asleep. Lucas carries her to her own bed and we go downstairs to eat. On the way, I gather my jeans from the bathroom floor. In the kitchen, I throw them away.

"There's something in the pocket," says Lucas, freeing the cork from a bottle of Italian red. "I heard something."

"A dirty dime Alice found on the pavement. I didn't really want her to pick it up."

"Not my money you're throwing away, then?"

"I wouldn't do that."

"I read somewhere that you are in the top one percent of the world's richest if you don't pick up anything less than a dime on the street."

"That's not much of an accolade."

"I guess it's the same if you throw money away."

"Are you trying to make a point?"

He hands me a glass of wine. "Not really."

"You were going to tell me something about Agat."

"Yeah. Angie rang earlier. Agat's in a bad way. She's in the hospital for now. They'll attempt to operate, but it doesn't look good."

"That's sad."

He nods, thoughtful. "Angie said Agat's been rambling on about Bonny, and Alice, that's why she called me."

"Alice?"

He hesitates. "Agat gave up a child for adoption when she was sixteen. Turns out, over the years, she convinced herself it was Bonny."

I stare at Lucas. "Was it?"

"Not a chance. Think of the age difference."

"How can you be sure?" Agat being Bonny's mother would explain a lot.

"Angie persuaded Agat into DNA tests when

Bonny died because things, as you can imagine, got out of hand."

"What was the conclusion?"

"No conclusion, meaning the tests were inconclusive."

"So?"

Lucas bites the side of his right thumb, something I've never seen him do. "I always thought that, maybe, just maybe, Agat was Bonnie's *grandmother*."

"Why?"

"I once suggested it to Bonny. She went ballistic. I thought she was going to kill someone."

"*Kill someone*?"

"Me, or Agat, yeah. She went mad. Insane."

"She protested too much. Is that what you mean?"

Lucas shoves his hands into his pockets and nods, head down.

"Poor Agat," I say. "How dreadful for her."

"She was okay with it for a while, but over the last six months I guess the tumour was growing, and affecting her reason. She's telling everyone in the hospital that she is Bonnie Dalton's mother, and insisting that she is Alice's grandmother. Who knows? But Angie thought it best to tell me."

I lift my wine glass and sniff. The bouquet is glorious, the colour deep garnet. I close my eyes and sip. Heavenly. Putting the glass on the counter I open the bin. I'm drinking expensive Italian wine and throwing away money. This isn't right. I bring out the jeans, covered in scraps of fishy dinner Buster wasn't here to eat. Serves me right for not recycling. I almost give up but, holding my breath, I poke two fingers into one side pocket—nothing—and then the other—also nothing. One back pocket is torn right off and hanging by a thread, and the other...

"Honestly, why does the damn dime have to be in the last pocket I—" This is no dime. I pull out the object.

A key.

Chapter Thirty-One

Not any key, but the key to the sea horse door. Another key, because Lucas used mine to open the door this evening and it's lying on the table at the bottom of the stairs. I know, because I've just seen it there.

"Lucas?"

"Mm?"

The key is attached to a decomposing cork and…

I lift it closer to my eyes to make sure I'm actually seeing what I'm seeing.

A diamond ring. A large, round-cut solitaire in a tarnished setting.

Bonny's ring.

If it's lost, you can find it.

"Lucas?" I turn away from the bin, closing it on the ripped jeans that have given up their prize, and face him. "Look what I found."

He strolls over to see what I'm holding. To say he does a double-take doesn't cut it. It's more like an electric shock. He stares at the key in my hand for a moment, looks up at me wild-eyed and pale, and then back at the key. He steps back, recoiling, and then leans forward to look again. He prods the key with a forefinger, here in the palm of my hand, and picks it up, letting the diamond ring dangle.

"God," he whispers, walking to the table, mesmerized. He sits heavily in a chair and lays the key and ring in front of him like an expert with a rare treasure on *The Antiques Roadshow*. Head in hands, he stares. Helpless, I look on. I can barely imagine what he's feeling.

Eventually, he speaks. "Where did you find these? How?" His voice is rough, and unsteady.

"When I was chasing Buster through the undergrowth." I go on to tell Lucas how I thought the one and only sea horse door key had fallen out of my jeans' pocket during the scramble. "I was overwhelmed with relief to find it, even in the chaos. Imagine if I had lost the only key to that door."

"You have no idea what this means."

Don't I? Do I? My mind's in replay. If Agat hadn't finished knitting the bunny, Alice and I wouldn't have driven out to her cabin with the Halloween cookies, Agat wouldn't have given Alice the duck for Buster…and that damn key and ring would have lain half buried in the compost of the shore, forever. I shiver to think I almost threw it away without knowing, after finding it without knowing. Serendipity gone awry.

"Does it prove anything?" I ask, because I can't see that it does.

He nods. "Oh yes. To me, it proves everything. Bonny went for a swim, meaning to come home. That's what I need to know."

Buster, in his near-death throes, has handed Lucas his salvation.

Lucas is quiet for the rest of the evening, distant and thoughtful like he's undergoing some sort of change. I let him be. This is something he has to get through by himself.

Something.

We go to bed early folded in each other's arms, falling asleep face-to-face, heart to heart in the darkness. When I wake I have no idea of the time, or how long I've been asleep. It's like silence has woken me; it's too quiet. I move Lucas's arms off my body and get out of bed, careful not to disturb him. At the window, I open a shutter a few inches and look on a scene that takes my breath away. The full moon hangs ice-white over a ragged sea, eerie behind a slanting veil of heavy snow. I've never seen snow at sea level before; it's magical, and disturbing, like there's something wrong with the planet.

"What?" Lucas grunts from the bed.

"It's snowing."

"Mm." He rolls over, turning his back. I get into bed and snuggle behind him. He's so fast asleep he doesn't even complain when I warm my cold feet between his calves.

"Lara?"

Right. Not so fast asleep after all. "Sorry about my feet."

He turns around again, dragging the bedding with him.

"Hey!" I whisper, clutching my share. There's a brief fight for territory, and we settle, him pulling me to his chest, running a hand over my hair, the back of my neck, my shoulder blades, and ribs. He touches my stomach, stopping there.

"Lucas?"

He breathes out long and slow. "Are you too scratched and stinging to—"

"No." I squeeze closer, pressing myself to his body, drinking his heat.

The release of tension in Lucas's hand, sliding further, downwards, between my legs, and the heat of his kisses drives me to the shimmering edge. Next second I'm on red alert. Lucas is different. He's strong and tender, and utterly committed. Together, his tactical intensity, the buzz and thrill of rising climax, the swift, exquisite power and release of simultaneous orgasms followed by the effervescent aftershock, equal the most beautiful few minutes of…

Of my life thus far, come to think of it.

Something's different. Something's happened. I glance at Lucas, facedown in the pillow next to mine.

Something's got to happen.

I think it did. Except it wasn't *something.* It's everything.

Everything just happened.

Lucas surfaces by turning his head to face me. "That was different," he murmurs.

I stare at him in the dark, feeling rather than seeing his eyes holding mine. "Different?"

"How was it for you, Ms. Fairmont?" he asks, in a deep, mock-television-interviewer voice.

Neither mechanical, nor studied, nor textbook. "Perfect."

"Please elaborate. How perfect, Ms. Fairmont?"

"As perfect as one of Queenie's gorgeous eggs."

He drops the voice. "Huh?"

"Boiled, Lucas. Boiled."

The bedding rustles and pulls tight. He's up on one elbow. "What the hell are you talking about?"

"Soft and hard in all the right places."

He smothers a big laugh, shaking the bed. I reach out and touch his face, "And you, Lucas? Was it great for you too?"

He's quiet for a long time, but I know he's staring at me with those brown-diamond eyes.

"What?" I cuddle up, but he pushes me away, holding me by the upper arms like he can see me in the dark.

"Lara? Something's different."

He felt it too. I stare back. "Different?"

"You—I don't know how to say this—but sometimes, no, actually always, all the times we've been together, you've..."

"I've what?"

"Sex with you is fantastic, Lara, don't get me wrong. It's wild. It's perfect. The best, but..."

"But?"

"You always hold something back. It's like there's a small, vital part you don't give."

I hold my breath. "Which part?"

"The best part. The part I want most. Tonight you were fully in the moment with me. Not distracted like you're hiding something, holding a secret, unwilling to give me everything."

Everything.

"Tonight, Lara, you were mine. All mine. You gave it all."

"You too."

We slide across the small area of sheet that lies between us and wind our arms around each other. I slide a leg between his thighs.

"We should get some sleep," he says.

"Can I tell you something first?"

"Sure."

I move my head back, so I can see the shimmer in

his eyes.

"I love you, Lucas." I hold his face, and kiss his mouth. "I love you. I love you forever."

Chapter Thirty-Two

There's snow in London, but nothing like the dump they had in Maine in early December, a few days before I left.

I'm catching up with friends in the few—hopefully—days left before Julie gives spectacular birth. My parents are home, briefly until the New Year when they start a lecture tour in Canada, so that's a relief. It's great to see Holly again, and to meet Alan, of course. What fun to go shopping together along Oxford Street, under the Christmas lights, dusted with light snow. How homely to sit in a cosy pub beside a crackling fire and drink mulled wine with carol singers. To hear the familiar rumble of the engine of a London black cab, to breathe the warm, dusty breath of the Underground, and marvel at the astonishingly lavish festive windows in Selfridges. I love it, and I've missed it. However, to tell the absolute truth, something's missing. Well, maybe not that, but...I feel like a visitor. I'm welcome, all is familiar, yet I belong somewhere else. Suffice it to say I think about Lucas *all* the time, and Alice most of the time.

Holly's got a few days' work left before she heads south to her parents in Surrey. After our last lunch of the year in a wine bar near Liberty's—it feels strangely like a significant farewell, like I'm never going to see her again—she comes with me all the way to Piccadilly, to a picture-framing studio in Half Moon Street, where I have something waiting for collection. Perhaps she feels the same.

"What's that?" she asks, peering over my shoulder.

I run my fingers over the glass. "A sea horse I got in Maine."

"Stunning. I adore the frame."

"It's like a renaissance drawing," says the framer himself, handing back my credit card.

"I know."

"Who's it for?" Holly asks.

"Me."

Holly has to go. We say goodbye while I wait for the picture to be packed.

"Phone me, Skype me, email me, SMS me," she calls, waving from the kerb as she gets into a taxi.

"I will, I promise. You too. Happy Christmas!" I blow kisses and wave until she disappears into the sleet.

"What can I bring you from London, for Christmas?" I asked Lucas, at the airport.

"You. Just come back. Please."

I slid my hand around his waist and put my head on his chest. "A herd of moose wouldn't keep me away."

"Promise?"

"Promise." I drew back, squeezed his hand and we kissed each other goodbye.

"What would you like for Christmas?" I asked Alice.

"A sister," she said, without hesitation.

"Oh, darling, I can't give you a sister."

"Then a brother."

"Perhaps we can arrange one or the other for Alice's birthday?" Lucas's eyes rested on me, keen. I didn't look at him. I bent to kiss Alice. "Be good. See you very soon."

"See you at Christmas."

I leave the framers and walk back to Regent Street, buying everything Barbour for Lucas, and half of Hamley's for Alice.

Julie gives birth quickly and easily, surprising everyone after the monumental build up. James George Simon—Jamie within days—enters the world two days after his due date, serene, wise and wrinkled. Julie adores him immediately—we all do—and Derek is smitten. Julie's positively bovine, her obsession with breastfeeding broken only by heartfelt complaints about not being able to consume alcohol. We put away gifts of champagne for Julie and Derek to enjoy at a later date and Dad goes out to buy more, so we can celebrate and be festive all at once.

My mother sensibly brings Christmas forward by a week.

"In case you have to be somewhere on the actual day, Lara."

"Meaning what?" I ask.

"You Skype those American people every few hours. Why not just go back to Maine and be with them?"

On the eighteenth of December, we have the works. Roast turkey and all the trimmings, plum pudding—containing money—included. The following day we eat a mammoth lunch and attend a carol service at a local church. After a supper of leftovers we spend the evening watching Christmas shows on television, handing Jamie around like a game of pass the parcel.

The days pass slowly, dragging on cocktails,

pudding and port parties, and a stream of visitors popping in to see Jamie, to squeeze in a few mince pies and a glass of mulled wine while they're at it. All such fun, but there's somewhere else I'm longing to be.

That said, what loser would be sitting in an airport on Christmas Eve? That'll be me, in twenty-four hours, thanks to Hurricane Somebody who may well bury the east coast of the USA in a million tons of snow overnight, thereby delaying my flight.

In the end, it's not too bad. We get underway in light snow at Heathrow, a couple of hours late, warned that visibility problems on the other side of the Atlantic may cause a diversion. I cross my fingers on take-off, hoping the pilot will spot the runway at Logan Airport, and spot it in time for me to get a connection to Portland. Actually, glancing at the thick cloud pressing on the window, I hope he can spot America—that's how bad it looks.

Tired, excited and nervous for some reason, I nevertheless sleep most of the way, dreaming of bright gold leaves overlapped by crimson, lying in the falling snow. By some incredulous miracle planes *can* still fly in and out of Logan, and—vitally important—grope their way to Portland. There, at last, I am overjoyed to find Lucas and Alice, both bundled in coats and gloves, wearing red and white Santa hats, waiting for me in the arrivals hall.

"I feel like I've been away for years." Muffled by Lucas and Alice's joint hug, I know I'm back where I belong. "I couldn't wait to get back."

"We couldn't wait for you to get back either, could we, Alice?"

Alice smiles up at me. "Daddy's got a present for

you."

"I've got some for Daddy and you," I tell her.

"Daddy's one for you is very small."

"Alice." Lucas picks her up. The concourse is crammed, and we're being shoved on all sides in the storm of noise and humanity all around. "Remember what I said. It's a secret."

She nods, solemn. "You mustn't tell," he reminds, "any of the secrets, or the surprise will be spoilt." She wriggles with excitement, bursting to tell, and buries her face in Lucas's neck.

There's heavy snow, but the Jeep is wearing snow tires so we drive straight into Lobster Cove, the most festive and twinkly town on the eastern seaboard, I'm convinced, without delay or mishap. Christmas lights sparkle along the waterfront, there's a giant spangled, glittering tree near the gazebo on the town square, every shop front is decorated, and each front door displays a wreath of pinecones, red ribbons, and greenery, at the very least. Lucas drives all the way through town, so Alice and I can see the lights, then turns around and heads back. We end up at Frenchman Bay B&B.

"Lucas, why are we here?" I ask.

"Small power problem at Blue Rocks. We had an outage, so we'll stay here for a few days."

"What? For Christmas?" I ask, but Lucas doesn't hear. He's out of the car getting my bags out of the boot. I look at the façade of Frenchman's. It's pretty, with green shutters, a wide porch, and Adirondack chairs on either side of each door, but doesn't do justice to my fantasy of a first, perfect Christmas in Maine. I'd imagined a huge, festive, grocery-shopping spree, and a tree in the hallway at Blue Rocks, as high as the gallery.

I've got several boxes of decorations in my ridiculously enormous baggage pile—for which I was charged overweight. There are Christmas lights, and a nativity scene for Alice, charged with glittering angels. I've got velvet-trimmed crackers from Harrods, a ruinously expensive Stilton from Fortnum's, a bottle of ancient port from Berry Bros., and—

Lucas opens my door. "Out you get."

I step out of the car and follow Alice inside, disturbed. Something's not right.

"Lucas, where's Buster?" I ask.

"At the house."

"What about his meals?"

He hesitates, or does he? "I went to feed him before I drove to the airport. He's fine."

"Did you enjoy visiting Buster today?" I ask Alice, while Lucas checks me in at the desk.

"I didn't see him," she says. "I stayed here and played with Gigi."

I glance at Gigi, preoccupied behind the reception desk. What's going on?

Lucas takes me to the suite of adjoining rooms he's booked, telling me he has to go out. He won't tell me where. "It's a secret. I'll take Alice. She's got a carol-singing play date later with Grace and Ben, here in town."

"When will you be back?"

"In about an hour. Have a rest meanwhile. Take your time." They go, leaving me alone.

I sit on the bed, unsettled, staring into the bathroom. I should unpack, relax, lie in a hot tub for half an hour and forget about Blue Rocks and the power outage.

I can't, because there's a fiery ring of leaves swirling in my mind. I call Skeet for an immediate pick-up, grab my coat, and go.

En route, no amount of prodding or probing will get Skeet to reveal any Lobster Cove scandal I might have missed. Surely, surely he'd drop a hint if Blue Rocks had burned to the ground in my absence. He concentrates on the icy road and keeping the windscreen clear of falling snow. We drive in through the gate and there, right in front of the sea horse door is a large red vehicle. The fire chief, I knew it!

Once I'm closer, I see it isn't. It's an electrician's van, that's all. Skeet waits. First I plod around the outside of the house, knee-deep in snow, soaking my boots and trousers, knowing full well that while the driveway side of the house looks perfect from the outside, the sea-facing side will be gutted. At the front, I walk across the hidden lawn, head down, leaving a trough in my wake. At the top of the little steps to the beach, where the old gate is bolted shut, I take a deep breath, turn my back on the growling sea, and look up.

There's nothing wrong.

Blue Rocks is fine, on the outside. I go around the front, where the sea horse door is wide open, freezing the house. In the hallway, reaching up to the gallery is a giant pine tree, growing in a pot, quite bare. What a shame. A man in a red overall emerges from the kitchen, surprised to see me.

"Hello," I say. "How's it all going?"

"Fine. Can I help you?"

"I'm only here to check on the cat."

"The big black guy? He's been in and out of the basement all day long. It's warmer there."

"Thanks," I say, turning to go. "Happy Christmas."

"Happy Christmas, ma'am." I go ōut onto the porch, he closes the sea horse door behind me, and Skeet drives me back to town.

Oops, I walk straight into Lucas in the reception area of Frenchman's. He sees me, but he's on the phone, listening with intent, a sombre expression on his face. He finishes the call and walks over.

"Where were you?" His eyes are too serious.

I smile. "It's a secret, but if you must know, I went out to Blue Rocks."

"Why?"

"To see that it hadn't burned down while I was in London. To check Buster is still alive."

He stares at me. I can't read his eyes. "But—"

"I worried about those…that leaf pattern Agat left. I looked it up. The closest reference I could find indicated it could have been a—"

"A fire symbol. I looked it up too."

"You did?"

"I was worried."

"Was there a fire at Blue Rocks, Lucas?"

"Almost."

"What happened?"

"The fire alarm woke me a few nights ago. Smoke was coming out from behind the panelling upstairs."

"Which panelling? Where?"

"In your bathroom. I got Alice out of the house, called the fire chief, and it was all over very quickly."

I must sit down. Luckily there's a sofa right behind me. "So the fire wasn't anywhere near you or Alice?"

He closes his eyes briefly. "She was sleeping in your bed. She missed you, so I let her sleep there. The room was really smoky, but I got her out before she woke up. But yes, yes, she was close."

I don't know what to say. I gaze at the people walking in and out of the reception space, disconnected, like I'm busy with an out-of-body experience. "Were Agat's leaf circles some kind of warning?"

"No. The fault was electrical. Product failure on a part that should have been recalled—"

"But Lucas—"

"It had nothing to do with Agat," says Lucas the Engineer, and I don't know whether to believe him.

"You can't live like this. Looking over your shoulder all the time, suspicious of every sign, every gesture—"

"Lara, I don't."

"I do!"

"You won't have to any more," Lucas says, his face set. "That was Angie on the phone. Agat died this morning."

"Oh." I look up at him. There's no relief in my heart, only sadness. "Was it...peaceful?"

"Yes, because Angie finally gave in to her insistence that she, Agat, was Alice's grandmother."

"Agat died believing that?"

"She did, and it made her real happy. Angie said she died at peace, a beautiful smile on her face."

"How lovely."

"That's what I thought." Lucas sits next to me, taking one of my hands in his. "In hindsight, Agat was only strange after she got sick. Before that, she was a really interesting person."

"You're very forgiving, Lucas." Worn out, I put my head on his shoulder. We sit together, holding hands, saying nothing, watching folk walk in and out.

After a time, Lucas speaks. "Let's go to the bar and have a big glass of an important, Californian red."

"Let's."

"We'll wait there for Alice to come back." He glances at his watch. "She shouldn't be long. Then we'll take her up for her bath, and put her to bed."

"I'll unpack."

"Gigi's available to babysit, so we'll go along to Merlot's for dinner, if you're not too tired."

I was, but not any more. "I'd love that."

"You might want to dress up a bit." He takes my hands in his, and studies them.

"All right." Warmth spreads through me and it's got nothing to do with the festive red and gold tea light flickering on the table between us.

Lucas's phone rings. It's the electrician. The system at Blue Rocks is up and running. It's been checked and triple checked, inspected and passed. We can move back first thing tomorrow.

"Let's go now," I say. "Tomorrow is Christmas Eve."

"We'll freeze. We'll go tomorrow, early."

"I'll need to buy groceries. Quite a lot."

"We'll do it on the way."

"That tree has to be decorated. All the food has to be cooked."

"Alice can't wait to help with everything."

"Have we got a gift for Buster?"

Lucas laughs. "My dad might come up from Florida for New Year."

"Why didn't you tell me that already! What other good news are you hiding?"

"Debra had the baby this morning."

"Lucas!"

"Debra and John are the proud parents of Elizabeth Alice."

"You should have told me immediately."

"I like to keep the best for last."

I gaze at him, smiling. "You are a beautiful, if wicked, man."

And that's what we do while we wait for Alice: tell each other things, put ideas out there for discussion, exchange views, and make plans, small and big, forge decisions like precious elements fitting this way and that, the stepping stones in the journey toward the start of our joined lives.

We never made it to Merlot's.

Epilogue

Bliss, to get away from the tail of winter in Maine, lovely as it is, although I wouldn't want to miss the spring. It's March, and I'm lying on a lounger in six inches of crystal-clear Indian Ocean on a private island in the Maldives. We're on honeymoon. Lucas swimming way out in the turquoise lagoon, and Alice less than twenty yards away, making a wonky sandcastle in the shade of a thatched umbrella. Who, in their right mind, would take a five-year-old on honeymoon?

I would. Lucas would. Besides, Alice presumed she'd be coming from the start, and believed Buster would be coming too—we had quite a time convincing her that he wouldn't enjoy himself. She wasn't interested in kind offers to come and stay from friends in Lobster Cove, from Debra and John, and even Grandpa. Although Lucas wanted to spend our honeymoon in Venice with the Vitruvian Man, I persuaded him otherwise. Venice, stunningly beautiful as she is, is no place for a five-year-old with all that open water, and not a blade of grass to be seen. We'll do Venice some other time.

Lucas proposed to me on Christmas Eve. We'd finished decorating the tree when he went down on one knee right there in the hallway, joined by Alice.

"Lara, will you marry me?" he asked.

"And me," Alice said.

Buster wandered in to see what was going on, and sat next to Alice. Faced by this row of people, I had to laugh.

Lucas surveyed his committee. "I think you've been outvoted, Lara."

"Yes," I said, smiling.

"Yes what?" Lucas asked.

"Yes to everything."

We were married ten days later, at the town hall, followed by a party at Blue Rocks that went on until sunrise. We invited everyone we knew in Lobster Cove and beyond, and every single person accepted, and came, and enjoyed themselves. There was one exception: Julie. She stayed in London with Derek and Jamie—the most perfect and beautiful baby in the world, wouldn't you know?—and watched the proceedings on Skype. I missed her, felt—feel—disconnected right now, but we'll have plenty to share one day soon.

Lucas comes back to shore, standing up in the clear water and wading, knee-deep to inspect Alice's masterpiece. He is glorious—tall, wide-shouldered, lean, dark-haired and so deeply tanned, all over, he's been mistaken twice for a local. I gaze at him, loving him with all my heart, and touch my stomach with the fingertips of my left hand, looking down at my wedding ring, a hoop of square-cut sapphires, each a different colour blue or purple. "All the blues of Maine" was the brief to the jeweller, Lucas told me, and the result is meaningful and utterly beautiful.

Lucas kneels next to Alice and begins the salvage operation as warm water laps the base of her castle's walls. I'm no engineer, but I envisage a moat. He's been sketching, filling up that fat sketchbook I caught him doodling in all those months ago, when I stood in his studio and suggested my job at Blue Rocks was done. "No need. What's the rush?" he said and I'm overjoyed I didn't. Frankly, he's brilliant at design— creative, artistic and practical. Last December, when I went away to London, he bought a plot of land further up the coast, on the other side of the yacht club, and that's what he's sketching—a house for that land. Architecturally, it's breath-taking: a modern classic with all the beautiful details you can see on many of the lovely old houses and mansions of Lobster Cove.

He calls it The Sea Horse House and says we'll transfer the sea horse door there, if we move out of Blue Rocks. It's not his only project. Agat left her little house to Alice, and Lucas will renovate that, and rent it out to holidaymakers. It's full of character, imbued with local culture, and I know he'll incorporate all the best elements of Agat's legacy, and make it beautiful. That's what he does: he makes things beautiful. Even stuff like ugly old oil rigs and my messed-up, one-time failure of a life.

"Thank you for waiting for me," he says, often. "Thank you for being so patient."

I did wait for him. I waited for him to choose me, and to say he believed in me. I met Lucas, and instantly my life was better.

Lucas wants to sell his company and sell Blue Rocks. He claims the house belongs to a part of his past on which he's locked the door. He says it was an overly ambitious project, explains that he doesn't want the memories any more. Actually, the house isn't called

Blue Rocks now. I had the weather vane replaced—that poor, pierced mermaid—with one made by a local craftsman in Lobster Cove, and the house simply became The Mermaid House instead.

"Why a new mermaid?" Lucas asked.

"Because she's prettier, and Alice likes her." Deep down inside, I admit it's an homage to Bonny. She trapped Lucas, but she also set him free. She wasn't of this world, and she isn't now. However, she will always be Alice's biological mother, represented by the lovely bronze mermaid swimming above the grey roofs of the house Lucas once loved, in the blue ocean of the sky. Quite apart from anything else, as Alice's stepmother, I'd prefer her to remember her natural mother as a mermaid, rather than an egg.

Me? I am the sea horse, a creature of this world.

A cheer goes up. Lucas and Alice celebrate the resistance of the sturdily reinforced castle as a tiny wave trickles into the moat, posing no threat whatsoever. I lay my hand flat on the warm skin of my stomach and close my eyes. We won't be able to give Alice a sister or brother this birthday, but I'm pretty sure she'll have someone to play with by the next one.

A word about the author...

Gina Rossi was born in South Africa and grew up there. She now lives and writes romance in the Channel Islands, happily married with four grown-up children in the UK. She is a member of the Romantic Novelists' Association (RNA) and the Romantic Organization of South Africa (ROSA). *The Sea Horse Door* is her fourth novel.

Thank you for purchasing
this publication of The Wild Rose Press, Inc.

If you enjoyed the story, we would appreciate your
letting others know by leaving a review.

For other wonderful stories,
please visit our on-line bookstore at
www.thewildrosepress.com.

For questions or more information
contact us at
info@thewildrosepress.com.

The Wild Rose Press, Inc.
www.thewildrosepress.com

Stay current with The Wild Rose Press, Inc.

Like us on Facebook

https://www.facebook.com/TheWildRosePress

And Follow us on Twitter
https://twitter.com/WildRosePress